Praise for

EVERYWHERE EVERYTHING EVERYONE

Everywhere Everything Everyone examines the power
of freedom and the precariousness of control, both in
civilisation and in the everyday lives of individuals. There
are unsettling echoes of contemporary issues of race, class
and threatened social liberties. It is an influential first novel
from a grand new voice.
– Claire Atherfold, *Readings*

A fast-paced tale with twists and turns to entrance the
reader, with well-developed, credible characters [in a]
situation [that's] scarily possible. A powerful young adult
debut novel from award-winning playwright Katy Warner.
– *Blue Wolf Reviews*

A story of compassion, a story of the power of community
and a story of hope. It shows that truth and love can
conquer all – even if it takes a long time.
– *Educate Empower*

A fast-paced and very realistic story of corruption and the
power of resistance. [The author's] messages are clear and
timely: Stand up for what you believe in – there is always
hope. And never allow fear-mongering and ignorance to
dampen your capacity for compassion.
– Deborah Kelly, *CBCA Reading Time*

For Mum

Everywhere Everything Everyone
published in 2019 by
Hardie Grant Egmont
Ground Floor, Building 1, 658 Church Street
Richmond, Victoria 3121, Australia
www.hardiegrantegmont.com

 A catalogue record for this
book is available from the
National Library of Australia

Text copyright © 2019 Katy Warner
Illustration and design copyright © 2019 Hardie Grant Egmont

Illustration and design by Jess Cruickshank
Typeset in Galliard 10.5/16.5pt by Kerry Cooke

Printed in Australia by Griffin Press part of Ovato, an Accredited ISO
AS/NZS 14001 Environmental Management System printer.

3 5 7 9 10 8 6 4 2

The paper in this book is FSC® certified.
FSC® promotes environmentally responsible,
socially beneficial and economically viable
management of the world's forests.

EVERYWHERE
EVERYTHING
EVERYONE

KATY WARNER

Hardie Grant

EGMONT

PART ONE

CHAPTER 1

I wasn't going to make it.

Curfew was about to kick in and there was no way I'd be where I was meant to be in time. I tried to run faster. I was meant to be at home, indoors, like everyone else at nine o'clock. Instead I was outside, running down the middle of the street and wishing time would just stop.

The bus had dropped me off and the driver had said, *Got far to go?* And looked at her watch like she was making a point. I told her, *Nope, not far,* which wasn't a complete lie. Besides, what was she going to do? Offer to drive the bus to my front door? I don't think so.

So I ran.

My backpack hit my back, bounce-bounce-bounce, as the world quietened down around me. There was no-one outside. No cars or buses or bikes or people walking dogs or kids screaming in the broken-down playground or orders for

3

burgers and fries being made in the drive-through or couples out for evening walks just cos it was a nice night. Everywhere was silent, everything closed and locked. Everyone was where they were supposed to be.

Except me.

I could feel people watching me from their windows. *Look at her,* I imagined them saying as they shook their heads, fingers itching to call the Emergency Line as soon as the clock ticked over to nine. Then the Unit would turn up and do whatever it was they did to people who were out after Curfew. They'd call me a Disturbance. Or maybe a Potential Threat. That would be much worse. Once you were a Potential Threat it didn't take much to lose the Potential part of the label.

I didn't want to think about what happened to Threats.

I begged my legs to move, *move,* but all they wanted to do was stop. I wished I'd left my backpack behind. It was slowing me down. I could run a lot faster than that. Correction – I *had* run a lot faster than that. Once I was all about being the first over the line and blue ribbons and crappy fake gold medals and people cheering my name – Santee, Santee, Santee – but that was a long time ago. Now I was just that Weird Girl they all ignored. (*Don't talk to her,* Tash had told the kinda-cute new boy only a couple of weeks before. He'd noticed the drawing I was working on and said it looked interesting. *Interesting? What the hell does that mean?* I'd said and he'd laughed and was about to say something more when Tash swept in from nowhere and dragged him away. *Don't talk to her.* She said it so I could hear it. *She's a freak.* They always made sure I could hear it. Me and the new boy hadn't spoken since, though he'd caught my eye a couple of times and I'd smiled. And he'd smiled back. So there was that, I suppose.)

My crappy apartment block came into view and it took all I had not to turn around and run in the opposite direction. The tired concrete building loomed over the bitumen. Rows and rows of tiny windows peered out onto another identical block, and another, and another. So many eyes. In the dull light they kinda looked like a pack of monsters. Hungry, watchful monsters that would swallow me up. I kinda wished they would.

I heard the Unit patrol car siren.

Curfew.

I ignored the stitch in my side and the fact Mum was going to kill me and ran into the mouth of the monster.

Home.

'Don't you ever, ever do that to me again. You hear me? Never,' Mum hissed in my ear.

I could tell she wanted to shout but she couldn't because that's not what we did. Shouting was not allowed in our flat. We were surrounded by too many eyes and ears and Good Citizens who were keen to do the Right Thing. I was three minutes late, maybe five. Depends on your clock. Mum considered this The End of the World but even then she wouldn't raise her voice. I wished she would.

'What the hell were you doing?' Astrid demanded, frowning. My big sister had slipped into Mum mode. She did that a lot, despite the fact that our actual mother had the whole Mum thing down pretty well. When we were little, people thought it was funny and cute, but I'd always known it was just Astrid's way of proving she was better than me.

'I just …' I searched for the right words but knew anything I said would sound like bullshit. I felt my face burning and avoided their eyes. 'I lost track of time.' Even I thought it sounded like a lie, which it was. But not entirely.

'Where?' Mum said. 'Where were you when you "lost track of time"?'

She always asked the right questions. I stared at the TV, hoping for something that would distract her. The News was on cos it was always on at that time of night. The words *Breaking News!* and *Live!* scrolled across the screen and I saw images of the Unit in riot gear, ready to storm a building full of Threats. The building was only a couple of blocks from the deli where I worked on weekends. I shivered. I walked past that building every Saturday and never gave it much thought, and now it was about to be ripped apart by the Unit. What had the people inside that building been planning to do? Another bomb on another bus? Another car speeding into another crowd? I felt sick thinking about it even though I should have been used to it by now. There had been heaps of Threats identified lately. And more attacks. Unexpected. Violent. And always close enough to our neighbourhood to scare us.

Everyone was frightened. All the time. Including Mum. I finally looked at her. She'd sunk into her old armchair and was rubbing her forehead like she was exhausted. I hated seeing her like that and I hated being the reason for it. I wanted to reach out and hug her, crawl into her lap like I had when I was a kid and cuddles made everything better somehow. But I didn't.

'We didn't know where you were,' Mum said.

'I sent you a message,' I mumbled. That was the truth. The message itself wasn't so truthful. I'd told her I was finishing a project at school. Lie. I'd written, *Be home after dinner 7.30 ish.* Also a lie. She'd responded with three kisses: *xxx.* According to Mum that meant I Love You. It had made me feel bad but it hadn't stopped me. I'd figured she wouldn't find out. I was wrong. Of course.

'Santee,' Mum said and this time she didn't hiss but sounded disappointed, which was actually even worse. Part of me wondered if that was her plan. But still, as bad as I felt for lying to her, I couldn't tell her the truth. What was the point? I was home and I was safe and if I'd told her where I'd been she'd just lose it. She always did when I tried to see Dad.

I looked back at the TV. Shots had been fired. *From inside, from inside,* an excited voice said over the footage, and my stomach lurched. The Unit opened fire. The screen went black for a moment and then we were back in the studio with the smug News anchor. I wondered who was in that building. Had they been watching the News? Did they know the Unit had them surrounded and that they were supposed to come out with their hands up? Did any of them survive?

We saw reports like that every day. At first it had been a shock and we'd stand around the TV and cry. Now the shock might have gone but the fear had grown and grown. So when Our Leader, Magnus Varick, and his men in suits announced all these rules to keep us safe, we followed them. Like Curfew. We were too scared not to. Plus, they said it was to protect us.

But that didn't stop the bad stuff from happening. And it always happened on our side of the city, where thousands of people were crammed on top of one another in little apartments and burnt-out cars were left near the abandoned factory and the dead-end streets stank in summer. The bad side. The good side was where people had more money and better jobs and the apartment blocks weren't towers of concrete and nothing bad ever happened. Whatever. The bad side wasn't the bad side to me. It was just where we lived. And it had its own good things, like the cafe where people chatted in all kinds of languages while music spilled out of passing cars and mashed together in a mix of beats and bass, and the graffitied walls that were like some sort of free art gallery, and the delicious smell of bread from the bakery in the mornings, and the brightly lit restaurants families crowded into on Sundays, and the park where dogs ran freely, and the cinemas with their over-buttered popcorn and cheap movies. But most importantly, it was full of memories of Dad.

It was home.

As if she could read my mind, Astrid said, 'You were trying to see Dad again, weren't you?'

I glared at her. She looked like she'd just won a prize and it made me want to hit her. But I didn't. At least I had the guts to try to see him. I was the only one who did. And that made me better than Astrid. So I ignored her. 'I didn't mean to be late.'

'Santee ... ' Mum started to say something and her voice made my stomach twist. She wasn't whispering anymore. 'It's not about you being late.'

'What is it then? What?' I snapped, and Mum flinched, just a bit.

'We've spoken about this. You are not to go there.' She was about to launch into a lecture, but I didn't let her. I'd heard it all before.

'You don't give a shit about him. You never go to see him. You never want to talk about him. Maybe you're happy he's gone.' I wasn't shouting, but I was close.

'I'm not arguing with you about this, Santee,' Mum said.

'See! You never talk about it.'

Mum took a deep breath and let it out slowly, her lips in a tight straight line, her eyes unblinking. 'Santee. You know it's not safe to go out there,' she said in a low, quiet voice. 'So from now on, you go to school and you come straight home. And you go to work and you come straight home. That's it. That's your life now. OK? Nothing else.'

I knew I should shut up but I've never been great at taking my own advice. And so I didn't shut up – I laughed. Not a friendly, ha-ha, isn't-that-funny laugh, but a mean, screw-up-your-nose-and-curl-your-lip laugh. Cos, seriously, Mum was grounding me. *Grounding* me? Didn't she realise my whole life was basically one big grounding anyway? All our lives were. You couldn't actually *do* anything here. Everyone was too fricking scared. Scared to make too much noise. Scared of their neighbours. Scared to speak up, to be heard, to say anything. And I was tired of being scared. I was over it. My chest felt tight and the room was hot and I couldn't hold it in any longer. 'I'm over this bullshit,' I shouted.

'Santee!' said Astrid, as loudly as she dared, in *that* voice. The one that always made me want to run away because I hadn't done anything wrong and it's not fair to be stuck with two mothers – my actual mother and my big sister. There was no space, no room, for me to just *be*.

'Bullshit,' I screamed. Mum and Astrid stared at me, mouths open but silent, as I ran into my bedroom. I slammed the door and threw myself onto my bed and hated myself.

I shared a room with Astrid because we didn't have a choice and after I'd screamed into my pillow and punched it a couple of times, she snuck in. She acted like I was some kind of bomb that would explode in her face. Maybe I was.

'Stop being an idiot,' she eventually said. 'I saved you some dinner.'

'Not hungry,' I lied, and rolled over to face the wall.

She sighed like an old lady as she sat on the edge of my bed and rubbed my back the way she always did when I lost it. 'We all miss him, you know.'

I knew that. Logically. Of course. How could anyone not miss him? He'd been gone for almost three years now, since I was thirteen, but it felt like forever. I couldn't understand why they refused to even try to visit him. They said it was dangerous and irresponsible, travelling all that way on my own. Making a nuisance of myself (Mum's words, not mine). Mum and Astrid made all these empty statements like, *We need to fly under the radar, we can't cause a fuss, we have to be careful.* And I got it. I understood. But I just couldn't, and wouldn't, put Dad behind me. I wasn't going to pretend everything was OK. Cos it wasn't.

They'd found out about me going there a couple of times and I'd promised to stop. But I didn't. I got better with my timing and planning and lying and I always made sure I was home before Curfew. At first I tried to go every month but it wasn't easy to get there and soon I was missing a month or two. And then, that morning, I realised it was something like four months since I'd been there and I felt like shit and couldn't stop thinking about him. I was at school, trying to concentrate, but I saw Dad's face and heard his voice in everything and everyone all day. So I went out there. I left class early, skipped out on a session with Beth and caught the bus that took me all the way to the outskirts of the suburbs. From the bus window I watched the houses make way for the bush. Or was it the other way round?

When I finally got off the bus my legs were wobbly and I felt like throwing up. I made my way down the long driveway of loose, hot gravel and joined the small crowd that had gathered by the fence enclosing the prison. They were always there. People like me, waiting and waiting for the moment they'd be allowed through the gates to the people they loved. That moment hadn't come. Ever. Well, not since I'd been heading there and not that anyone else in the queue could remember, anyway. But I still went, like all those others, cos maybe one day they'd let us in. And if I wasn't there when that happened … I didn't want him to think we'd forgotten about him. Dad had been in there for a long time.

At least, we assumed that was where they'd taken him that night. We never knew for sure, and we didn't know if they'd moved him. We were never told anything. All we had to go on were careful whispers, and we never knew if they were rumours or the truth.

As usual, the Unit Officers recorded my name, my address, took my photo. I knew the drill and did all the right things. I was polite and looked them in the eye, and when they asked why I was there I told them the truth, like I always did. *I want to see my father. Joseph Quinn.* Usually I'd search their faces for a sign of recognition but their faces were always blank and they'd say, *No visitors.* But that's not what they said today. They said, *OK.*

My heart stopped. OK. They never said OK. Before I could ask what they meant they walked over to the next person to go through the whole process again, and I truly believed I was going to see my dad. So I waited. Longer than I should have.

I explained it all to Astrid. The reason I was late. Waiting around too long because the Unit had said OK. It sounded so stupid when I said it out loud.

'I thought it was a sign,' I said. 'Or a code. You know?'

'Seriously, Santee? Grow up. They were never going to let you in,' she said, and the tone of her voice made me feel like a little kid. 'You can't keep going there. It's pointless.'

I knew she was right. Deep down I probably knew, even while I was outside the prison, that I wasn't going to see Dad. But I wanted to believe that it might, somehow, be possible. I didn't need Astrid being all Astrid about it.

'Leave me alone,' I said, and she did. She turned off the light and closed the door behind her.

I couldn't hear them but I knew Mum and Astrid would be talking about me, wondering where they'd gone wrong and why the appointments with Beth weren't working. I wanted to shout at them, *Stop talking about me!* Instead, I rolled onto my back, stared at the ceiling and counted from one to ten, slowly, slowly, and tried to Control That Temper the way Beth had taught me.

Beth was a psychologist. After I'd shoved Tash, who'd started it and totally deserved to be shoved, the school said I had to see Beth once a week. Mum agreed, I disagreed, but what I wanted didn't matter. And so I'd been seeing Beth for nearly three years and, for some reason, she'd been unable to change me. What a surprise.

In our first ever meeting Beth said I had to *Control That Temper* and count to ten in my head before I said something I would regret.

'Imagine white clouds gently rolling across a bright, blue sky. Can you do that? Can you try?' Beth had smiled and stared and waited for me to say something. I told her she was a moron, or something like that. Obviously, I didn't count to ten that time. But Beth just nodded and said she understood. It didn't take me long to work out she was quite good like that. You could throw all the crap you wanted at her, and her perfect smile and and her positive attitude and even her neat hairdo wouldn't budge. Although sometimes I'd catch her just staring and staring and it felt like she was looking right through me to the life she could have had if she hadn't become a school psychologist. Maybe a model. Or a News anchor. She could have done either with that hair and that smile. Blargh.

For once, though, the counting and the clouds worked and I thought how happy Beth would be when I told her that I'd done it. Controlled That Temper.

Better late than never.

CHAPTER 2

Mum might have banned shouting but she still knew how to make a lot of noise. And she did, at five o'clock every morning. She slammed drawers and doors and banged pots and if she was feeling particularly annoyed she'd start up the vacuum cleaner. It was her version of screaming, *Get out of bed!* I once suggested she could bring me a coffee instead. I mean, that's a civilized, calm way to get someone out of bed, right? She wasn't impressed.

I buried my head in my pillow to block out the noise and wished I didn't have to face the day.

'Good sleep?' Astrid said.

'No.' I watched her tuck her sheets into hospital corners. She was always trying to teach me to do that. Her bed, like her, looked perfect.

'Feeling better?' Astrid said.

'Nope.' I rolled over to face the wall.

'That's cos you're hungry, idiot. Come on.' And she whipped the blankets off me and hurried out of the room before I could throw something at her.

Mum had made me a bowl of porridge, which she never usually did. And she'd even put cinnamon on it like Dad used to when I was little and couldn't do that sort of thing myself. I mumbled, 'Thanks,' and Mum squeezed my shoulder.

'I couldn't handle losing you, too,' she said gently. 'I want to keep you safe. That's all, honey.'

'Sorry,' I said, because I didn't know what else to say. And it was true.

'You're still grounded,' Mum said. She kissed the top of my head before rushing off to iron her uniform.

The not-angry-just-disappointed version of Mum made me feel so much worse inside. The porridge felt like a rock in the pit of my stomach. I ate slowly and flipped through my sketchpad and tried to pretend I didn't have to go to school. The last sketches I'd done were of trees and leaves and stuff like that. I'd discovered this little hidden spot at school where I could sit and draw and think and be somewhere else for a moment while the others gossiped and laughed and did whatever it was they did at lunchtime. My sketches were kind of boring, the sort of thing you'd expect old people to draw, but I was trying to work on shading and capturing light. It wasn't really working. I hated everything I'd done. I decided I'd go back to my spot today to get some more practice in. Knowing I had that place to myself made the thought of school a little easier. Made me panic a little less.

'What are you looking at?'

I jumped. Mum was right behind me, peering over my shoulder. 'Nice work,' she said. 'Now move it.'

'How about we take the day off? Go to the beach? Hawaii, maybe.' I grinned. Mum didn't.

Despite everything, we were OK, the three of us. We fought and argued but we also told each other *I love you* and we meant it and we gave the neighbours very little to talk about. Well, Mum and Astrid held up their end of the bargain on that one. I tried, more or less. Mum was always worried about what they'd overhear but I didn't think it mattered cos they made up shit all the time anyway. Last month the guy from number four vanished, bam, like that, and all the neighbours said he'd been a Threat and was plotting something (they never said what – their imaginations weren't that impressive). But we all knew, deep down, he was a nice guy who always said, *Good morning,* and swept his balcony and jogged in the afternoons. Maybe it was the jogging they didn't trust. Or the clean balcony. Who knows? The neighbours stuck to their version of the man from number four being a Threat and we never stood up for him. We didn't say, *No, you're wrong, he's OK.* Mum said it was better not to get involved. I asked why and she said, *Don't start.* So I didn't. But I still thought about him now and then. Wondered if there was someone like me waiting for him by the prison gate.

Since the incident with the man from number four the neighbours had increased surveillance to ensure no other Threats appeared in our building. But I figured if none appeared they'd just make something up anyway cos, like they said, they were Good Citizens.

Mum stood in the bathroom doorway, watching me and making that impatient *tch-tch* noise she did. 'You've got two minutes,' she said.

I was trying to deal with the toothpaste I'd dribbled down my shirt and hair that wouldn't do what I wanted it to do. I only had to pull it back into a ponytail. Nothing fancy. You wouldn't think it would be so damn difficult.

Mum had this thing about the three of us walking to school together every morning. I'd never admit to Mum, but I kinda liked it. Walking with her meant the Unit was less likely to hassle us. And it meant I had company for a bit. It could be lonely at school, which was part of the reason I had to talk to Beth. I had an appointment with her that morning, which meant I'd miss part of double maths. So things weren't going to be entirely awful.

I hurried to the front door, chucking my books into my backpack as I went.

Astrid tried to stop me. 'Let me fix your hair,' she said.

'Hurry up, we're gonna be late,' I said in my best Astrid impression, and slipped past her.

'Your hair!' Astrid said.

'Don't care,' I lied.

A Unit Officer walked up the stairs towards us. Our stairs. His head bent down, his long legs taking two steps at a time. My heart stopped. A visit from the Unit was bad news. Like what happened to the guy from number four. And other things. I wondered if the neighbours had reported me for missing Curfew. I wouldn't have been surprised. I was ready to tell them exactly what I thought of them when the officer looked up.

It was Peter.

I'd never seen him in uniform before and it didn't look quite right. I waved at him and went to say, *Good morning,* but Astrid pulled my arm down.

'Stop it,' she said, squeezing my hand tight. 'We're not talking to him.'

Mum shook her head. It was nice that she was disappointed in someone else for a change.

Peter bounded up the rest of the stairs like a puppy. I imagined him licking Astrid's face when he got close enough. But Astrid pushed past him and stormed off. I wondered what the hell was going on with them. I mean, of course things had changed – the three of us were older now and no longer played stupid games on the slab of concrete we called the yard. Plus, we barely saw Peter anymore when once, not that long ago, we saw him all the time. But then Peter moved out and joined the Unit, while Astrid stayed and went to university. She was smart. He wasn't. That's the way it went.

'Good morning,' he said.

'Is it?' I said, because he looked so sad that I couldn't help myself.

Mum elbowed me. 'We haven't seen you in such a long time. We miss you, don't we, Santee?' she said, and I nodded. It wasn't a lie. 'You visiting your parents, love? I've been meaning to pop in and see them but you know how it gets, don't you? Anyway, I'm sure they'll be pleased to see you.' Mum was doing that chatty, chirpy thing she always did when she got nervous. She just talked and talked.

'Just, um, finished night shift, thought I'd drop by.' He

was being polite but he wasn't really with us. He kept looking over his shoulder in Astrid's direction.

'Well, it's lovely of you,' Mum said, but before she could really start up again Peter took off after Astrid.

He'd been chasing after Astrid since we were kids. *And not just when we play tag,* I used to joke. Even though the chasing thing wasn't really a joke. That was serious. That was love. Mum knew it. I knew it. Astrid ignored it. I'd never had anyone like me like that. Unless I counted the kid in grade three who ate glue and decided I was his girlfriend without asking me. I pushed him over at recess and that was it – over.

I tried to hear what Peter and Astrid were saying as they stood together in the so-called yard. Astrid's hands flew around like crazy birds while Peter studied his polished shoes.

'You have a choice …' Astrid said and she pulled Peter further away and dropped her voice so we couldn't hear. I tried to follow them but Mum stopped me. She was listening too, but trying to look like she wasn't. The neighbours, however, weren't quite as subtle. A few had emerged onto their balconies to catch the action.

'Good morning, Mrs Jackson,' I shouted, and waved with heaps of fake enthusiasm.

Mrs Jackson gave me a weak wave and disappeared from view.

'Santee,' Mum said.

'What? I'm being a friendly neighbour!'

'Let me fix that hair.' Mum turned me away from Astrid and Peter and started pulling at my ponytail. 'This hair, just as crazy as your father's …'

She went quiet. I wanted her to keep talking about Dad but I didn't want to upset her again.

'Did you bring a brush?' Mum said.

I laughed, *Yeah right,* and then she laughed and kept trying to get my hair to look decent.

I looked out through the security gate and onto the street and watched people going who-knows-where to do who-knows-what. Heads down, shoulders bent. No-one looked at the sky. *Today,* I thought, *I will look up when I walk.* I didn't want to become one of those people, broken by a day that had not quite begun.

'What's going on with you guys?' I asked Astrid when she finally joined us. There was no sign of Peter. I wondered if she'd melted him down into nothing with the same look she was giving me.

'Your hair looks better,' Astrid said.

I tried to pretend that I didn't care, but I did. A little. It was hard not to at my school.

There were schools closer to home than the one I went to. But the Quinns were smart. Or at least, Astrid was, and I got taken along for the ride. Plus, it helped that I was a fast runner – the school liked that because it made them look good. I could also draw, but the school didn't care so much about that. Anyway, Astrid made it into the good school on the nice side of the city and because of Opportunities (their word, not mine) I went there too.

We passed the identical apartment blocks that lined the roads. I looked up into the endless windows. Some people had put up colourful curtains or decorated windows with stickers or had bright flowers hanging over their balconies, as if they wanted to stand out. We didn't have anything like that. Mum liked it better if we blended in. It was safer that way.

There were more Unit Officers around than usual. In their patrol cars and on foot, walking around in small groups making everyone feel like they'd done something wrong. They were always watching. So were the cameras attached to buildings and streetlights. So were the helicopters that chopped up the sky. And the drones that quietly whizzed by. It felt so crowded living there among all those eyes. Even when I was alone I felt surrounded and on display. It was as if I was trapped in a glass cage and all these people were watching me, waiting for me to screw up. I wanted to stand in the middle of the road and yell something. Anything. But I couldn't, not with all those eyes on me, and so the feeling just grew and grew.

The garbage collectors hadn't been again and the bins on the footpath were overflowing. Even though it was early it was already hot and the smell had started to seep into everything and I was sure I was going to stink by the time I got to school.

Ahead of us, in the park with the graffitied slide I may or may not have added my name to last summer, a group of guys about my age had been stopped by the Unit. One officer was going through their bags and asking stupid questions while another patted down their arms, their legs, their chests. The guys were being so polite, all, *Yes sir,* and, *No ma'am,* and things they'd never say in real life.

Mum said good morning to an officer who was standing back, watching the scene. I don't know why she bothered, but then Mum was one of those people who smiled and nodded and said hello to everyone. Humans, dogs, stray cats. She'd comment on the weather to complete strangers. Tell parents their baby was beautiful. That kind of thing. I'd stand beside her, silently dying inside. I never understood how she could be like that with people she didn't know. Especially Unit Officers. This one just looked right through her. Blank-faced. Serious. I wondered if Peter was like that when he was out here, patrolling the streets in his stupid uniform. I couldn't imagine it.

We got to the part where Mum said goodbye and because she liked what she called Proper Goodbyes, we hugged and kissed cheeks and said, *See you tonight,* cos we all thought we would see each other tonight. We always did. I watched her walk away, shoulders bent, feet shuffling. Suddenly she seemed old.

Once, Mum would have come with us. She'd been an artist and had taught at the university with Dad. But then everything changed and Magnus Varick decided we didn't need art teachers anymore. So they gave her a job at the grocery store instead. She came home smelling like cabbage, her feet aching, her uniform stained with sweat. She would say things like, *A job's a job,* and, *The bills won't pay themselves.* She was right, but it didn't make it any better. Astrid and I always said we'd take care of her. One day. And then she could paint again and no-one could stop her.

'Poor Mum,' I said.

'I know,' Astrid said. 'Let's go.'

We headed off to catch the bus that would take us closer to school and university. Usually Astrid would stride ahead and yell out for me to keep up, but not that morning. That morning she walked slowly, arms crossed, head down. It was weird.

'You OK?' I asked.

She nodded without looking up. She'd been quiet since that whole thing with Peter and it was killing me not knowing what they'd said.

'How's Peter?' I said as casually as I could.

'How's maths going?' Astrid countered.

She was good, but I wasn't about to change the topic. 'You seemed kinda pissed off at him, that's all.'

'It's nothing,' she said. 'Sometimes I just feel … disappointed in him, you know?'

'Tell me,' I said eagerly. Astrid never opened up about this sort of thing. Ever.

And she wasn't about to now. Instead, she started walking at a more Astrid-like pace and launched into a boring monologue about the value of mathematics. Astrid was all about numbers and equations and stuff I hated. It wasn't that I couldn't do it, I just didn't want to. Astrid didn't think I had a choice. Not if I wanted to go to university, which I wasn't sure about – though the other options weren't so great either. If it wasn't university I'd have to work and there was no way I wanted to work at the deli for the rest of my life. Astrid loved studying and numbers and being organised. All the stuff they liked in a university student. One day, there would be a photo of Astrid like the one we had of Mum and Dad wearing black gowns and funny hats. Smiling. Proud. Astrid was smart, like them. And even though I knew she was looking out for me (in her own way), I was not in the

mood to hear all the reasons why I needed to Try A Little
Harder at school. Just being at school was hard enough.

'I don't want to talk about maths,' I interrupted. 'Tell me
what's going on with you and Peter.' I touched her arm, but
she pulled away.

'You know you've got toothpaste on your shirt, right?'
she said.

We were standing at the bus stop. A crappy wooden
bench under a tin shelter that got boiling hot in the sun and
leaked when it rained. I slumped onto the bench and waited
for Astrid to say something. Anything. She didn't.

'Was it something about Dad?' I said.

'No,' she said, like that was the end of it.

'Peter might be able to get information about him, didn't
you say that once? Weren't you going to ask him?'

'No,' she said again.

'Come on, Astrid. If there's something going on I have a
right to know. I'm not a kid. Tell me.'

But she said nothing. She was so frustrating. And
hypocritical. She had to interfere with my life, had to know
every little detail, but she never let me in on hers. It made me
want to throw my school bag at her. Shout at her. Pull her
hair. Anything to get something out of her – something other
than, *No*. I tried to do Beth's stupid breathing exercises but
my leg kept jittering, up and down, up and down, so I took
a marker from my bag and started drawing on the bench
instead. It wasn't one of Beth's techniques but it helped me
calm down a bit. I drew my sister's face. I gave her mean eyes
and was about to add some devil horns when Astrid noticed
what I was doing and demanded that I stop.

'No,' I said in the same voice she'd used on me.

She didn't find it funny – my impersonation or the drawing. She snatched my marker and threw it onto the road. I jumped up to get it but she held me back, hard. Harder than she had to.

'What the hell are you doing?' she said.

'Leave me alone,' I said, and tried to pull out of her grip.

'Stop being a little shit,' she hissed in my ear. 'You're going to get us all in trouble. Again.'

Everything stopped for a moment, and my eyes stung.

'Bitch,' I shouted in Astrid's face and she finally let me go.

I sat at the back of the bus, Astrid sat at the front. I knew I'd said the wrong thing but so had she, and I wasn't going to say sorry until she did. I watched the back of Astrid's head. Her shiny hair. Her stupid ribbon. Why did she still wear a ribbon? Wasn't she supposed to be an adult? I decided I'd cut all her pathetic girly ribbons into tiny pieces and throw them all over her neatly made bed. She was too old for ribbons anyway, I'd be doing her favour.

But then I saw her rest her head on the window and wipe her eyes and I knew she was crying. She always did that. Cried when it was *her* fault so it all became *my* fault. So *I* looked like the bad one. Seeing her like that twisted me up inside. How was it possible to feel sorry for her and angry at her at the same time? She was so frustrating. I closed my eyes and imagined the clouds and counted, slowly, slowly.

When I opened my eyes she had gone. She'd gotten off the bus earlier than usual so she could walk the rest of the way in the burning sun, just to make me feel even worse about everything. I imagined her that night, sunburnt and sad, telling Mum all about it. Mum would be disappointed in me. Again. I looked out the back window as the bus pulled further away. She kept her head down like all the other broken people around her. That was my fault. I'd done that to her. I pressed my head to the window and as I watched her get smaller and smaller, my chest felt tighter and tighter. I took out my phone and tried to text her: *Sorry*. But the message wouldn't send. I tried again and again and it still wouldn't go. And that's when I realised the bus had stopped, just like that, in the middle of the road.

CHAPTER 3

We all had to get off the bus. It was going no further. A line of Unit patrol cars with their lights flashing – *Stay back, stay back* – blocked the way. Officers paced in front of the cars, talking into radios and watching the growing crowd. Nobody was getting through that blockade any time soon.

Some businesspeople in expensive suits demanded to know what was taking so long because they were Very Important People with Very Important Work to do.

'What's the hold up?' shouted a guy with a leather briefcase. Other people joined in. And despite all the shouting, the Unit somehow kept their cool. I tried not to think about how different it would be if it were people on my side of the city, only a bus ride away, shouting at officers like that. The Unit had guns. You didn't shout at people with guns. I'd learned that the hard way. But I guess the hard way wasn't something these people had to deal with. They'd never been stopped by the Unit just for walking down the street. They'd never been harassed by them. Searched and questioned and terrified of accidentally saying the wrong thing.

To these people, the Unit meant protection. The Unit was there to serve them, look out for them, keep them safe. I suppose that meant they could speak to the officers however they wanted.

How long is this going to take? I have a meeting. Let us through. They sounded exactly like the kids at school: rich and self-important. I wanted to tell them to shut the hell up. The officers said nothing, just let them get louder and more annoying.

'Geez. Someone tell them to shut up already,' said someone behind me.

I smiled a bit and started to say something like, *You read my mind,* as I turned around, and it was him. The new kid. The cute one. The one who'd called my drawing *interesting* and not spoken to me since. Not a word. But now he stood right next to me and grinned like we were old friends. I couldn't finish my sentence and just stared at him like a freak.

'Santee, right?' he said.

'Yeah.'

'I'm Z,' he said, and held out his hand, which was bizarre. I mean, who actually does that? Handshakes were for politicians and important people in suits. Not me.

'Hey,' I mumbled and my face grew hot as I awkwardly shook his hand. What kind of name was *Zee?* Seriously?

'It's Zac, really,' he said. Maybe he actually could read my mind. 'I'm trying get Z to stick, you know, new school and all that ...' His voice faded away like he didn't know what to say next. Neither did I. So we just stood silently, side by side, as the crowd grew louder.

In the distance but close enough to shut everyone up, there was a burst of gunfire. Almost like fireworks. But not as fun. I wrapped my arms across my face, covered my ears. Waited for it to stop.

'You OK?' Z asked me quietly.

I dropped my arms. 'Yeah,' I said like it was no big deal. 'Are you?'

'Sure, yeah, sure, uh-huh,' he said.

He obviously wasn't but then neither was I, not really, so I didn't push it.

Everything had gone very, very quiet.

The air fizzed.

The officers told us, *Be calm, don't panic, we're dealing with a serious Threat situation.*

Drones hummed overhead and captured our faces. A record of who was there. I wondered if we'd be on the News with a scrolling caption – *Terrified Crowd.* The man with the briefcase pushed past me as he made his way towards the back of the crowd. Suddenly he wasn't so eager to get to work. Funny that. He dropped his briefcase and sat down, head in hands. He looked smaller now somehow.

They weren't used to it, the people who lived on the good side of the city. That sort of thing didn't happen over here anymore. Magnus Varick made sure of it after the attack that tore up the city years and years ago. That's when he created the Unit and the Curfew and the stop-and-searches and the cameras. All for our security. Some people used to complain about it but now everyone was grateful. That's what we were told, anyway. Even though I don't think the people on my side felt the same way. At all.

On the night of that famous attack I was at home. All of us were there. We had finished dinner and it was my turn to do the dishes. I was being a real brat about it and they left me in the kitchen and went to watch TV. I was still ranting about how unfair everything was when Dad shouted, *Santee, quick*, and I thought he was just playing a stupid joke on me to get me out of my mood. He did stuff like that sometimes. But this time, he wasn't. He wanted me to see the news. The city had been bombed. Multiple locations. Collapsed buildings and burning cars and screaming faces filled the screen. A shiver ran through me. My whole body went cold and I hid my face in Dad's chest.

'They don't need to see this, Joseph,' Mum said and she used his full name so she was serious.

Astrid and I went to bed but we didn't sleep. We whispered and cried and wondered what it meant. We could hear the hum of the TV all night. The next day, everything felt extra quiet but somehow the world got up and kept going. Over the next few months Magnus Varick made lots of speeches about our city and the state's security limitations and expectations and plans for improvement and how it wasn't good enough. People seemed to really like his speeches but they made Dad shout a lot and Mum would say, *Not here, not in front of the girls*.

My fingers shook as I texted Mum to let her know I was OK.

I knew she would be worried. I pressed send but it wouldn't go. I shoved the phone back into my bag. *Piece of crap*.

Z gave me his phone and said, 'Try mine,' and I did but all I got was that little exclamation mark telling me *Error! Error!*

'Shit,' I said.

'Network must be down,' he said.

Nah, really? I thought. But I said, 'Thanks,' and handed back his phone, which was a hell of a lot newer than mine. The screen didn't even have one crack in it.

'Sorry,' he smiled.

What was I supposed to say now? Ask about school? His favourite class? Teacher? It all sounded so dumb in my head. I looked around at the crowd. We must have stood out, me and Z, in our school uniforms. I wondered if he felt as out of place as I did, surrounded by all those suits with their takeaway coffees.

'Reckon this'll be you one day?' I said.

'What?' he said.

'You. In a suit. With your briefcase and coffee and shiny shoes.'

'Nah. No way.' He laughed. 'How about you?'

'Yeah. That suit, there, is my dream,' I said, and pointed to a woman in the brightest, shiniest pink suit I'd ever seen. It was so bad it was actually kinda good, and I laughed.

He didn't.

'That's my aunty,' he said.

My stomach dropped and I started stumbling around for the right words, but then he started laughing. Like really, really laughing, and saying stuff like, *You should see your face,* and he went on and on like he'd made the funniest joke in the world. Seeing him laugh made me laugh and we tried to

32

stop, but the more we tried the funnier everything seemed. I hadn't laughed like that in the longest time.

When we finally calmed down I heard the couple near us talking really loudly.

'I bet it's one of them, from over there, causing all this trouble. As usual,' the woman said as she sipped her coffee.

The man agreed with her and they started going on and on about how bad it was *over there*. How everyone from *over there* was a Threat. As if *over there* was a whole other planet, not a place where people lived and worked and had families and friends. People like me. I felt myself boiling up inside. Who the hell were these people with their ugly suits and loud opinions? Who did they think they were?

'What the hell's your problem?' I said.

The couple turned around.

'Excuse me?' The woman's face turned bright red. 'What did you say?'

'You're both full of shit,' I said.

'OK, OK, sorry – she doesn't mean it, she's not feeling well.' Z tried to pull me away, but I shook him off.

'I'm fine,' I snapped at Z. 'It's these two who are the arseholes.'

'Care to repeat that?' The man stood up a little straighter, his face blotchy and sweaty, and I wondered if he was going to hit me, or Z, or maybe both of us. 'Come on, tough girl, speak up.'

There was a lot more I wanted to say but right then my mind went blank. I wanted them to know how wrong they were but the right words wouldn't come, and static buzzed in my head, and all I could think of was the last time I'd tried speaking up and how it had made everything worse because I always made things worse, and Mum's voice in my head said, *Be careful, don't make a fuss,* and I clenched my fists as the static buzzed louder and louder and it felt like I was underwater. Drowning. My chest got tight like it was strangling my heart and I knew, I just knew, that I'd screwed up any chance I might have had with Z. I looked up at the sky and started to count in my head and when I got to ten I heard the man speak, and it sounded like he was underwater too. *What's wrong with her?* he said. And I let go of the sky and realised everyone had heard him and they were all staring.

At me.

'Check her backpack!' The woman's voice was shrill as it rippled through the crowd. People slowly edged away. *She's hiding something in her backpack. What's she doing? What's wrong with her?* They thought I was a Threat. I could hear it in their whispers; see it in the way they backed off. They thought I was carrying a bomb that would shatter them into tiny pieces.

'Officers!' the man shouted. 'We need some help here!'

I had to get out of there but my legs were like concrete.

And then I felt a hand on my shoulder. It was Z. He was still there, right next to me.

'I know a detour,' he said. He grabbed my hand and my body sparked. 'Let's go.' And we did. Hand in hand.

CHAPTER 4

The city was a tangled maze of roads and alleyways and I had no idea how it all fit together but Z obviously did. It didn't take long to lose the noise of the crowd. We slipped down an alleyway and I leaned against the cool bricks to catch my breath and slow my brain and get back to some version of normal. Whatever that was.

'Sorry about all that,' I said, without looking at him.

'Why are you sorry?' he said.

'Um, I think my mum would call that *causing a scene.*' I waited for him to say something, but he didn't. He stared at me with this look on his face, like he was trying to figure me out. I'd seen that look before.

A week ago we'd all been in the library when Beth came to pick me up for our chat. Usually I'd slip out and no-one would notice. But not that day. That day, Tash made a big deal about it. *Don't worry, everyone,* she said in this really exaggerated voice, *Santee's getting her meds. We're safe!* And everyone laughed. Everyone except the new kid. Z. He just sat there with that look on his face. In our session, Beth asked me to consider what I was doing to make my peers so antagonistic (her words, not mine). *There's a common denominator*, she said. There always is, right?

Now I said, all cool and casual, even though I didn't feel like that at all, 'You just gonna stare at me all day?' and tried to laugh. Z kept looking at me and my head pounded in the silence.

Finally he said, 'Those people back there, they're dick-heads. But it's not their fault, and it's definitely not your fault. It's the Unit and the whole Regime. It's their fault. You know that, right?'

'Regime?' I said softly, hardly believing the word was coming out of my mouth. Hardly believing Z had said it, just like that, as if it were nothing. I hadn't heard anyone say it since Dad had been taken away.

'That's what it is –'

'You can't say that,' I said, because it was true. No-one spoke like that about Varick and his government. It wasn't allowed. Who was this guy?

'But you know that's what it is, right? A Regime.'

'I know I should keep my big, stupid mouth shut,' I said, looking at the security camera above our heads.

Z smiled up into it. 'Ready for that detour?' he asked.

It wasn't like I was dying to get to school, but what else were we going to do – sit there all day? No thanks. So I followed him through the alleyway (which, until that moment, I never knew existed) and out onto another street.

The sound of helicopters and sirens drowned out the city's usual noises. Everything seemed slower somehow, like some kind of heavy blanket had been draped over the city. We slipped down another alleyway that looked exactly the same as the one we'd been in. I was sure we'd just done a circle.

'You sure you know the way?' I asked.

'I've got a good sense of direction,' Z said. I raised my eyebrows. 'No, I do. It's my thing.'

'Your thing?'

'Have a bit of faith, Santee,' he grinned.

'Dork,' I said, and gave him a nudge. I didn't say *cute* dork but that's what I really meant. Because he was.

Here's what I learned about Z during our detour:

One – He thought he was a lot funnier than he was and, because of that, you had to laugh. So maybe he actually was funny?

Two – He liked to talk, a lot. Mainly about absolutely nothing.

Three – He knew his way around the city.

Four – I liked being around him.

We eventually stopped in front of a wire fence.

'Here we are,' Z said.

I wondered if I'd have to re-evaluate Number Three on my things-about-Z list because at that moment he didn't seem to know his way around at all. His detour had taken us to a vacant block between some high-rise buildings. The sign on the wire fence said KEEP OUT but I didn't think anyone would want to go in there anyway. It was just a pile of weeds and rubble. Z peeled back a broken bit of fence as if he were holding a door open for me, like he was from one of those old-fashioned black-and-white movies.

'Um,' I said. 'The sign.'

He shrugged. 'You coming or what?'

'The. Sign.' I pointed at it for emphasis. But it didn't matter. He ignored me and the sign and crawled under the fence. On the other side he stood, did a stupid, elaborate bow and waited for my applause. I stared at him through the wire.

'Tough crowd,' he said.

'That is totally illegal,' I said.

'I do it all the time.' He was still grinning.

I couldn't help it: I liked his grin. I liked the way he didn't give a crap about the KEEP OUT rule, which did seem kinda pointless. I liked the fizz in my stomach at the thought of breaking the rules with Z.

'There's no cameras here,' he said.

'So, perfectly safe then?' I said.

'Maybe.'

I pulled back the wire, pushed my backpack through and crawled under the fence and into the empty block. He held out his hand and helped me back to my feet and I liked the way his hand fit into mine but I could feel my face glowing, hot hot hot, and murmured a thanks and busied myself wiping dirt from my knees, hoping he wouldn't notice.

At the far end of the block were two boring office buildings, grey and windowless. I wondered who the hell would want to work there. Not that they had a choice. Everyone had their job to do and Good Citizens did what they were told.

There was a narrow gap between the two ugly buildings and, of course, that's where Z went. We had to turn and sidestep our way through, my back up against one wall, my nose almost touching the other, and above us a slice of blue sky. It felt as if the walls were closing in on me.

'You OK?' Z whispered.

'Are you?' I said. I kept my focus on the little piece of sky. It helped.

We shuffled along like that until the space opened slightly and we could walk a little easier. Facing forwards. I kept my eyes on Z. Noticed how his dark hair was shaved at the back of his head, the way it made a V shape, the muscles in his neck.

Helicopters flew overhead. The wailing sirens grew louder as we moved through the gap. It sounded as if Z had led me right into the middle of the Threat situation we were trying to detour around. Maybe he had. I could feel the panic rising in me. Maybe Z was being a Good Citizen. Maybe all that stuff he'd said was just part of his act to get me to trust him and say things I shouldn't and now he was going to hand me in, tell them I was a Potential Threat and then go to school and be the big hero. The gap was getting wider and the exit was getting closer and the noise was getting louder and louder and I knew we'd be seen by someone soon.

Unit patrol cars shot past in a flash of blue and red.

'I thought this was supposed to be a detour?' I tried to keep my voice normal to hide my nerves.

'It was, I mean, I …' As he turned to face me his words were swallowed up by the whirring of a helicopter. Closer this time. Too close. We stared at each other in silence while we waited for it to pass. He looked as nervous as I felt.

There was something about that look that made me relax a bit despite the noise. I was being paranoid, as usual. Of course Z could be trusted. I looked at him and started to notice stuff I didn't really want to notice. Like his eyes, and the way they seemed to smile before his mouth did, and how he bit his bottom lip, and the scent of his deodorant or cologne or whatever it was guys wore. It smelled good. Had I remembered to put deodorant on that day? Suddenly I was worried that I stank of sweat.

'I'm just gonna take a look,' Z said, moving towards the exit.

He stuck his head out between the buildings and just as I was certain it was going to get blown off right in front of me, he turned back, looking pretty impressed with himself. 'It's fine,' he said. 'Come on.' And, as much as my legs didn't want to, I followed him out onto the path.

We were near Unit Headquarters. A huge, menacing building full of people who were meant to protect us. But I never felt particularly safe or protected when I had to walk past it. I'd put my head down, walk a little faster to get out of its way, as if it were some kind of sleeping dragon that might wake up and burn me alive.

Right then, Unit Headquarters wasn't sleeping. It was crawling with people and noise. I'd never seen it look like that before. Officers coming and going, patrol cars screaming up to the entrance and collecting official people in uniforms and then taking off again, helicopters and drones watching overhead.

Z and I put our heads down and walked as fast as we could.

CHAPTER 5

We stood outside the school.

'Told you I knew a detour,' Z said.

I tried to smile, tried to say something funny, but my stomach had twisted itself into knots. Even on a relatively normal day it was hard for me to walk through those doors and into that place. I had stood on that exact spot, the patch of grass between freedom and hell, and stared at the building so many times before. It was always the same – that feeling like you want to throw up and cry and run away all mixed into one huge ball of anxiety. I hated it – the feeling and the place.

'You OK?' Z said.

'Sure,' I said.

'Liar,' Z smiled. Number Five on the list of things-I-learned-about-Z was the fact that he actually noticed stuff.

It was quiet. Everyone was already in class. Our school did not tolerate tardiness (their words, not mine) and there would be Consequences. There always were. Like my weekly chats with Beth.

'Santee!' And there she was. Beth. She stood at the entrance gesturing at me to Get Inside Now.

'Beth! Imagine seeing you here,' I said, as if I was one of her friends at brunch. I imagined Beth did things like brunch.

She crossed her arms, unimpressed. Beth never laughed at my jokes. But Z did. It made me smile like an idiot and forget, just for a moment, the dread I'd been feeling.

We slowly headed towards the main doors. His hand brushed mine as we walked but I didn't look at him to see if he did it on purpose. Beth sighed and shook her head like, *What am I going to do with you.* 'My office. Now,' she said. 'And Zac – I'll catch up with you later.'

She click-clacked in her heels through the doors and we followed.

'You know Beth?' I said.

'Yeah. We chat,' he said. 'Every week.'

'Why?' I asked quietly.

'Gotta get my meds somehow, don't I?' he grinned.

Beth had tried to make her office warm and welcoming but the chairs were hard and even on a hot day the room was kinda freezing. She'd hung pictures on the walls. Landscapes of faraway places. Forests and waterfalls and beautiful sunsets. I think it was supposed to make you feel calm but it just made me worry that I would never get to see a place like that in real life. Ever.

'Want to tell me why you were so late this morning?' She sat in front of me with her notepad and pen, ready to record my answer. She wrote everything down. All the things I said, and didn't say, were recorded and filed away.

'Blockade,' I said.

Beth scribbled some notes, then stopped and stared at me. Full-on eye contact. Silence. That's what Beth did. It was her tactic: creating awkward silences so I'd talk and fill the gaps with too much information. But I was used to it by now and said nothing.

'And?' Beth finally spoke. It felt like I'd won something. Point to me. 'How did you get through it?'

'Um. The bus wouldn't go any further so we had to walk around it,' I said.

She raised a perfectly shaped eyebrow and made a note. 'And ...' she prompted. But I wasn't playing. 'Santee,' she said sweetly, 'remember what we agreed? Open communication.'

I hadn't agreed to anything. The open communication thing was just another one of Beth's theories about me. According to her, if I practised more open communication I would experience fewer outbursts. She had given me a pad of paper and a pencil and told me to write down everything I thought. Everything. *Get it out*, she kept saying, *open communication*. Instead, I drew stick figures dying elaborate deaths – jumping off a cliff to the pointy rocks below, or being eaten by a shark or flattened by a train. That kinda thing.

She didn't make me use the pad anymore. But she stuck with her theory.

'OK then,' she continued, 'tell me about Zac.'

'Z,' I corrected her.

'Yes, sorry, my mistake,' she said. 'So, you two are friends now? Yes? Santee and Z?'

I smiled in spite of myself; a tiny smile, but enough for Beth to notice and scribble something in her notepad.

Crap, I thought. Point to Beth.

The class was quiet, all heads down and writing furiously. I showed Mr Lo the blue slip that meant I was allowed to be late and there was nothing he could say. He grunted and shoved a paper into my hand. A maths test. Of course. Mr Lo was such a fan of the surprise test it became more of a surprise if we didn't have one.

I sat at the back of the class and stared at the page of numbers. Once, I would have been able to hide in the Art Room when I felt like this. Ms Francis, with her crazy big earrings, would always let me hang around. She got it. Or she used to. There were no art classes anymore. And no more Art Room, with all its colour and mess. It had been turned into just another dull classroom.

I watched the rest of the class working through the test, punching numbers into their calculators, looking as if they knew exactly what to do. I rummaged through my backpack for my things.

'Shhh,' Tash said loudly.

The irony wasn't lost on me but still I said sorry and she rolled her eyes at me.

'Sorry,' I said again.

'Santee!' Mr Lo snapped.

I put my head down and pretended to be working on a solution. The numbers and symbols danced on the page and I couldn't hold them in place long enough to figure out what to do with them, so I stopped trying and started drawing instead. My lines took shape and became Z's eyes. What the hell? What was wrong with me? I scribbled over them.

Class dragged on and on. My head ached. The pain pulsated right behind my eyes. I squeezed them shut. Maybe Mr Lo would let me get a drink. I raised my hand, but he was reading. Or asleep. I couldn't tell.

'Sir?' I said.

'Shut up,' Tash hissed.

I was about to tell her where to go when the siren started. *Lockdown. Lockdown. Lockdown.* The familiar voice of the school's automated security system started up. The sirens whirred. I winced. This was not helping my headache.

Mr Lo sighed, slowly pushed back his chair and stood. 'All right, folks,' he said. 'Let's do this.'

The lockdown drills weren't the most annoying thing about school but they were definitely in the top five. We could expect to go through the whole hide-under-your-desk bullshit at least twice a week. More if there had been a recent Threat situation.

Mr Lo locked the door, turned off the lights and shut the blinds while the rest of us struggled to get under our desks. I never fit properly – my legs stuck out at weird angles, my neck bent weirdly. It was stupid and uncomfortable. We were all way too big for this kind of thing. There was a thump. Someone said, *Shit*. Someone else giggled. It happened every time.

'Quiet,' Mr Lo shouted.

But nobody was quiet. It was like the siren flicked a switch that turned everyone into idiots.

'Maybe it's the real thing this time,' someone joked.

'Hope not,' Mr Lo said from beneath his desk. 'Cos you'd all be dead by now.' That made the class shut up. For a second. At least.

I couldn't find Z. I wasn't expecting him to be my new best friend but stupid Beth with her stupid theories had made me believe, just for a second, that I might at least have someone to hang out with during lunch. But I didn't. I gave up searching for him and headed towards the girls' bathroom. I didn't feel like drawing, not now, and thought I'd just spend lunch in a cubicle. It was pathetic but there were some days when it was easier to stay out of everyone's way.

I pushed through the students in the hallway. They hung out in their groups, talking and laughing, bitching and gossiping. Whatever. I was one of them once. It was such a long time ago that I could hardly remember that version of myself: the Santee who had friends, and never had to hide in the toilets at lunchtime.

'Santee!' Tash's voice sang out across the hall.

She was standing with her army of friends right near the bathroom. I put my head down and pretended not to notice everyone watching as I turned and headed in the opposite direction.

'Eating lunch in the toilet again, Santee?' she called out.

I ignored her and kept walking. There were other bathrooms. I didn't need Tash's bullshit. Not that day. Not any day.

'Your dad still in jail?' Tash shouted.

I froze. The hallway suddenly went very quiet.

'Leave me alone,' I said. I tried to sound calm but my voice wobbled. I had to get out of there.

'We all know your dad is a Threat,' she said. 'Or *was* a Threat. Have they killed him yet?'

The walls closed in on me. Everyone was watching, listening, waiting for me to lose my shit. I turned to face her. Tash crossed her arms and stood there smirking, daring me to do something I'd regret. I clenched my fists. My blood boiled and bubbled and my head pounded.

'You can't be too careful with Threats,' Tash said. 'Better safe than sorry.'

I punched the closest locker. Bang. Someone cheered. *Wooohoo.* I'd given them what they'd wanted. Tash's friends fussed around her as if she was the victim.

'Santee,' she said like she was speaking to a two-year-old. 'Calm down.'

My fingernails cut into the palms of my hands. I took a deep breath in through the nose and out through the mouth, like Beth had taught me. I tried to imagine white clouds and a blue sky but it was hard to get my thoughts together under the flickering fluorescent lights. All I could think was how much I wanted to hurt her. I wanted to punch her and keep on punching and never stop.

'She's probably a Threat, too,' Tash told the crowd. 'Like father, like daughter, you know?'

I took a step towards her.

The hallway got smaller.

The crowd got louder.

They yelled and cheered. I couldn't hear what they were saying; it was just noise, like a huge waterfall rushing through my brain. My jaw tightened. My whole body tensed up. Everything fizzed like static. I took another step.

And then he was there. Just like that, standing in front of me, holding out a sandwich. 'Wanna go halves in this?' Z said as if there was no-one else around.

What the hell was with this guy? I gestured at what was happening, at what he'd walked into.

'Hey, Riley,' he said, and waved to someone across the hall. The guy waved back awkwardly. 'So,' he said, returning to me, 'sandwich?'

I looked around. Suddenly no-one was watching me or laughing or cheering on my craziness. They had all gone back to their own groups and conversations. Tash's friends had crowded around her as if they were protecting her. They were all hugging and whispering and shooting me worried glances. But that was it. It was like Z had magically diffused the whole situation with his stupid sandwich. Just like that. The static lifted and I came back to earth.

My hand was bleeding. Just a little. I'd taken some skin off the knuckles with my locker punch. Idiot. I shoved my hands into my pockets and hoped Z hadn't noticed.

'Be careful, Z,' Tash said in her singsong voice as she and her friends walked past us. 'She is so weird.'

'I like weird,' Z said, and shrugged.

I didn't know if that was a compliment but it made me smile. I smiled even more when I noticed a red blush start to creep up Tash's neck.

'Tash?' I said in the same singsong voice she'd used on me.

She stopped. Her friends stared me down. But Tash wouldn't look at me. She kept her eyes down, and I could see that her face had turned bright red, like her neck. I knew it made her self-conscious. Once, we would have laughed about it and all of us would have tried to turn her extra-red.

They'd been my friends once, too. Even when the Unit had arrived on our streets and Curfew had been put in place, everything else stayed pretty much the same. We still had birthday parties and hung out after school and had sleepovers. Until things started to change. My friends started saying, *No, sorry, we're not allowed, we can't come to your place. It's dangerous*, Tash had said. And I didn't understand. Cos my place was just where I lived. It was my home. Even if it was the place where they'd found the Threats. Even if it was the wrong side.

Tash had been the last of my friends to stop visiting.

All the mean, smart-arse comments I'd been preparing vanished. I took a deep breath.

'My dad – my parents, Astrid, me – all of us. We really liked you,' I said. 'You were like part of the family.'

Something crossed Tash's face. An expression I couldn't quite place. Before I had a chance to work it out she had turned and stormed out of the hallway, followed closely by her friends.

I'd finally said something.

CHAPTER 6

We sat at the edge of the school oval. The younger kids were running around and attacking each other with sticks. Some of the bigger guys were trying to play a serious game of soccer and yelled at them to piss off. I picked the crust off the sandwich and rolled it into tiny crumbs.

'You OK?' Z said.

'Yeah,' I lied and took a bite of the sandwich as if to prove it. But my eyes filled up with tears. I blinked them away. It was always like that. I could hold all that stuff inside until someone was nice to me, and then it would all spill out. Anyway, that was something else I learned about Z: Number Six – he was generous.

And it was because he was kind and generous, and I was all emotional, that I told him about my dad. I never talked to anyone about Dad.

I told him there had been four of us: me, Astrid, Mum

and Dad. I told him how Mum and Dad had been artists. That Mum would come home with paint under her nails and in her flyaway hair and how finding it there made her laugh. I told him how Dad would always stay up late, hunched over his glowing computer screen, and I'd always try to stay up as late as him but I never could. In the morning, Dad would drink black coffee and I'd always want some and he'd say, *Just a sip*, and I hated it but pretended to love it because he did. Then one night, real late, the door crashed open and the Unit stormed in and Mum screamed this scream that didn't sound like her at all and Dad kept saying, *It'll be all right, it'll be all right*, over and over and there was yelling and pushing and they grabbed Dad and dragged him away and I wanted to run after him but Astrid held my hand really, really tightly and then they were gone and it was quiet.

Empty.

Dad never came back and Mum never talked about it.

That was it.

'And Tash?' Z said.

'She used to be my friend, but after that, yeah ...' I shrugged like it was no big deal even though it was. She'd probably been my best friend (if you believe in that stuff) and then, just like that, she wasn't.

Z pulled up bits of grass and tore them into tiny pieces. 'That's shit,' he said.

'Who needs friends?' I tried to joke. 'Gives me more time for my *interesting* drawings.'

He laughed loudly, like he didn't care who heard him or what they thought. I liked that. 'Hang on,' he said and went through his bag as if he had suddenly remembered something. He pulled out a sketchpad and, without a word, handed it to me. I flipped through the pages. They were filled with drawings. Careful, delicate pencil work that seemed to zoom right in on people; a hand with bitten-down nails, the creases in an old man's forehead, the wrinkled toes of a baby. He was good. Really good. I looked back at him but his head was down, concentrating on ripping up the grass.

'Wow,' I said.

'I'm working on it,' he said, and showed me a page where he thought he'd messed something up and another where the proportions were, in his opinion, all wrong, even though it looked perfect to me. 'There's this spot I like to draw and I thought maybe you'd like, I dunno, go with me today? After school? Hang out?' he said.

I could feel the heat rise up in me and hoped I wouldn't turn red like Tash. 'Sure,' I said, like it wasn't a big deal. Except it was. For me.

I hadn't forgotten I was grounded but I tried to work around it; I told myself Mum would understand, that she'd be happy to know I had a friend. I mean, in our chat Beth had even said this was a *good development* and *friendship enhances emotional wellbeing* and surely Mum wouldn't argue with that? But still, I planned to get home way before her shift ended. Then she would never have to know. That seemed to be the best solution. Because I really wanted to go. I liked him, and I'd never liked anyone before. Not that way. So I made myself believe it would be OK.

Z was standing out the front of the school. I watched him as I headed out the main doors. Everyone was stopping and talking to him as they left for the day. He was all, *See ya tomorrow buddy,* and, *Have a good one,* and laughing and joking around. Z, the new kid, had way more friends than I'd ever had and I'd been at that school since forever. He was just better at that stuff than me, I suppose. Plus, it probably helped that rumours of being a Threat weren't constantly swirling around him.

'Hey!' he broke into a smile when he saw me, and his smile made me smile, and I couldn't get that smile off my face.

We started walking. The blockade had cleared and things seemed to be back to normal.

'So, where are we going?' I said.

'Just gonna pick up my car and then we'll head to the spot,' he said.

His car? That guilty feeling lurched in my stomach. I tried to ignore it and smiled at Z and said *cool* or something pathetic like that. But it wasn't cool. I really wanted to go, but I was freaking out. If Mum ever found out I'd been in a *car* with a *boy* who may or may not actually have a licence … I tried to push her disappointed face out of my mind. Mum would never need to know about the car, I told myself. It would be fine.

Z chatted easily about nothing as we walked through the city. Past the stores and office blocks, past the billboards of Our Leader, Magnus Varick, with his charming smile, past the big screens that played an endless cycle of breaking news. *Network still down!* was the latest message scrolling across the screens.

We crossed the cool, calm park that bordered the city. On

the good side. Of course. The park felt out of place, sitting there among the shiny city buildings. It was all lush green and trees and fountains. Dad and I had run up and down the wide, open space when I was a kid, desperately trying to fly this kite I'd been given for my birthday. We never managed to make it fly.

'That's home,' Z said, pointing to a nice apartment block that looked out onto the park. It was one of those old-fashioned blocks, painted yellow with shutters on the windows and little balconies covered with brightly coloured pot plants. It had a garden out front and a big old tree and it looked warm and inviting and I wished I lived in a place like that. 'And there's Red.' He pointed again, this time to a beaten-up car parked on the side of the road. It definitely looked like Red had seen better days.

He unlocked the passenger door, jumped in and slid across to the driver's seat. He gestured for me to follow. I ignored Mum's voice echoing somewhere in the back of my mind – *you're grounded* – and got in the car. I wanted to go with him. And I never got to do what I wanted. There were so many rules; I just wanted to break one. Or two.

'So, you're allowed to just go for a drive, whenever you want?' I said.

'Not technically,' he said.

I felt a surge of something run through me, like a fizz of electricity. He grinned as he started the car, and the feeling got stronger.

CHAPTER 7

The passenger window wouldn't open and the radio didn't
work and my seat slid backwards every time he hit the brakes
but, according to Z, that was all part of Red's charm. I was
nervous. Not just because I thought the entire car was going
to fall to pieces as we drove. But also because we were alone.
It was just me and him.

'I know what you're thinking,' he said. I really hoped he
didn't. 'You think Red is a shitty name for a car.'

Red was a shitty *car* full stop, but I didn't tell him that. I
laughed, relieved, and said, 'Nah, it's just an obvious name.
I mean, Red? Really? Why not Dorothy, or Dolores or
something?'

'Those are good names,' he said.

'I know,' I said. 'I'm good at naming things. Like, um,
see that dog?'

It was a border collie or something, bounding along next to its human, excited to get into the park.

'Robert,' I said.

'Robert?' he said. 'Really?'

'What? It's a good name for a dog.'

Number Seven on my list of things about Z – he laughed really easily. It didn't take much to make him laugh, loudly and like he meant it, as if you were hilarious when really you were probably just a bit weird. But he never made me feel like he was laughing at me, and that was a nice feeling.

'My sister picked the name. And cos she's the boss of everything, I went with it. Like always.'

'Sounds like my sister,' I said. Thinking about Astrid brought back that guilty feeling and I checked my phone for the thousandth time that day in case the network had suddenly come back to life. It hadn't, and so my apology sat in my phone, unsent and unread.

Z drove very carefully. He slowed down when the signs told him to and kept two hands on the wheel and his eyes constantly flicked from road to mirror to side mirror and back again. I wanted to remember all those details so I could tell Mum how responsible he was if it ever came up.

I watched as the city became the suburbs, which then gave way to warehouses and factories and paddocks of yellowing grass dotted with sheep and cows. There was more room out here. The roads were wider and the sky seemed bigger. The sun flickered through the trees and made everything look like it was in strobe light. I closed my eyes and concentrated on breathing and tried not to think about the nauseous feeling that was coming over me in waves.

'Hang on,' Z said. 'We're almost there.'

Of course Z had noticed I was about to be carsick. He noticed everything.

I felt the car slow down to a stop and stumbled out of it as quickly as I could. My skin was clammy and my lips tingled and I didn't know what to do with myself. I crouched in the dirt and put my head in my hands and repeated, *Do not throw up,* over and over again in my head like some kind of mantra until I felt Z's hand on my back. The thought of throwing up in front of someone I actually liked, someone who might actually like me, was more than embarrassing. What a way to kill the moment before the moment had even happened.

'Santee,' he said quietly.

I looked up. He handed me a water bottle. I tried to smile a thank you but I felt sweaty and cold and hot all at the same time and I just wanted him to leave me alone for a moment. He must have got the message because he disappeared and I took a sip from the bottle and splashed some water on my face and took deep breaths of the hot, eucalyptus-scented air. Eventually the feeling started to fade and I could actually take in the surroundings. I knew the place. We were in the National Park, where people had hiked and climbed and biked and made out and camped and wandered until it was considered unsafe for reasons unknown, fenced off and forgotten. I'd been there when I was seven or eight for a class excursion. We sat in the dirt and sketched purple wildflowers and magpies and collected gumnuts and leaves that had fallen from the trees. That was a long time ago, though. Everything had changed since then. Except, it seemed, that spot.

Z had parked right at the edge of the lookout – a small clearing off the dirt track that wound up through the bush. From there you could look out over a valley of trees. The only thing between us and the drop below were a couple of big rocks and fallen tree trunks. I hoped the handbrake was one of the things that actually worked in Red. Z sat on the bonnet, pretending he hadn't been watching me trying not to be carsick. I joined him.

'Sorry about that,' I said. I was dying inside, but at least the moment had passed.

'When I was a kid I threw up all over Mum's laptop,' he said.

'No, you didn't,' I said.

'We were on this long road trip and I told her to pull over, but she thought I was joking so she didn't and then, bam, out it came. It was pretty impressive. All over the back seat. And her laptop was next to me so, yeah, I killed it. With my vomit.'

I didn't know if his story was true but it made me laugh. And that made me feel better.

We sat on the rocks at the edge of the drop, our sketchpads on our knees, pencils ready. But we were too busy talking to actually draw. Z stretched out, using his backpack as a pillow, and stared up at the sky as he spoke about moving from his old school – cos it was a bit shit (his words, not mine) – and the movies he liked and the comedians he admired and the books he'd read. He looked so relaxed and conversation seemed so easy for him. Of course it did. I mean, he was Z. He was always smiling and people liked him and that made me wonder why, exactly, he'd wanted to hang out with me at all. I started to panic; perhaps he brought a lot of girls to this spot. Maybe it was just a line. Maybe this whole thing was some kind of joke. I was such an idiot. Of course I shouldn't have agreed to go with him; he was basically a stranger. A good-looking, popular, funny stranger who probably had a list of girls he'd brought here, and here I was, just another name he could tick off. Someone he'd laugh over with that Riley guy and his friends the next day.

'Look at that.' He sat up quickly and pointed to the sky. There was a hawk, hovering, circling in on its prey. He took his sketchpad and pencil and started scribbling. And he was so excited about a bird that all of my worries vanished to nothing. He was a dork. A cute dork who liked to draw and, maybe, just maybe, liked me. 'You gonna draw or what?' he said.

And I did.

I stared at this big, old tree, trying to find a place to start. Her trunk was bruised and scarred and home to thousands of ants. I squinted up into her branches and watched as the light crisscrossed through, changing the colour of the leaves as it did. I only had a pencil but even if I'd had all the colours in the world I wouldn't have been able to capture that light. I never could. I took a photo of the tree with my phone so I didn't forget. I also snuck a photo of Z as he sketched, bent over his pad, biting his lip, concentrating. He was so into drawing he didn't even notice me do it. I wished I could be that focused but my mind kept wandering and my hands kept shaking and, in the end, I gave up trying to draw and lay back on the rock, using my backpack as a pillow the way Z had. I'd almost forgotten what quiet sounded like. There were no sirens or helicopters, just birds singing to each other and the hot breeze pushing through the trees. The warmth of the rock radiated across my back and the sketchpad slipped from my hands.

'Shit.' I woke with a start. I was sure I'd only closed my eyes for a second. I sat up quickly.

'Welcome back, sleepyhead,' Z said.

I felt my face grow hot. I hoped I hadn't been snoring, or drooling in my sleep. I pretended to search through my bag for something and wished I could climb inside it.

Z sat down beside me. 'Show me what you drew.'

'Um, no,' I said, and shoved my battered sketchpad into my bag. I really needed a new one. I was running out of pages and the cover was falling off, but they were expensive and not really a priority when there were nights we had to eat porridge for dinner or nothing. 'Yeah, I was doing more napping than drawing,' I said.

'Sleeping Beauty,' he said.

'Shut up,' I laughed and shoved him, gently. The way Z looked at me made my heart thump and as he moved in closer I wondered if this was the moment he would kiss me or I would kiss him, and I wasn't sure how it worked or if my breath smelled OK or what I was supposed to do with my hands. It was like something just sort of took over and I moved towards him and felt my eyes close.

'Here,' he said, and handed me his sketchpad. 'Swap.'

'Yeah, OK, sure,' I said quickly, hoping he hadn't noticed that I'd almost kissed him. Idiot. I gave him my sketchpad thinking it might distract him from my bright red face and wobbly voice. Idiot, idiot, idiot.

He opened the book gently and really looked at each sketch before he turned the page, and there was something about the way he did that that made me feel special. I loved drawing but I never thought I was all that good at it. Not like my parents. Not like Z. So I just did it for myself. Beth said it was a way to channel my energy (her words, not mine) and maybe she was right. But Z's sketches were next level – there was the hawk and the detail of a dried-up leaf and it all looked so realistic. I wondered if he felt sorry for me, now that he was really studying my attempts at drawing. I looked up and locked eyes with him. He'd been watching me and he had this expression on his face that I couldn't quite work out.

'What?' I said. 'What?'

He didn't say anything for a while.

'You're an artist,' he finally said. I expected him to start laughing, like it was some kind of joke. But he didn't. He meant it.

'Nah,' I said, and avoided his gaze.

'You are.'

I shook my head. 'No,' I said, 'I'm really not.'

I grabbed the book out of his hands, stuffed it into my backpack and stood up. 'We should get out of here,' I said.

I wasn't an artist. No-one was. Not anymore. It wasn't something the State liked all that much, so they took it away. I mean, we still had *art*, of course. There was a big gallery near the university. It was full of old paintings trapped inside ornate golden frames, landscapes and still lifes and scenes of men returning from war, and statues of naked bodies carved out of marble and stuff like that. I used to wander around that gallery and think that maybe those artists were trying to tell me something, you know? Like maybe there were hidden messages in the way they chose to position that particular orange in that particular fruit bowl on that particular table. I mean, did the white tablecloth in the still life mean something? Or was it just supposed to look pretty?

'Yeah,' said Z after I'd explained my theory to him. 'It all means something.'

'I dunno,' I said. We sat in the car, ready but also not ready to head home. 'I mean, the stuff is amazing, right? Like, totally realistic. But I don't think it means anything. I think they prefer it that way.'

'Who?' Z said as he started the car.

I shrugged. I wasn't meant to say stuff like that. Anything negative anyone said about the government, no matter how small, could be twisted into something massive and suddenly you were a Potential Threat even though you'd only complained about the crappy art gallery. I trusted Z, despite only spending a few hours with him, but Mum's constant worrying had made me paranoid about that sort of thing.

The sun had moved and the birds had changed their song and I was freaking out about getting home. I had definitely left it much later than I had planned. Z was reversing the car out when suddenly, just like that, it stopped. Dead. Nothing. He pulled on the handbrake.

'What the hell?' I said, or maybe I shouted. Just a little.

He shook his head and muttered something like, *This happens all the time*, but he wasn't smiling or laughing when he said it. He tried to restart the car but Red wouldn't budge. She just made this awful whirring noise, over and over. We sat there, silent. This. Was. Not. Happening.

CHAPTER 8

We weren't going anywhere. Red had given up on life. We looked under the bonnet for some kinda clue but we were both useless when it came to cars. He slammed the bonnet shut, apologised, kicked Red's front tyre, apologised again (to me or Red or perhaps both of us) and then stood on the rock and swore into the sky (and Beth told me *I* had impulse control issues?). Seeing Z's breakdown actually helped me keep it together. A little. And I wondered if this was how Astrid felt with me being the way I was all the time.

'We could walk?' I said. 'If we start now we might make it before Curfew.'

'No way,' Z said. 'It'll take hours.'

'We should try. Maybe we can hitch a ride? Someone might take pity on us.'

'Or the Unit might pick us up,' he said.

He was right. It wasn't worth the risk. We'd have to stay.

Z said something but I wasn't listening, I was freaking out inside and I didn't want him to notice just how scared I was. I moved away from him, leaned against the gum tree and watched the breeze move through her branches. It looked as if she were nodding at me. *Yes*, I imagined her saying, *you are an idiot, Santee. A big, stupid idiot.*

'I'm so sorry,' Z whispered beside me.

I reached out and squeezed his shoulder. 'Not your fault,' I said, cos that's exactly what Z would have said to me, had it been the other way around.

Every ten minutes or so Z tried the engine, just in case. Not that we could have gone anywhere even if Red had miraculously sprung back to life – Curfew had definitely started. As often as Z checked the car for signs of life, I checked my phone. There was still no network but I wrote out long, apologetic messages anyway. I imagined Mum and Astrid pacing the floor, panicked and stressed, and it made me feel sick. I closed my eyes and counted one to ten, slowly, slowly.

When he was sure, really-really sure, that Red was actually dead, we got out and sat on the bonnet (it was all she was good for now) and watched the sky turn dark and fill up with stars. In different circumstances it would have been nice, maybe even romantic. I didn't think I was into romantic stuff until I sat there with Z. Having him close made it a little easier to push Mum and Astrid from my mind. It was probably terrible to do that, to stop thinking about them, but there was nothing I could do except chill and wait.

I put my hand near Z's. Or maybe he put his hand near mine.

'My mum's gone,' Z said suddenly. I didn't know why he'd said it and I made a stupid *oh* noise cos I didn't know how I was supposed to respond. I was no good at that stuff. I looked at him but he was focused on the stars. He cleared his throat. 'Sorry,' he said, 'you don't need to hear this.'

'Yeah I do,' I said. 'Tell me.'

And he did.

'Mum was a journo and she was always getting into trouble with the government, you know? Varick hated her,' he started.

'Magnus Varick? Our Leader, Magnus Varick?' I interrupted.

'Yeah, him,' he said.

I raised an eyebrow without meaning to.

'Not him personally but him, his people, you know what I mean.'

'Sorry,' I said.

'We'd get weird phone calls in the middle of the night. A couple of times someone threw bricks through our windows. And they slashed Mum's tyres. That kind of thing.' He said it so matter-of-factly, like this sort of stuff happened to everyone. 'She wrote articles that made people ask questions, and they hated her for it.'

'What sort of questions?' I said.

'Like, OK, she wrote this thing asking why the elections were stopped and how does stopping elections actually keep anyone safe. How is that in anyone's best interest?'

'That's quite a question,' I said carefully. 'What's the answer?'

'That Varick is a corrupt arsehole.'

I didn't know what to say to that. I mean, it's not as if I hadn't heard it before, especially from my dad, but to hear Z say it so casually, like it was no big deal, was something else.

'They called her a Potential Threat cos of that article but she didn't care. She always said that the angrier they got, the closer she was to the truth. She was real tough.' He smiled a little. 'Varick's reported as calling her a pain in the arse.'

'Really?' I said.

'Yeah. She was fierce.'

I liked that. That word. For his mum.

'Anyway,' he continued, 'they closed the newspapers down. You remember when they did that?'

I nodded. I remembered. I also remembered not thinking much about it, not back then. Nobody did.

'Mum kept writing, even without the newspaper, but then they started blocking websites and shutting it all down and so ...' his voice faded away to nothing. He rubbed his hands over his face. For a moment everything was still. All I could hear was the humming of the insects.

When he finally spoke, his voice was clear. 'There was a car accident and they told us she died. But I think they took her. Like they took your dad.'

'I'm so sorry, Z,' I said.

We sat there, not saying anything, and it felt completely OK – that silence with him. His fingers brushed the side of my hand and it sent shivers up my arm and through my body and my heart thumped so loudly I was sure he would hear it. I turned to look at him at the same time he turned to look at me and he smiled that smile that made me feel like I was melting and I tried to smile back but my lips were trembling and then I was moving closer to him as he moved closer to me and my body sparked and my eyes closed and his lips found mine and we kissed, softly and deeply, and I never wanted it to end.

CHAPTER 9

The cold and mosquitoes meant we slept inside the car. Or tried to. We talked and laughed and kissed some more because it was difficult not to, now that we'd started. If I was about to be grounded forever, I had to make the most of this night. I might never see Z, or anyone, ever again. Mum would make sure of it. But right then I didn't care cos there was this new feeling bubbling inside me and it made it easy to smile and feel like, maybe, everything would work out.

Z fell asleep before me and I stared out the windscreen, into the black nothingness of the bush, and replayed the stuff he'd said about his mum. She sounded amazing. Of course she did. I did the same thing when I talked about my dad. My memories of him were like those perfect paintings in the gallery, framed in gold.

I looked over at Z, quietly snoring beside me. I wanted to gently wake him and say *I found you* because that's how it felt. Like this was something that was meant to be. Me and Z. But I let him sleep and wrote another long, apologetic message to Mum instead. It wouldn't send.

It was still dark when our alarms went off. My neck ached from the weird angle I'd slept on and I knew I had morning breath. My mouth was dry and I needed water but we'd run out. I slipped out of the car before Z and stretched and sighed loudly and tried to wake up. I wasn't sure what to say to Z. The night before had been so easy and it had all just sort of happened, but now everything felt a bit awkward. Maybe he'd only kissed me cos he felt sorry for me or something. What if he hadn't even liked kissing me? I didn't really know what I was doing and maybe I was terrible at it. I knew I was overthinking things. But I couldn't help it. All that stuff I'd felt the night before was quickly being replaced by panic.

'Good morning,' Z said.

'Hey,' I muttered, covering my mouth in case he could smell my breath and be even more grossed out by me than he probably already was. I didn't know what I was supposed to do. Act like nothing had happened, or say something? But what would I say? *How about those kisses?* My mind was racing when, out of nowhere, Z pulled me into a tight hug.

I hugged him back and I wanted to stay like that, and not face the real world, forever. Well, with a proper bathroom and toothpaste and water and food and stuff but still, just me and Z and nothing to worry about. He kissed the top of my head and those little sparks started fizzing inside me all over again.

'Is this weird?' he said as he took my hand. We started walking down the steep track towards the road.

'Not yet,' I said, and laughed, and he laughed, and I tried to stop worrying and overthinking and just breathe.

Our plan was to find a ride as soon as possible and, preferably, before the Unit found us. The Unit would have a lot of questions about two kids, in school uniform, walking the streets at four-thirty in the morning. The thought of facing angry parents *and* the Unit was too much – Mum and Astrid were going to be enough for me to deal with as it was. According to Z the walk to the city would take about six hours and from there I'd catch the bus home – so I wouldn't get to Mum until about eleven, which was crazy. We had to take the first ride we could. No question.

'We could run, that'd take some time off,' I said, and started jogging to warm up.

'Nah,' Z said.

'Just till we find a ride,' I said, and took off, slowly, waiting for him to catch up.

'I'm useless at running,' Z shouted behind me.

And he wasn't exaggerating. He actually was useless. And it was hilarious. He kinda shuffled his feet and swung his arms around madly. I doubled over laughing. Z finally caught up and started laughing too and we just stood there on the side of the road, laughing our heads off until we could start walking again.

We were lucky cos it didn't take too long for someone to take pity on us and pull over. A small delivery truck with a cartoon cow painted on its door. I thought we could trust a cartoon cow. No serial killer would drive something that looked so cute. Would they? The driver leaned across to the open passenger window.

'You right?' she yelled over the idling engine.

Z and I looked at each other. He shrugged. I nodded. She sounded like a nice enough, normal enough person. We climbed in.

We didn't talk much, which was fine with me. Z, being Z, attempted small talk and asked the driver all these questions about milk and yoghurt and cheese. She mumbled one-word responses – *Yeah, nah, dunno, maybe*. In the end Z gave up and we bumped along in silence. I don't know who was more relieved, her or me.

But then she suddenly pulled onto the side of the road, muttering to herself. I looked at Z. He shrugged, raised an eyebrow and didn't seem concerned at all. I, on the other hand, thought we were about to be murdered. Thought the whole delivery driver thing was an act, and that she probably had a truckload of bodies in the back, all of them lured in by the cute cartoon cow …

'Check this out,' she said as she got out of the truck.

'What the hell is going on?' I whispered to Z.

'Come on,' he said, and undid his seatbelt.

I shook my head. No way.

'Hurry,' she shouted from the roadside.

'It'll be fine, I promise,' Z said. 'Come on.'

I followed him out of the truck, still convinced something bad was going to happen.

And I was right.

Armoured vehicles and tanks rumbled down the road, one after the other after the other. They cast a shadow over us, shook the earth under our feet, made me feel so small and insignificant. And scared. What the hell was happening? Even when the riots happened there had not been that many tanks. The three of us just stood there, numb and speechless as the convoy passed by. Z reached for my hand and squeezed it tight.

CHAPTER 10

We stood on the side of the road long after the monsters had disappeared from view. The sky had finally woken up and was full of reds and purples. *Red sky in the morning, shepherd's warning.* My grandma used to say that. It never made sense to me until then.

The driver went back to her truck. We could hear her on the radio. *Come in Ron,* she kept repeating, *do you read me?* But Ron didn't answer. All she got was static.

We drove on in silence. I kept hold of Z's hand, or maybe he kept hold of mine.

'Reckon all that's for a drill or something,' the driver suddenly blurted out. It was the most we'd heard her talk. We nodded in agreement – it was a logical, perfectly reasonable explanation. Of course that's what it was. A drill. The government showing off. Reminding us how tough they

73

were. But as much as my brain wanted to believe it, my gut kept twisting and nagging at me. Something was off.

She dropped us off near the sparkling shopping mall that Mum and Astrid and I never went to cos who could actually afford any of that stuff? Not us. From there I'd be able to find my way to the bus stop and get the number twelve and I'd be in a heap of shit but at least I'd be home.

I stood with Z, trying to find the right thing to say to him. *Thanks for last night? Good luck with your dad? You're a great kisser and I'd like to keep doing that with you.* It all sounded lame in my head, so I said nothing, just waited for him to break the awkwardness the way he always seemed to. Except this time, he didn't. He kept his eyes down, studying his shoes. I wondered if I should just go. Walk away. Maybe all that had happened between us didn't mean he actually liked me. Maybe I'd got carried away with that feeling of something almost like freedom. Maybe it was all a huge mistake and he just wanted to be friends and I'd stuffed it all up. Taken it too far. Like I always did. I didn't know who I was angrier with – me or him. *Screw it*, I thought, *you can't kiss someone and then let them walk away, right?*

'You just gonna stand there?' I said.

He looked at me.

'You can't just go all quiet on me,' I said. 'You can't ignore me. It's not fair. Not after everything –'

I stopped myself. I could feel the heat rising in me and knew I had to calm down. It didn't matter. He was just a boy. Why the hell did I care so much?

'I'm going to come with you,' he said.

'What?'

'It's my fault, Santee, and I should be the one to explain it to your mum.'

'No way,' I said, but I couldn't help smiling because – Number Eight on my Z list – he was truly a nice guy. Which probably sounds clichéd but it's the truth. He was actually really, really nice and it was kinda sweet that he thought he could explain anything to my mum. Mum wouldn't listen, she'd be too busy being disappointed and then killing us. Both of us.

We started walking towards my bus stop.

'Maybe I can offset some of the damage?' he said. 'I'll charm her. I can be charming, you know.'

'You? Charming? Really?' I laughed.

He pretended I'd stabbed him the heart. We were joking and laughing and being idiots and then …

Everything changed.

There in front of us was a wall.

A wall.

We stopped.

We could go no further.

It didn't make sense.

I could see it, I knew it was there, but I didn't *believe* it was there. It was like my brain was having trouble keeping up with my eyes. Or something. This was not right. This was not happening. Everywhere I'd ever been, everything I'd ever known, everyone – it was all about to change. Nothing was ever going to be the same again.

They'd split my world in two.

PART TWO

CHAPTER 11

Tall, solid concrete blocks made a wall that cut the road right down the middle. Barbed wire was sprawled across the top of it like evil icing. We followed the wall further along the road, looking for some sort of opening. I couldn't breathe properly. My heart hammered, fast, fast, fast, in my chest. There had to be a way through. There was life over there, on the other side.

My life.

I started to run the length of the wall. I could hear Z struggling to keep up but I had to keep going. I had to get to the end of this nightmare.

The roads were eerily empty. Up ahead, traffic lights flashed amber. Anyone who drove through them would have a head-on collision with the wall. Maybe that wouldn't be such a bad thing. Maybe a car or a truck or a bus could smash through the concrete and break through to the other side. If

I'd had a car I'd have tried it. At that moment I would have done just about anything to get home.

The wall followed the road and then made a sharp turn, cutting off another section of the city. And then: there, up ahead. A gap. No wall. Not yet. Cranes were moving massive chunks of concrete into place and people in fluoro vests and hard hats shouted to each other over the noise. Barriers with flashing signs that said WRONG WAY GO BACK and a heap of barbed wire blocked the way, as did the Unit Officers who stood nearby, but still, there was no wall there.

That was my way through. It had to be. I could jump the barbed wire, outrun the Unit and sprint all the way home. Me and Mum and Astrid would cry and hug and kiss each other and they'd say, *Never do that again*, and I'd be grounded for the rest of my life, but I'd deal with it. And I'd never do anything to hurt them again. Ever.

My chance to get home was right there. I tried to ignore the barbed wire's sharp, shining teeth as I sprinted closer.

'No.' A woman in a fluoro vest and hard hat approached me from the other side of the barbed wire. She had one of those handheld screen things and a walkie-talkie that hummed with voices I couldn't quite understand.

'I've got to get through,' I said. 'Please.'

'No,' she said again. Behind her were the armed Unit Officers, and beyond them, more concrete slabs were going up. Were they closing me in or out?

'What's going on?' I said, my voice wavering.

'Get out of here,' she said, and turned away as if that was it. End of conversation.

'Hey!' I shouted after her, but she kept walking.

'What did she say?' Z finally caught up and stood by my side, out of breath.

'Nothing,' I said. Everything was twirling around inside me and I didn't know if I wanted to cry or scream or run or fall to the ground and sleep for a million years.

'Hey!' Z shouted at the woman. 'Hey! Come back!'

She ignored us and started what looked like a Very Important Conversation with the Unit Officers. One of the officers looked over her shoulder, right at us. It was like he was trying to stare us down or read our minds or memorise our faces so he could add us to the Potential Threat list or something.

'Excuse me,' Z waved to the officer.

The officer's gun glinted.

Z waved again. 'Can you help us?'

What the hell? I pulled his arm down. 'Let's go,' I said.

'You sure?'

I didn't think there was a choice. The way the officer watched us, the way the woman with the hardhat dismissed us, the barbed wire, all of it made it pretty clear we were definitely not meant to be there.

'There'll be another gap, further down,' I said, and turned to go.

But suddenly we weren't alone. Just as we started to move away we saw them, coming in from all directions. People. They looked like a crowd of zombies, all shuffling together, some pointing at the wall, some half asleep, confused. My heart thumped, thumped, thumped. I looked at Z, his eyes wide and unblinking as the crowd started yelling and then, suddenly, they were running towards us. A stampede rushing to the barbed wire. We were swept up in the sea of bodies, and tried desperately to keep hold of each other and not drown as we all crashed up against the barrier.

A woman slipped. I heard her scream as she struggled to pull herself out of the barbed wire's razor teeth. She thrashed and kicked and screamed but no matter what she did, she couldn't get free. Someone reached for her arms and tried to pull her up but she yelled out, *Stop, stop, stop.* The Unit just watched and waited. For what, I didn't know, and I didn't want to find out. I had to get the hell out of there. There were too many people. Too much noise and heat and blood boiling. I grabbed Z's hand and started to weave past people, away from the wall.

'Wait,' Z said. He pulled me back, pointed to the other side of the barrier.

'Mum?' I whispered.

It wasn't Mum, but she might have been there, somewhere, in the crowd that had gathered on the opposite side. We pushed closer to get a better look and I searched for a familiar face or shape or voice. Everyone began shouting out to the other side. They screamed, *I'm here, I'm here.* And I found myself screaming too, *Astrid* and *Mum,* and, *Santee, I'm here, tell them Santee is here.* I wanted someone, anyone, to know who I was and where I was and maybe, somehow, get a message to my family. But all the voices mashed together and I couldn't hear any words coming back from the other side. I couldn't hear my name or Mum's voice or anything. It was all just a mangled mess of desperate cries and my throat felt full of razor blades from all the yelling and it was no good, no good and I pressed my hands to my eyes to try to stop myself from crying.

A woman pushed past me carrying a bundle and, as she approached the barrier, I realised it was a baby and she was attempting to pass it over the barbed wire to the other side. The Unit was gesturing *no, stop, no* and the baby was wailing but still she kept trying to get it over. And then I heard a man say, *Go, go, go,* and a group of people cleared a path through the crowd and tried to get a run-up in order to jump the fence and one got caught in the barbed wire and it must have hurt because over all that noise I could hear his noise the loudest. And another made it and was madly unravelling his clothes and his skin from the barbed wire and there was a lot of blood. I thought maybe I could get across, too. I knew I could run faster, get a better run-up than he had, jump further. I had to try. I had to.

'Don't do it,' Z said, as if he'd read my mind.

I wanted to say something smart and funny back to him but I couldn't think of anything. There was too much noise, too many bodies. I looked at the barrier again. I could jump it. I knew I could. But the Unit was advancing, guns raised. The first man was still struggling in the wire and someone else slipped as they tried to help him and the metal teeth pushed deeper into his skin and he howled in pain. Someone else had covered the barbed wire with clothing, like padding, and was helping people up and over. Some ran straight into the Unit and were handcuffed, others darted around them and made a run for it. We cheered them on. *Run, run, run.* But it didn't last. The Unit lost patience and started firing their guns into the air, then into people's backs as they tried to run away.

I saw them fall to the ground, arms splayed and legs twisted, heads hitting the bitumen. Frozen in a final attempt at escape. Just like that.

That could have been me, I thought. And I sunk to the ground, crouching, head in hands, and let the tears fall.

Everyone stopped shouting and pushing and jumping and baby-passing. Everyone stopped everything except getting the hell out of there. Guns will do that. Suddenly no-one was quite as brave or outraged as they had been. Instead, they shook their heads and threw up their hands in disbelief and wiped at wet eyes and said how awful and terrible and bad it all was. But nobody *did* anything.

They left the scene.

They left the bodies on the ground.

They turned away from the blood and the sobbing and what might have been the only slice of hope to be found in the wall.

CHAPTER 12

Everywhere we went, people stared silently at the wall. We saw cars and buses abandoned, engines left running and doors flung wide, as drivers and passengers stood on the road and just looked. Mouths open. No words. Numb. We tilted our heads back and looked up at the endless wall until our necks ached. Drones hovered overhead.

We wandered in a daze, neither of us really able to put together a sentence, let alone figure out what the hell was happening. I thought we might get some information from the big TV screens that constantly showed the News all through the city. There was one in the square that sat between expensive restaurants and sleek office buildings. We made our way there through streams of people, all heading to the wall looking excited, or terrified, or maybe both.

A small group had gathered in front of the screen. Nearby stood some Unit Officers. I couldn't tell if they were watching the people or the News. Maybe they didn't know what was going on either, and needed the News as much as we did that morning.

The News was showing images of the wall. A drone must have filmed the entire length of it. It looked like a scar running through the city and beyond. Then it showed us the parts of the wall still being built, and the high security checkpoints and the heavily armoured Unit Officers who patrolled them. Slabs went up quickly, efficiently, one after the other after the other, sealing us off or in or whatever the hell it was doing. Even with the proof of it right there on the screen, I still couldn't believe what I was seeing.

Magnus Varick's face appeared on the screen. People called him handsome and I suppose he might have been, to some, but not to me. Not at all. He had this giant smile full of glistening white teeth – a smile that never quite reached his eyes. His hair was a wave of grey and he always looked perfectly put together. When Varick spoke, people listened. They always had. Even before he became Our Leader, Varick was a powerful man, rich and important and always in the news. Now he made the News.

It felt as if everyone stood a little straighter, a little taller when he appeared on screen. Z muttered something under his breath. I looked at him and whispered, *What?* He just shook his head.

Varick stood on a podium on the lawn outside Parliament. Around him were men in dark suits and high-ranking Unit officials. You could tell because their uniforms were much more full-on than anything I'd seen on the officers on the street. All gold chains and buckles and medals and crap like that.

'Good Citizens,' Varick said, and paused for the usual response.

'Our Leader,' people on and off the screen replied in unison. I mumbled along with them. I'd always hated saying it. It felt awkward and weird and I couldn't understand why they'd started making us do it. Mum would say, *Just go with it, Santee, stop asking questions.* Z must have felt the same as me about it. He rolled his eyes and kept his mouth shut. I hoped nobody noticed.

'Today is a very special today,' Varick continued. He spoke clearly, slowly, as if explaining something to a bunch of preschoolers. 'The Safety Border is a temporary measure designed for your protection and security. Sadly, after uncovering even more Threats in our city we have had to implement this difficult yet necessary initiative. We do this for you, Good Citizens. Thank you.' And the people on the screen clapped and Our Leader nodded.

That was it? What did that even mean?

'Liar!' a woman screamed, and threw a can at the screen. Cola burst out of it and fizzed everywhere.

The Unit Officers snapped into action. They pushed us roughly out of the way and tackled the woman to the ground. One pressed his knee into her back, another held her legs down, another kicked her in the ribs. She screamed and screamed and I wanted to help her but didn't want to end up like her and I couldn't look and yet I couldn't look away. And then someone was moving towards them yelling,

Stop, stop! and they sprayed something in her face and she cried out and stumbled away.

After that, everyone became very, very quiet, even the woman on the ground. They lifted her to her feet but she couldn't stand on her own. She kept flopping over like she was asleep, and when they tried to make her walk her head lolled forward like she was watching her toes drag across the ground.

'Get out of here,' the Unit Officers shouted angrily as they stuffed her into the back of a van. 'Go home.'

Home.

I couldn't go home.

But Z could. I grabbed his arm and started walking. In all that was happening I'd totally forgotten that Z had a dad who would be just as angry and worried and upset as my mum.

CHAPTER 13

Z punched a complicated series of numbers into the security pad that unlocked the entrance to his apartment block, and we stepped into the foyer. Like I said, Z lived in a really nice place. I mean, for starters, there was a *foyer*. And every apartment had a welcome mat at the door and it felt like they meant it. *Welcome*. The whole place just had that feel, you know? Outside Number Six were pot plants and a garden gnome who sat on a little toadstool with his fishing rod. He was perfect and ridiculous and I kinda wished he were Z's but we walked right past him.

'What's his name?' Z said.

'What?' I said.

'Your thing, you know, about naming things. What would you call the gnome?'

I had nothing. I shrugged and Z said we should call him George and I tried to laugh but nothing came out.

We stopped at the next door. Number Seven. There was no welcome mat there. Just a dried-up pot plant. Z hesitated.

'You OK?' I said.

'Yeah,' he said, and grabbed his keys, but he hadn't even put his hand near the lock when the door was flung open.

'Bloody hell,' a voice bellowed, and Z was pulled into a massive bear hug. The man was either embracing Z or squeezing the life out of him. Perhaps both. The man cried and Z mumbled, 'Sorry, sorry,' and it sounded like he was crying too.

I wondered if Mum was waiting just inside our door, too, frantic and scared and imagining the worst. I bit my lip and looked away. Z's neighbour from Number Six stood in her doorway, watching the scene unfold. She smiled and nodded before disappearing back inside.

'This is Santee,' Z said. 'Santee, this is my dad.'

He held out his hand the way Z had at the blockade. It seemed like a lifetime ago. Z's dad wore an expression that you only ever see on parents: a mixture of relief and anger and love and disappointment. It's a complicated face. My mum and Z's dad were pros at it.

'Sorry about all this, sir,' I said, and shook his hand.

'OK,' he said. 'Let's get inside.'

Z and his dad went in. I didn't know if I was supposed to follow them or not. I waited, awkwardly, in the corridor.

'Santee,' Z's dad called out, 'close the door behind you.'

I walked behind them down a long hallway. The walls were covered in family photographs and brightly coloured paintings.

'Zac!' A girl ran towards Z and jumped into his arms,

nearly knocking him down. 'I hate you so much,' she said, but she was laughing and crying and hugging him as she said it.

'Sorry,' he said again.

She broke off from the hug and pushed him away to get a better look at me. I smiled, but she didn't. She crossed her arms and looked me up and down.

'Who's that?' she said.

She must have been only nine or ten years old. Her hair was a mess of curls and she wore cat ears on her head and a mismatched combination of a skirt over a dress over jeans. Others might have described her as cute, but I had the feeling she would have hated that word. She had way too much attitude to be called cute.

'Hey,' I said. 'I'm Santee.' Even as I spoke I realised how lame I sounded. Like I was trying way too hard to be friendly. I was so bad at that sort of stuff.

'This is Mila,' Z said. 'My sister.'

'Nice to meet you,' I said, and went to shake her hand like the rest of her family had done. I thought it was their thing. But she pulled a face as if she were allergic to me.

'Santee's my ... my friend, from school,' Z said.

He gave me a little half smile and raised his eyebrows and I had no idea what to make of it.

'What's she doing here?' Mila asked Z, as if she didn't want to speak to me directly. I guess she blamed me for her brother going missing all night, so I couldn't really blame her for hating me.

'I can't get home,' I said. 'Cos of that wall.' My eyes suddenly became hot with tears. I stared up at the ceiling and tried to blink them away. As I did, I felt arms wrap around me and looked down to see it was Mila hugging me.

'Sorry,' she said, and it took all I had not to burst into proper tears right there in front of everyone.

There is nothing that makes you miss your family more than seeing other families in action. Even the really crap families who don't talk much and kinda hate each other. Not that Z's family hated each other. And that just made the whole I-Want-To-Go-Home feeling even worse. Z's family sat at the table together. His dad made us bacon and eggs for breakfast and kept saying, *You must be starving,* and giving me sympathetic looks. It was so much food, more than we ever had at home, but all I really wanted was Mum's porridge with cinnamon. As we ate, Z told our story – minus the kissing – and they all listened. His dad said we'd made the right choice to stay there overnight and Mila patted me on the shoulder and said, *Don't worry, you'll be OK, don't worry.*

My mind wandered to Mum and Astrid. I imagined them pacing the floor as they waited for me to come home last night, jumping at every siren that screamed past our block, neither of them able to sleep or eat. I thought about them heading out as Curfew lifted, but instead of finding me they would have found the wall.

'Is the network working yet?' I blurted out. I needed to know if I could at least call Mum, tell her I was alive and safe and would be home soon.

'No,' Z's dad said. 'Nothing yet.'

They continued talking as I pushed the eggs around my plate. I was hungry but I couldn't eat. The food felt weird in my mouth. I couldn't swallow. It all felt so wrong.

'You don't like eggs?' Z's dad said gently. 'I can make you something else. Anything you want.'

'No, sir, it's fine,' I said. 'Thanks.'

'Sir?' he laughed. 'You guys hear that? Santee called me *Sir*!'

He seemed to think this was a big joke. I could feel my cheeks burning and wanted so badly to just leave, get out of there, go home.

'Ignore him,' Mila said. 'He's so immature.'

He stopped laughing. Mila made a *tch-tch* noise and shook her head like she was disappointed in him. Who was the parent here?

'Sorry Mr … um … Mr …' I couldn't remember Z's last name.

'Driver. But no, you can't call me that. Mr Driver? Ugh. No, that's no good. Call me Diggs.'

His kids groaned and rolled their eyes.

'What?' he said.

'Your name is not Diggs, Dad,' Mila said.

'Yeah, it is,' he insisted, but they kept laughing at him.

'His name,' Mila explained patiently, 'is actually Douglas.'

'Diggs is my nickname,' he said. 'Everyone calls me that.'

'You're too old for nicknames, *old man*,' Z laughed.

'Our old, *old* papa,' Mila joined in.

'Hey, hey, hey,' Diggs laughed along with them. 'I'm young at heart.'

They kept laughing and talking and despite everything else, it was nice just to sit among that noise. Z kept sneaking me looks and smiling, as if he were checking in on me, making sure I was OK. Then he'd get swept up in their family jokes again. It was pretty much the opposite to my house. At home it was all about being quiet and careful. Here they made as much noise as they wanted and nobody seemed to care what the neighbours heard or thought. The conversation moved to me and they asked an endless stream of questions about my family and home, which I tried to answer but wasn't in the mood for. I pretty much let them do the talking. It was easier that way. My mind kept drifting back to the wall, to the bodies on the ground, to the blood and barbed wire. I squeezed my eyes shut and tried to block out the images and focus on what they were saying.

I discovered Diggs had a good job (like I couldn't tell just by looking at their apartment) at the television studios and Mila was some kind of genius who could not only play the violin *and* the flute but also solved algebra equations 'for fun'.

'Seriously?' I said.

'I like to keep busy,' she said like she was much, much older than she was.

'Wow,' I said, genuinely impressed.

'Are you two in a relationship?' she said, proving again that she was a thirty-year-old stuck in a kid's body.

Suddenly I didn't care that I couldn't eat. I stuffed my mouth with toast and dealt with it. Anything was better than having to answer that question. I snuck a look at Z. He shrugged. Grinned at me. 'I'm gonna get some more orange juice,' he said.

'That's not an answer,' Mila said, but Z ignored her and left both of us wondering what he thought the answer was.

CHAPTER 14

Diggs said I was to stay with them, for as long as I needed. I said, *Thanks,* even though it seemed like such a tiny word for such a big deal.

'It's the least we can do, Santee,' he said.

Z and Diggs cleaned up while Mila showed me around the apartment. It was huge. I couldn't understand why anyone needed so much room, but it must have been nice not to step on each other all the time like we did at home. They even had an extra room for guests and I wondered why something like that needed to exist but was happy it did. Mila proclaimed the guest room *Santee's Room* and I got the feeling that once Mila decided on something no-one dared argue.

She grabbed an armful of clothes from her wardrobe, told me I could wear whatever I liked and showed me the bathroom, where she said I could take as long as I wanted.

I took Mila at her word and stood in the shower for way too long. If I'd been home Mum would have knocked on the door. Home. I drew swirls in the condensation on the shower screen. I felt bad thinking it but it was nice here, in their big apartment with the pretty bathroom and fluffy towels.

The hot water ran cold and my fingers turned into shrivelled puffs, but I just stood there. The cold pellets of water felt good against my skin.

I forced myself out of the shower, dried off and looked through the pile of clothes. Mila's clothes were, of course, Mila size but there was a purple-and-pink striped dress that almost worked. I put it on and felt like an oversized ten-year-old, but at least I was out of my school uniform. And clean. I'd never imagined it was possible to feel so grateful for clean clothes.

I found Z and Mila sitting in front of the TV, watching the News. A state of emergency had been called, meaning no school and no work Until Further Notice. Usually, a no-school notice would have made me very, very happy, but there was nothing to be happy about today. Except, it seemed, my outfit, which they all found totally hilarious. Z kept cracking up whenever he looked at me.

'What?' I said, smiling in spite of myself.

'Ignore him,' Mila said. 'You look beautiful.'

And something about the way she said it, so sincerely, made me crack up laughing, too, and I felt a little better.

It didn't last long.

Of course.

Here's what the News told us:

One – It was not a wall and should not be referred to as a wall. It was henceforth to be known as The Safety Border.

Two – The Safety Border had been designed to minimise movement of potential Threats and increase our safety, hence its name.

Three – The majority of Threat activity was on my side of the city, and Varick's government had no choice but to separate Potential Threats from Good Citizens to ensure Safety For All.

'For all? Safety for all? Bullshit!' I didn't mean to shout but I couldn't help it. 'Sorry,' I mumbled. I felt stupid. I knew I wasn't supposed to say stuff like that, especially not around people I didn't really know. And even then, it was better not to take chances. That's what Mum had always told me.

I noticed Diggs standing in the doorway. He'd heard my whole outburst. I felt my stomach turn. I apologised again. 'Nothing to be sorry about,' he said, and I relaxed a little. I definitely wasn't at home anymore.

He watched the News with us. No, he didn't watch. He commentated. Throughout the animated graphs and numbers that popped up on the screen to prove the increase in Threat levels from That Side (*my* side) and interviews with Good Citizens telling the camera why they felt so much better now the Safety Border was in place, Diggs had something to say. It went like this: *Crap, lies, bullshit, don't trust them, full of shit*. It didn't make any sense to me – I mean, how could he say that stuff when he worked at the studio where the News was filmed? I had so many questions and I couldn't keep them all inside the way I was supposed to. So I didn't.

'Don't you work at the TV studios?' I asked Diggs.

'Yep,' he said. I must have looked confused, cos I was. He leaned in like he was letting me in on a big secret. 'Know thyself, know thy enemy,' he said.

'OK,' I said slowly, even though I had no idea what the hell he was going on about.

We spent that first day stuck inside the apartment, which wasn't as bad as it sounds. Z gave me some of his clothes that fit me a whole heap better and Mila showed me some of her stuff on the violin (she was good) and we watched TV and talked crap and it was OK. I mean, if I couldn't be at home at least I was somewhere safe. I worried a lot about Mum and Astrid but Diggs told me he'd work something out. And I believed him. What else could I do?

That night, I sat on the bed and realised I'd never slept in a room on my own before. I missed having Astrid right there, in the bed next to mine. It felt weird. I didn't know how I was supposed to fall asleep.

Z knocked. 'You awake?'

I jumped out of bed and opened the door.

'Here,' he said, handing me a sketchpad and pencil case, 'you looked like you were about ready for a new one.'

'Thanks,' I said.

We stood there for a moment cos I wasn't sure what to say to him even though we'd just spent almost twenty-four hours straight together.

'Awesome,' I said, and immediately wished I'd come up with something, anything, better. Awesome? Why had I said that? I'd never said *awesome* in my life.

'Goodnight,' he said, and disappeared into his own room.

Of course. *Goodnight*. Idiot. That was what any sane, normal person would say in that situation. Goodnight. Or thank you. Or both. *Thanks Z*, and *Goodnight, Z*. Easy. Maybe a kiss on the cheek. A hug. Something. Idiot.

CHAPTER 15

In my dreams that night I was tangled up in barbed wire, just like the woman I'd seen at the wall. I woke, sweating and cold, and reached out for Astrid. It took a moment to work out she wasn't there and I wasn't at home. And the barbed wire wasn't really ripping my skin apart.

We'd always shared a room. It was tiny, so I'd only have to reach across the gap between our beds to shake her awake when I'd had a nightmare. She would always tell me everything was OK and that always helped me get back to sleep. The older I got, the less I'd had to wake her. The nightmares stayed but I could deal with them knowing she was right there, next to me. She made me feel safe. Now I was on my own, in a room I didn't know, on a bed that didn't feel right, in a house that wasn't ours. And I was thirsty. I felt shy about sneaking around the Drivers' house in the dark. I didn't want them to think I was snooping or stealing anything from them (except their goodwill) and my imagination went a little crazy with all these stupid ideas about what they'd think I was up to until I threw back the sheets and made myself get out of bed.

I tiptoed towards the kitchen, hesitating at Z's door. His light was on and I imagined him sitting on his bed sketching, completely unaware of how late it was. I could have just slipped in. Said something like, *You can't sleep either?* He would laugh, say, *Come here*, and I'd join him on the bed and … I stopped. Why the hell was I even thinking about stuff like that?

Diggs was sitting at the kitchen table. Next to him was a bottle of scotch. He downed a glass and, with shaking hands, refilled for another round. It looked like he'd had a few rounds already. I went to head back to my room. But he saw me.

'Santee,' he said unsteadily. 'Sit down. Have a drink!'

'No, thanks,' I said.

'You OK?' he said, when really, I should have been asking him that.

'Just wanted some water,' I said, wishing I had stayed in bed after all.

He stumbled out of his chair and banged around in the kitchen for a glass. It took all his concentration to fill it with tap water and, in different circumstances, it might have been funny. But right then all I wanted was to get out of there.

'Sit,' he said. He thumped the glass on the table and sat down.

He looked so sad, as if his face belonged on a Lost Dog poster or something. I felt kinda bad for him, sitting there on his own, so I sat. He smiled. His breath smelled like booze. He said he wanted me to know something, and I thought, *Hurry up with it so I can get outta here,* but he was talking slow, as if it were a big effort to get the words out of his mouth.

'It's important,' he slurred, 'so you've gotta listen.'

'Sure,' I said, even though I wasn't sure at all.

He cleared his throat and wiped his forehead before pouring another scotch. 'The Regime took my wife.'

That word again. *Regime.* No-one actually said it, even if that's what we thought of Varick and his party. It made me uncomfortable, hearing Diggs say stuff like that so loudly and so freely. But Diggs didn't notice. Right then, he was in his own world, and I was just the unlucky audience.

'She spoke out and they hated it,' he continued. 'They want to break us, control us, kill anyone who gets in their way.' He slammed his glass on the table and the brown liquid sloshed over the sides.

I wasn't sure what I was meant to say so I just nodded.

'They're greedy, power-hungry bastards and they, they want to destroy us, kill anyone who gets in their way.' He started repeating himself, getting louder with every word.

I made a move to get Z but Diggs said, *Listen, listen, listen,* and I tried to tell him that maybe he should get some sleep but he just laughed in my face with that stinky, hot breath and kept going on and on, making zero sense until, thankfully, Z appeared.

'Dad,' Z said. 'Time for bed.'

'Zac, Zaccy, Zac,' Diggs rambled.

'Come on,' Z said and tried to lift him from the chair.

'Fuck off.' Diggs swung out and pushed Z to the ground.

Everything seemed to go very, very still. I wanted to disappear. Vanish. Melt into the floor.

Z called Diggs all kinds of things I knew he'd regret later on. I didn't know where to look or what to do. Z never looked at me, not once, but his face was full of shame and sadness and anger and I wanted to tell him, *It's OK, let's just go back to our rooms and leave him out here.* But Diggs wouldn't stop ranting.

Z finally scrambled to his feet and moved close to his dad. 'You are pathetic,' he said in a voice that I didn't recognise. Cold and removed and not the Z I thought I knew.

'What did you say?' Diggs stumbled.

'You're –'

But he never finished his sentence because Diggs slammed him into the wall, hard, and shouted, *You little shit,* or something and Z laughed and that made it worse cos Diggs raised his fist and I really thought he was going to punch him in the face and I wanted to go home so bad it hurt.

'Dad.'

Standing in the doorway was Mila, ghostly, silent, arms folded across herself in a hug.

Diggs let go of Z and, as he did, let out a howl like I'd never heard before. And Z, silently, as if it was something he was totally used to, put his arm around his deflated father and half-dragged, half-carried him to his bedroom.

I was shaking as I tried to clean up the mess Diggs had left strewn across the table.

'I can fix it up in the morning,' Mila said gently.

I nodded cos words weren't really working for me right then.

'You wanna sleep in my room tonight?' she said.

I did.

Mila pulled out a thin mattress from under her bed but insisted that was for her and that I had to take her bed. I lay down among the stuffed toys and cushions and stared up at the glowing stars on her ceiling. She reached out in the dark and squeezed my hand. Maybe she needed me there for her nightmares just as much as I needed her there for mine.

CHAPTER 16

I didn't want to leave Mila's room. I could hear them all out there, talking loudly like nothing had happened the night before, and for a second I wondered if maybe I'd dreamed the whole thing.

'You coming out?' Mila stuck her head in the doorway.

'Yeah, sorry,' I said, and scrambled out of bed.

'You have nothing to apologise for,' Mila said as she slipped into the room and closed the door. 'But we do, and I am absolutely mortified that you saw that last night. I'm sorry.'

Mortified? What sort of ten-year-old says *mortified*? When I was ten I don't think I'd have been able to spell it let alone use it in a sentence. But here she was. Mila. Staring at me with her kind, bright eyes.

'Are you OK?'

'Yeah,' I lied and smoothed down my hair self-consciously. It always looked a bit crazy in the morning.

'You're very brave,' Mila said. 'Just thought you should know that.'

It wasn't true. Not even a little bit. But it was nice to hear it, anyway. 'How about you?' I said, changing the subject. 'Are you OK?'

'You don't need to worry about me.'

And there was something in the way she said it that made me think she was right. She gave me a quick hug before pulling me out of the room, insisting I had to eat breakfast.

Diggs kept calling it a road trip but, really, we were just going to pick up Z's car. Or we were going to try to. I kinda doubted Red would be going anywhere, to be honest, except maybe the tip. We piled into Diggs's car, which didn't have a name but did have air-conditioning and windows that you could open *and* close. To watch the three of them together, you'd never imagine anything out of the ordinary had happened the night before. Mila called shotgun for the front seat, Z jumped in the driver's seat as if he were going to drive, and Diggs told him, *No way, buddy,* and laughed. They all seemed perfectly fine. Normal. I wondered if, perhaps, Diggs's drunken behaviour *was* their version of normal. That seemed to make it so much worse. Still, none of them were talking about it and I wasn't about to bring it up, so I played along and pretended we were going on a drive.

The roads were deserted. The News had *strongly advised* that everyone stay indoors *until further notice* and it looked like everyone had listened. Except us. All I wanted to do was

107

watch bad TV and try to contact Mum and wait for all of it to be over. But that wasn't an option. According to Diggs, we needed to get out of the house or we'd go stir-crazy.

And so we went on Diggs's road trip.

After a while, Z stretched his arm across the back seat and his fingers softly brushed my shoulder. Maybe a road trip wasn't such a bad idea after all.

Mila controlled the music because, One: she was Mila and, Two: those were the shotgun rules in this family. She filled the car with classical music, which is not the type of thing you'd expect a ten-year-old to choose but exactly the type of thing you'd expect from Mila. I'd never really listened to that sort of stuff before. Beth had wanted me to try it, *For relaxation purposes. Just try it out*, she'd said, *for me.* The next week I'd told her I'd tried but it didn't help. She'd looked disappointed. And I'd felt a bit bad cos I'd lied to her. I hadn't tried it at all.

But when I was there, in the car, I realised maybe Beth had been onto something. I closed my eyes and let the music wash over me, and while it didn't make me relax (because who could relax in this situation?) it did seem to quiet down my mind. My brain had been on this non-stop loop of worry and questions and replaying everything I'd done wrong to end up in this situation and how and why and what the hell was I going to do ... but Mila's music kinda turned all that down for a bit somehow.

The waves of violins were interrupted by the *whoop-whoop* siren of a Unit patrol car.

Diggs swore loudly and pulled over. 'It'll be all right,' he said. I couldn't tell if he was reassuring himself or us.

He wound down the window as the officers approached. There were two of them, because they always came in sets of two. One of them stared in through the back window, right at us.

'Good afternoon, Officer,' Diggs said to the officer at his window.

'You know why we've pulled you over today?' She, like her partner, wasn't smiling.

'Nope, no idea. Why don't you tell me?' he said, and grinned. Like father, like son.

'Step out of the vehicle.' She sounded tired and over it.

'Oh, come on,' Diggs said, cos he didn't seem to know when to give up. 'We're just out for a family drive. Kids go nuts stuck inside all day. You know how it is.'

'Out,' she demanded. 'Now.'

Something about her tone made Diggs shut up and get out of the car.

'Dad,' Mila said, and reached for Diggs, but Z gently put his hand out to stop her. When she turned back to her brother, I could see she was trying not to cry. It broke my heart, seeing her look like that, and I squeezed her shoulder and said, *It's all right,* even though I wasn't sure if it was.

The officer walked Diggs over to the patrol car. We swivelled around in our seats to catch the action out the rear window. We could see the officers talking and Diggs nodding a lot, but we couldn't hear what was being said. Diggs looked very serious, hands clasped in front of him as if he were posing for a formal photo. Mila sniffed loudly.

'He'll be OK,' Z said.

'Promise?' she said, wiping her eyes.

'Promise.'

Diggs's laughter carried into the car. The scene had turned into something much friendlier. The officers were smiling and laughing with Diggs. It looked like they were old friends. Then he shook their hands and headed back to us, giving them a little wave goodbye before getting in the car.

'Arseholes,' he said, the smile still plastered across his face.

He waved again as the patrol car whizzed past us. As soon as they'd gone, his smile disappeared. He leaned over to Mila and gave her quick hug, murmured something into her hair.

'What happened?' I whispered to Z.

Diggs overheard me. 'I worked my magic,' he said as we pulled back onto the road.

'It's his job,' Z said. 'Cos he works at the studios.'

'People are idiots,' Diggs added. 'I just have to tell them I'm a director. Give them my card. Name-drop a couple of celebrities. Give them a bullshit showbiz story. Ask them if they've thought about a career in television, because they have the right look for TV – "The camera will love you." That kind of thing. They eat it up. Idiots.'

I watched him in the rearview mirror. He might have made it all sound like a big joke, but his face told a different story. The others laughed along with him. Maybe they didn't notice the way he kept rubbing his temples, the look in his eyes. They'd got to him, those Unit Officers, even if he wouldn't admit it.

As soon as we were on the windy tracks of the National Park we saw them. A group of people hiking through the long grass, their backpacks weighing them down. Diggs slowed the car to a stop and called out the window to check that they were OK. They gave the thumbs-up and kept walking, but Diggs wasn't satisfied.

'Stay here,' he said, and got out of the car.

We looked at each other, then rushed over to join him. The hikers didn't seem too thrilled about chatting with Diggs until they saw us. Once we arrived, they relaxed a little.

'These are my kids,' Diggs said. 'I told them to wait in the car.'

'But whoever listens to old Dad? What would he know, right?' the man at the head of the pack said. He gave the kid standing next to him a playful punch and the kid said, *Ouch*, and looked totally embarrassed.

They were a family: a dad, his son and two cousins. He told us they'd been visiting their grandparents and stayed the night. Next morning ... well, we all knew that story. And now they were trying to get home.

'Not trying. We actually are going home,' one of the cousins said. She was older than the other kids, and she looked bored, as if talking to us was completely beneath her. I knew that look. I got it at school. A lot.

'This is all my idea,' she said. 'It's simple. They haven't finished building the wall out this far. You can see it on the News. So, we'll be able to get around it. Easy.'

It sounded good to me. I mean, if there was a way around the wall, maybe I could get home, too.

'Could I come with you?' I said.

The girl just looked me up and down like she was judging me.

'What?' I said, making myself taller and meeting her eye.

Z pulled me away. 'You can't go with them.'

'Yes, I can,' I said, and was about to return to the bitchy girl and her sneering face when Mila and Diggs stopped me.

The three of them surrounded me with this expression on their faces that said, *Are you out of your mind?*

'Not a good idea, Santee,' Diggs said.

'If they don't die out here, they'll get arrested at the wall, or worse,' Z whispered. I suppose he didn't want to hurt their feelings.

'Look at them.' Diggs gestured to the group. 'You reckon they know what they're doing?'

It was true. They didn't look like the most experienced travellers with their overstuffed backpacks and sunburnt faces. But, still, they had a plan to get home. Surely that was better than waiting around for the unknown?

A drone buzzed across the sky, jolting me back to reality. Out there, surrounded by nature, it was easy to forget to be careful. In the bush there was no need to worry about interfering neighbours or security cameras or the Unit. And so you could forget people were still watching. They always were. Always. Even out there. Eyes in the sky. If not drones, then helicopters. Even the magpies seemed to sing out, *We can see you.*

I watched the drone disappear into the blue sky. Mum would want me to Be Careful. That was always her advice, even though I'd never really listened to it.

'You coming?' the girl yelled impatiently.

I told them no and that was that. The family waved goodbye and continued, single file, on their mission.

'You know you can stay with us for as long as you need to,' Diggs said.

'That's a promise,' Mila added.

Red was where we had left her. Of course. Diggs and Mila worked under the bonnet checking oil and water and stuff like that. They told Z to stay away, that he'd done enough damage already.

We sat on a rock and looked over the bush that stretched out below us. I was looking for the family – I wanted to catch a glimpse of them, wanted to know they were OK and still on the right course. I really hoped Z was wrong. I wanted them to make it.

'You made the right decision,' Z said.

I shrugged. I still wasn't convinced. I started to replay all the things I should have done differently. Maybe I should have taken the chance and gone with them. Why hadn't I at least given them a message to take to Mum? Why had I gone off with Z in the first place? Once my brain started the *why-didn't-I?* game it was hard to snap out of it. I thought of how Beth would say, *It's unhealthy to dwell in the past,* and how I should, *Focus on the future.* It was a bit hard to focus on the future with a stupid wall blocking your way, though. I thought I'd ask her about that if I ever went back to school.

I hugged my knees to my chest and closed my eyes. I imagined the clouds rolling by and counted one to ten slowly, slowly in my head. I got to five when I felt his hand on my arm. Gentle. Reassuring. I turned towards him and moved a little closer. He put his arm around me and pulled me in. I rested my head on his shoulder. I was sure he'd be able to hear my heart thumping. It felt good, sitting like that. Like maybe everything could end up being OK after all.

He kissed the top of my head. My heart felt like it wanted to jump out of my mouth. I turned to look at him. Heart thumping. Lips tingling. Shaking. I closed my eyes. He cupped the side of my face.

'We did it!' Mila shouted, making us both jump.

Red burst back into life with a sputter and then a roar. That car always had the worst timing.

CHAPTER 17

'What the actual hell is going on?'

'Crazy.'

'Nah, nah, it's like … surreal. Don't you reckon?'

'It's messed up. Totally messed up.'

I sat on the couch and watched Z and his friends talking over each other. Now and then one of them would give me this sympathetic look, which kinda made me want to scream, but mostly they sounded pretty excited about the wall. And that made me want to scream even more. They analysed and argued like it was a debating topic for a school project, not something that actually affected some of us.

Riley had turned up first. Knocked on the door and scared the shit out of me because people only knocked like that if they had bad news or were the bad news. He was neither. He was Riley. And he was *totally stoked* (his words, not mine) that there was no school for a few days.

'Oh, hey, Santee?' he'd said awkwardly, and gave Z a look I couldn't quite work out. 'What are you doing here?'

'Me and Z got married and moved in together,' I said. 'Didn't you know?'

Z cracked up laughing and Riley looked at me like I was some sort of contagious disease. Number Nine on my list of things I learned about Z: he didn't change around his friends. He was just Z, and I liked that.

'Santee's my girlfriend,' Z said, like it was no big thing.

I felt my face grow hot.

'I mean, if she wants to be, we haven't really talked about it, I mean it all kinda happened and, um,' he stammered, and blushed, which made my heart ache just a bit.

'Shut up,' I said. 'Boyfriend.'

And that was that: it was official. Well, maybe. It was a weird thing to be confused and happy and nervous about when there were way bigger things going on. Way bigger.

Anyway, Riley was there and then Will turned up and Gen and Bas and Imara and I think I'd forgotten how popular Z was. I mean, all these people just showed up to say hi and see how he was going and hang out. No-one ever dropped over to our flat anymore. I wondered if, when this was all over, Z would come and hang out at my place – or would he stay away, too?

Z's friends were OK. I didn't know them well enough to say I didn't like them but I did hate how clueless they were. I sat there as they ate junk food and laughed at in-jokes I didn't get and got all excited over their stupid theories about the wall. I didn't say anything cos I was trying to not be the Weird Girl they all thought I was. I didn't want to prove them right by going off, like I had in the past. But it was hard.

I liked Z. A lot. More than a lot, if that was even possible. But I didn't fit in with his friends. 'I'm going for a walk,' I said suddenly, interrupting Gen's story about her chihuahua or her cat or maybe her baby sister – I wasn't really listening.

'I'll come with you,' Z said, but I told him no, he should hang with his friends, and left the house quickly before he could change my mind.

I didn't have a plan. Not really. I thought if I followed the wall I'd eventually find an opening somewhere, like what the family in the bush had told us. A fence I could crawl under or something. Like I said, there was no plan. There was just the need to get home. To see my family. To make everything better.

The wall looked even bigger than I remembered. I knew I wasn't going to find an opening. It was complete. And it looked as if it had been there forever.

I tried to climb it, shoved a foot against the concrete, but there was no grip, nothing to hold onto. My fingers slipped. I tried again, even though I knew it was pointless. I took a run-up, thinking I could leap onto the wall like some kind of superhero. Stupid. But I couldn't stop. Even though my fingers were burning and my body was screaming, I just kept running and running at the wall, bouncing off it, running at it again.

'HEY!' a voice stopped me in my tracks. 'MOVE ALONG.'

The Unit.

I took off, and ran and ran until my lungs felt like they were going to burst wide open.

The News was on because it had to be. As much as Diggs complained about it, he still seemed to follow the rules. Sort of.

'Good Citizens,' Varick said.

Instead of saying *Our Leader*, Diggs burped loudly, which made Mila giggle. Mum had always made us repeat the response. *It's respectful*, she would say. But that wasn't it. She was worried the neighbours might be listening. That didn't seem to be such an issue in this house.

Varick was making a Special Announcement. He sat at his impressive desk in front of an impressive bookshelf stuffed with impressive books. You get the idea. He smiled gently, calmly, like he was about to tell us a bedtime story.

'Tomorrow we will open the Checkpoints and allow Citizens with the correct identification to be reunited with their families,' he said.

'What?' I almost screamed, and shuffled closer to the TV to make sure I'd heard him correctly. There weren't many Checkpoints in the wall and the ones that did exist were for Unit access only. They were so heavily guarded and terrifying that no-one would have even imagined trying to get through them.

'Worryingly, it has been brought to my attention that a small number of Citizens have ignored Section 28B of the Movement Act. These people are not where they are supposed to be. They have broken the law.' Varick kept his steady gaze directly at the camera. It was as if he was

118

looking through the screen and right at me. 'Whilst I am not condoning their actions, I do believe in family. It is one of the pillars of our society, making us a better and stronger people. And so, I am offering immunity to those who need to cross the Safety Border to be reunited with their families.'

I kinda expected him to add something like, *But not you, Santee – you don't deserve your family.* He didn't, of course. He talked about *necessary measures* and *reasonable demands* and *protection* and *prosperity* and other empty-sounding words. I wasn't really listening. My mind was racing. I was going home.

'You can't go,' Z said.

'Bullshit,' I said, and laughed, cos I assumed he was trying to be funny.

He wasn't.

'It's not safe, come on, you know that. Remember what happened at the fence?'

Of course I remembered. When I closed my eyes, I'd see the blood on the barbed wire, hear the screaming baby. It was something I'd never be able to forget.

'People are going to get hurt,' Z said. '*You'll* get hurt. I don't want you to get hurt. So you can't go. Please.'

I stared at him. Speechless. No-one spoke. I looked at Diggs but he was pretending to watch the News. Even Mila wouldn't make eye contact with me. What the hell was going on? Of course I'd be going to the Checkpoint. They were all crazy to think I'd miss that chance to get home.

'I appreciate everything you guys have done,' I said, and tried to steady my voice, 'but I want to go home. I have to.'

'It's not safe,' Z said.

'You don't know that.'

Diggs turned off the TV and stood up. 'He's right. You'll stay here. OK? For as long as you need to. You're important to Zac, so you're important to us. Simple.'

'Thank you,' I said, still trying to hold onto a little bit of calm. 'But I'm going.'

'No,' Diggs said, as if it were final.

'Diggs, come on, you can't –'

He walked out of the room before I could finish. Just like that. Conversation over. I looked at Mila for backup, but she still wouldn't look at me.

'Really?' I said.

'Sorry, Santee,' Mila said. 'I think he's just worried about you.'

'And you, Z? You're just worried about me?'

'Of course I am,' he said. He looked hurt.

'You can't stop me from going home!' I shouted, so Diggs would hear me, then stormed into the guest room and slammed the door.

CHAPTER 18

I woke early the next morning. I didn't need anyone's permission to sneak out. That's why it's called sneaking out. And that was why I was going to do it. Partly cos I didn't want to fight with them and partly cos I didn't want to say goodbye.

That night, Z hadn't knocked at my door to check on me or say goodnight or anything. I tried not to think about it too much. It was easier this way. Just leave. Get out of there.

I folded the clothes they'd lent me and piled them neatly at the end of the bed. I was back in my school uniform, which felt kinda weird after living in Z's jeans and T-shirts. But I wasn't going to start thinking about that, either. I made the bed (Astrid would be proud), left a note that said THANKS FOR EVERYTHING (I was crap with words) and crept out of the bedroom.

The apartment felt dull and grey in the early morning light. I wandered through the kitchen, where I half expected to find Diggs, drunk and passed out at the table. Or Z, stuffing his face with toast. Or Mila, setting up her music stand and asking me if I wanted to hear her play the violin or the flute. *Which one, Santee?* I hesitated before unlocking the front door and slipping out into the hallway.

'You're up and about early.'

I jumped.

'Sorry, love,' the woman said. It was their neighbour. The woman from Number Six. She was watering the collection of pot plants that surrounded George the Gnome. She shuffled towards me. Grey hair, glasses, fluffy pink dressing gown and floral slippers. Like some kind of walking sofa. 'I always give his a little something,' she said, and watered the very dead-looking pot plant at Diggs's front door. 'Don't tell him. He'll get cross at me. Say I'm interfering. You know what he's like.'

I nodded. Yes. I knew what Diggs was like. I mumbled something about being in a hurry and rushed off down the stairs, but it was too late – she'd heard me.

'Santee!' Mila shouted.

I considered pretending I hadn't heard her. I could have done that, I suppose. Just kept on walking. Not looked back. But I didn't. Mila's voice was impossible for me to ignore. The realisation hit me as I watched her skip down the stairs: she was kinda like a sister to me. I wiped away the tears that had abruptly filled my eyes.

She was not happy. She said I was irresponsible and inconsiderate and impetuous and other words I didn't think a ten-year-old would ever use.

'I'm discussing your behaviour,' she added. 'Not you, as a person, but your *behaviour*.'

It was difficult not to smile but that would have just upset her more. So I nodded and said I was sorry. Because I was. Kind of. Still, she had to understand why I was sneaking out.

'If you were me, wouldn't you try everything you could to get back to your family? Wouldn't you miss them?'

'Yes,' Mila said, and then she fell quiet for a moment. 'I miss Mum so much it hurts,' she said finally, her voice small and soft.

'I know,' I said. When I thought of Dad I'd imagine he was in a cell, locked up but alive. And as much as I hated that, I could still feel a little hopeful that I'd see him someday, somehow. Mila didn't have any of that.

'We're coming with you,' Mila said.

'What?'

'To the Checkpoint. There's no way we'd let you go without saying goodbye.'

We?

And there he was. Z. Almost tripping down the stairs in his hurry.

'I brought supplies,' he said, holding up a paper bag of snacks. 'Could be a long wait.'

I didn't know whether I wanted to yell at him or kiss him. The night before he hadn't listened to me at all, hadn't cared what I'd wanted to do, and now he was willing to come along even though he was sure it wouldn't be safe.

'Don't bother,' I said coldly.

'I'm sorry,' he replied. 'I was being a stupid overprotective dickhead last night.'

'Yep, you were.'

'I don't want anything bad to happen to you. And I was being selfish cos I – I like you, a lot, and I didn't want you to go because who knows when we'll see each other again,' he said.

He was right.

'I'm sorry,' he added quietly.

I hugged him. Tight.

'Does this mean you forgive me?' he said.

'Yes,' I said and kissed him without even caring where we were or who saw.

'Gross,' Mila said. 'Can we go now? Please?'

CHAPTER 19

The Checkpoint was located at a section of the wall near the university. The one Astrid used to go to. That old ivy-covered building had remained on the 'right' side of the wall. Of course. On a normal day the lawns would be full of students with their heads in books or typing on laptops or having smart conversations. On this day it was empty. But across the road, in front of the wall, stood a mass of people. So-called law-breakers like me who just wanted to get home. Home. It was so close. I couldn't believe it. All I had to do was step through the terrifying Checkpoint and I'd be there. But first I had to join the huge queue. It looked as if some of them had ignored Curfew and camped out overnight, which was a bit like cheating, and I wished I'd thought of it. But then, seeing the bits of cardboard they'd slept on made me pretty grateful that I'd had the guest room. My room. Santee's Room. I wondered if Mila would keep calling it that, even when I wasn't there anymore. I kinda hoped she would.

Unit Officers were everywhere, ignoring us even while they watched us, if that makes sense. They kept shoving people away from the wall like it was some fragile, precious thing we might accidentally break. If only it were that easy. *Move back, move back*, they shouted. And everyone did. No-one was about to argue with the Unit. Not that day.

I imagined Mum and Astrid waiting in an identical crowd on the other side. Or maybe Mum would have stayed home, just in case. She was always careful. Perhaps it would just be Astrid at the wall, and we'd walk home together. She and Mum wouldn't be angry, just relieved, but I'd still say, *Sorry*, a million times over. I'd mean it, too. And I'd be a better sister and daughter and I'd help out more and take maths seriously and keep my temper and cook dinner and never give them anything to worry about. That's what I thought about as I stood in the crowd at the Checkpoint.

It sounded like a party. Everyone was happy and talking and someone had brought a guitar and people sang along to old songs and I never thought I'd see so many people that excited about heading back to the wrong side. Maybe the wrong side wasn't so wrong after all? We weren't all bad. No-one in the crowd seemed like a Threat. They were just normal people who wanted to go home.

The excitement calmed down as the hours passed and the heat increased. The heat seemed to bounce off the wall and slam through our skin. Mila sat on a piece of cardboard, her head on her knees.

'Maybe you should take her home,' I whispered to Z.

'I'm fine!' Mila said and sat up a little straighter. 'We have to stay until you've made it through.'

'Waiting is so boring. You should go,' I said.

What I didn't tell them was that if they stayed they would make me cry. I knew it. I was a mess of emotion. And I didn't want them to see that. I didn't want Z's last memory of me to be full of snot and tears.

'Sorry, Santee. You heard her. We have to stay,' Z said, and shrugged.

There were lots of rumours flying around the wall, all these ideas about what was going on and why. It was a socio-economic experiment. Or an army drill. Or there had been a huge Threat incident that they needed to contain. That one scared me the most because it was the most credible. Something could have happened on my side of the city because something *always* happened there. A bomb threat. A hostage situation. A shooting. If something like that had happened again that would definitely explain the wall. The people on the nice side of the city always got mad when stuff like that went down, as if it affected them more than us. They'd say how unsafe they felt and more security cameras or Unit Officers or drones would appear. Maybe this time, instead of all that, they'd made the wall.

'You're all wrong!' a woman sitting near us said loudly. 'Blind and stupid. All of ya.'

People shuffled away from her. They shot her anxious looks. Some told her to be quiet.

'Ever think maybe Varick's just an arsehole who wants to keep control?' she said. 'Power and greed. That's what this is.'

'You sound just like my dad,' Mila said, and both me and Z told her to shush.

'Your dad is a smart man,' the woman said, and laughed.

'Would you like a snack?' Mila said. 'We have sultanas.'

Mila filled the woman's hands with sultanas and started chatting away with her new best friend. Her name was Lizzie and she loved to talk almost as much as she loved snacks. She told us about her two dogs, who were waiting for her to return, and how scared they'd be, and wondered aloud if any of her good-for-nothing neighbours (her words, not mine) had fed them. She showed us photos of the dogs and we were all saying how cute they were when I realised the whole place had suddenly become very, very quiet.

I looked up and there, heading towards us, were more and more Unit Officers. Their faces were hidden under full helmets, their bodies covered in padded armor. Riot Officers. My whole body pounded in fear. *This isn't right, this isn't right*, I kept thinking.

They shoved at us and yelled, *Line up, line up,* but people got scared and confused, which made the officers even more frustrated, until they were almost picking people up and putting them into place. There was a lot of shouting and people fell over each other and cried out.

'Fascist pigs,' Lizzie spat at an officer who hit her, hard, with a baton. She fell down and officers surrounded her and I had to keep hold of Mila to stop her going in there.

When the officers cleared, Lizzie was nowhere to be seen and Mila started screaming her name and I thought, *What have I done?* I shouldn't have let them come. It was getting out of hand.

Somehow, among all the shoving and shouting, Mila and Z stayed with me. They each took one of my hands and we held on tight. We were all crushed up together and the heat was suffocating.

The officers walked up and down the line, telling everyone to have their IDs ready. Mila was helping me with my backpack when I felt a hand clamp down on my shoulder. Hard. It was an officer. I couldn't see his face, only my distorted reflection in his visor. I looked like a ghost. He pulled me out of the line and dragged me, roughly, away from the crowd. I opened my mouth but nothing came out. I could hear Mila and Z behind me, calling my name. Asking the officer, *Wait, wait, sir, please wait.*

I twisted around to try to reason with him. I wasn't going to miss this chance to get home. Not because of some idiot officer on a power trip. I kicked. I tried to squirm out of his grip. The officer just shook his head and continued to drag me further and further from the Checkpoint.

'Stop!' I said, my voice finally coming back to me. 'I want to go home.'

He pushed me into the grounds of the university and I could feel my body fizzing. 'Why are you doing this?'

I was probably causing a scene and being too emotional and pissing him off. All those things Mum always warned me about. But I didn't care. And I couldn't stop it. I wanted to pull his stupid helmet off his stupid head and kick him in the balls and stomp on his toes.

'Santee,' the officer said quietly.

Everything stopped.

'Get out of here. Now,' he said, and lifted his visor so I could see what I already knew.

It was Peter.

I almost screamed his name but he quickly returned to officer stance, tall and rigid and so unlike the Peter I'd grown up with. 'You can't be here,' he said.

'I have to –' I tried to explain, but he wouldn't let me finish.

'Go,' he said, and shoved me. It wasn't hard, but it caught me by surprise.

'What the hell?' I shouted. That was not the Peter I knew and loved like a brother.

'Piss off,' he hissed, and turned his back on me like I didn't exist. Maybe I didn't to him. Not anymore. I went to shove him back cos I didn't give a shit about his stupid uniform and his stupid job but Z and Mila gently pulled me away.

'Let's get out of here,' Z whispered.

I didn't want to go. I wanted to get back to the Checkpoint. Rejoin the queue. I had to. It was my only way home. And I was about to run back there, away from Z and Mila, when I saw them. The Unit. They were marching away from the Checkpoint, heading towards us. I panicked. Had they heard me shouting at Peter? Had they come to arrest me? Surely that wouldn't take so many officers. They had all moved away from the wall and onto the lawns of the university where they gathered in groups, hands on guns as if waiting for something. All their attention was focused on the queue.

I wanted to think this meant the Checkpoint was about to open. That they'd done their job, created the queue and now we'd be allowed to pass through. Orderly. Neat. The way they liked it. But it didn't feel right.

'Something's wrong,' Mila said.

I was going to say, *Yeah*, or, *Time to go*, or something like that. But I never got to say anything.

There was a dull thud.

A sound I couldn't quite place. Flat. Crack. Boom. The ground slipped out from under our feet. And then the smoke appeared. White and howling and filling up everything.

A bomb. In the crowd. Right near the Checkpoint.

The world turned into static. I could taste it, see it in the black spots that rippled in my eyes. I blinked and blinked. My whole body thumped. Time stood still and the earth jolted on its axis and I forgot how to move, how to breathe, and there was nothing but the humming of the static and I wanted to close my eyes and never open them again.

The static gave way to the screams and cries. Human but not human. The kind of sound that pierces the spine and hurts your bones and sits inside your skull echoing on and on forever. You can never forget that sound. Terror and pain all mangled together into one cry. And it grew louder and louder as the smoke billowed across the city.

There were people there, under that smoke. People we had just been waiting with, talking with, getting excited with. Lizzie. Children. Families. Grandparents. People who had only wanted to go home. People like me. I needed to get to them. To help. But the Unit moved in before I had a chance to get anywhere. They cut off the screams and the smoke with their sirens and lights. There was no way to get past them to the people who needed us, the people crying out for help.

Peter was gone. I remembered Astrid's words to him: *You have a choice.* He'd chosen to save me from what he must have known was about to happen. But he had also chosen to hurt all of those others. He was part of it.

Z and Mila were by my side, but we couldn't speak. It was as if my throat had closed over and my brain had turned to mush. And then we were walking, somehow, and I felt heavy and so, so tired as we walked through the university and back through the city and away from all the noise and screams and smoke. It all slowly faded away behind us, as if it hadn't happened at all. A kid rode her bike up and down the footpath. A man walked a tiny fluffball of a dog and said *good girl, good girl* as they trotted past. A couple in big floppy hats were pulling out weeds from their lawn. Two women laughed in the entrance to their apartment.

I wanted to spit in their faces. I wanted to tell them to wake up. *What the hell is wrong with you?* Shake them. Slap them. The world was breaking in two and they were all being so ... normal.

But I said nothing. None of us did. We just kept walking. I concentrated on staying upright and putting one foot in front of the other, cos if I fell down I wasn't sure I'd ever get up again. Or want to. The sounds of their screams clung to our bodies. The smoke stained our eyes.

Diggs was waiting for us outside the apartment. When he saw us he didn't say, *I told you so*. He didn't say anything at all. He just hugged us. Even me.

None of us could speak. And Diggs didn't make us. He fussed around. Got us water and sat us down and offered to make us something to eat, but eating seemed pointless. Everything seemed pointless. He kept touching Mila's head like he couldn't believe she was still there and he held Z's hand and I wanted my mum to touch my hair and hold my hand and tell me everything would be OK.

'Bloody hell, you lot.' A woman rushed into the apartment, dropped her bags and pulled Mila and Z into a massive embrace. 'You gave me a heart attack.'

She was a hurricane swirling between them, crying, then telling them off, then hugging them, then crying again. It was their neighbour. I thought of my neighbours back home. I wondered what rumours they were whispering to each other about where I was and what I was up to. I couldn't imagine them caring like this about me or anyone.

'Darling girl,' the woman said, and cupped my face in her hands. 'I'm Pip. And you gave me a bloody heart attack, you know that, don't you?' She pulled me into her arms. She smelled like soap and lavender.

'Is she your grandma?' I whispered to Z and he gave me an almost smile and shook his head.

'I am not anyone's Grandma,' Pip said. 'No thank you.'

And she hurried off to the kitchen to put some food together because she was having none of this not-eating business (her words, not mine).

That evening, the News reported the bomb as a Threat attack. They said, *This is why we need the Safety Border.* They said, *It could have been a lot worse.*

'This last-ditch attempt by the Threats to destabilize our security was swiftly controlled by the Unit,' the News anchor said. The footage showed the smoke, which didn't look as bad on TV as it did in real life. 'The Checkpoint operations were considered widely successful, with families now reunited.' And here the footage switched to smiling families embracing by the wall.

'I reckon that's about enough for one day,' Diggs said, and turned off the television. If he hadn't, I might have kicked the screen in.

Mila had fallen asleep on the sofa. She hardly stirred as Diggs scooped her up and carried her out of the room. My dad had done that. I used to pretend to fall asleep in the car just so he'd have to carry me inside and tuck me into bed. My eyes filled with tears and I tried to blink them away.

'Hey,' Z said gently, and pulled me into a half hug as we sat on the couch. I curled into him.

'How can Peter work for those bastards?' It was the first thing I'd said in hours.

'What?'

'He knew, he knew that was about to happen and he just let it ...' I'd been trying so hard not to cry, but up it came in huge sobs that ripped through my chest.

Z didn't know what to do. He was saying something but I was crying hard and I couldn't hear him and in the end he just held me. And maybe that was better than saying anything at all. We stayed like that until Diggs's voice, more quiet and gentle than I'd ever heard him before, broke into our little world.

'Santee?' Diggs said. 'Who's Peter?'

And somehow I managed to find the words and not cry, too much, as I explained how Peter had found me and dragged me out of that queue. And how the Unit had all retreated at the same time and watched, from a safe distance, as the bomb went off.

'I'm sorry, Diggs. We shouldn't have gone. I'm sorry,' I said. 'What if Peter hadn't –'

'But he did. Don't start that what-if game, Santee. You'll never get anywhere playing that one. Believe me,' he said.

That night, in the bed that wasn't really my bed, I tried to imagine the clouds gently rolling by. I tried to count from one to ten, slowly, slowly. *Calm down*, I imagined Beth saying. *Calm*. But Beth's clouds kept turning into smoke and screams and explosions. And the tears wouldn't stop sliding, hot and silent, down my face.

'I just wanted to check on you,' Z whispered from the doorway. 'Can I come in?'

He lay behind me, his body against my back. His arm reaching out across my chest, his hand holding onto mine. His heart beating into my spine. And I thought about how I shouldn't feel like this right now. Everything was so wrong and confusing, but I wanted him to be there. To feel his arm around me, his breath on the back of my neck, a constant reminder that we were alive.

CHAPTER 20

The network was back. Sort of. Heaps of websites now only displayed ERROR! messages. And those sites where people with more friends than me had shown off photos labelled BEST WEEKEND EVER or commented about how awesome or awful their day/lunch/coffee/best friend was didn't exist anymore. All that stuff had vanished into blank nothingness. Our phones let messages through and our emails worked but I got nothing from Mum or Astrid and had no idea if they were getting my messages or if some creep in one of the Security Offices was reading and blocking everything I wrote.

Varick didn't even pretend shit like that wasn't happening. He actually announced heavy surveillance of all communications (his words, not mine) as part of his Security and Safety Plan.

'If you've got nothing to hide, I can assure you that you haven't got anything to worry about. This is in the best interest of all Good Citizens,' he said, and everyone around him nodded. Everyone always agreed with Magnus Varick.

Z got a heap of text messages because he was Z and he actually had friends who wanted to hang out, as if this was a carefree summer break and not the hell we'd somehow landed in. Diggs had gone back to work but had been pretty adamant that we get outside and get some fresh air. Since the bomb, I hadn't wanted to leave the house. None of us had. It had been two days of not being able to get out of bed and staying wrapped up in the doona with the air-con on full blast and, even when the network came back to life, it was hard to get enthusiastic about anything.

'We're going to play soccer with the guys,' Z said, throwing me a pair of sneakers that were definitely not going to fit me.

I didn't want to go, but Mila did, and I hadn't seen her want to do anything lately – not even play her violin – so I agreed. We would play soccer with Z's friends and pretend that the world wasn't falling apart.

Riley and Imara were already there, kicking the ball back and forth between them. They looked happy to see us, even me.

'Are you OK?' Imara said, and it sounded like she actually cared, which was something I wasn't really used to from the people at my school.

We told them a bit about what happened. Well, Z and Mila did. I stood back and listened.

'Heavy, guys, that's so heavy,' Riley said.

Dickhead, I thought, but nodded and said, *Yeah, it was,* cos what was I going to do? Tell him he had no freaking clue and *heavy* didn't even begin to describe what we'd seen at the Checkpoint, let alone before that?

It felt good to run around and kick the ball. Somehow I managed to push aside the images that were keeping me up every night and the pain in my gut from missing Mum and Astrid and just focus on the soccer ball and running. Two things I could actually understand when nothing else was really making sense.

When I was a kid, Dad set up soccer goals in our shitty courtyard and we'd have these penalty shoot-outs, me and Astrid and Peter. It would get pretty competitive and usually ended in a fight. Dad would play with some of our neighbours. I'd hear them out there on warm nights, kicking the ball around and laughing and I'd sneak out to watch from the balcony. Dad was always the best at it. And I'm not saying that just cos he was my dad. It was true. Even Peter had said that.

Peter. The thought of him, yelling at me, shoving me, watching all those people …

The soccer ball hit the side of my head.

'Wake up,' Riley yelled, laughing, and Z jogged over in his awkward way to see if I was all right. I brushed him off and sat out for a bit, next to Imara and Bas, who were having some deep and meaningful conversation that quickly turned to silence.

'Sorry,' I said, and turned to go.

And that's when I saw the Unit Officers. There were maybe ten of them, sweeping the park and approaching random people for an ID check. It looked so familiar that for a moment it was as if I were back on my side of the city.

'What's that about?' Imara said.

'ID checks,' I said.

'Oh, are they doing that now?' Bas said. 'Have you got yours?'

'Maybe?' Imara said. 'Never had to worry about it before.'

Of course she hadn't. They had no idea, the people who lived over here. I always had my ID on me. Anyone from my side did cos you never knew when you'd be asked for it, and not having it was not an option.

Not far from where we were hanging out, a man was arguing with the Unit. 'I've got my ID, look,' he shouted. 'Look.' And he waved his plastic card around.

'Wrong ID,' the officer said.

'What?' the man was still shouting.

'You are currently in Region One,' the officer said calmly. 'But your address is in Region Two. This means you are now in direct violation of Sections 28B and 28C of the Movement Act. You haven't registered, so we have no choice but to take you to the Processing Centre.'

'The what?'

The man's friends started to argue too. They tried to explain there had been a misunderstanding and the man was a good guy and they would register him now, right now. But the Unit had already handcuffed him and were dragging him out of the park.

It felt as if everyone was looking at me, as if they all knew I didn't belong there, that the address on my ID was wrong. I felt sick. I was going to end up in a Processing Centre, whatever that was. I didn't want to find out.

'I'm not feeling well,' I told Imara and Bas. 'Can you let them know I've headed back?'

I started walking towards the Drivers' apartment and tried to ignore the panic washing over me.

'Santee! Wait! Santee!' Mila rushed up behind me.

'I'm not feeling well –'

'They took that man,' she said. She never missed a thing. 'Did you see? Did hear what they said?'

I nodded.

'Dad will know what to do,' she said as she put her arm around my waist, and we walked like that, together, to the apartment.

I was really freaking out. Mila rang Diggs as soon as we got inside and he said, *Leave it with me*, which was kinda ominous. I didn't want to wait for him to come home. I wanted to know what I was supposed to do if the Unit burst through the door, right then, and demanded my ID. Every second I waited felt like a second closer to being sent to the Processing Centre. Mila played her violin to calm me down and Z told me terrible jokes and held my hand and said it would all be fine but it wasn't until Diggs came home and I saw the look on his face that I could actually exhale.

He'd spoken to someone at work who'd spoken to someone who had a connection with someone else and it had been sorted (his words, not mine).

'What does that mean?' Mila asked, eyeing her dad suspiciously.

'I spoke to someone high up at the Citizens Office, told them Santee was like a daughter to me, and we wanted to help her out,' he said.

A daughter to him? Did he really think that? I mean, part of me liked that he thought of me that way but I also felt this pang of guilt, cos I was someone's *actual* daughter and I missed my mum so much.

'Here you go,' Diggs said and shoved a folded piece of paper into my hand. 'Temporary ID.'

I stared at the little square of paper and wondered how something so small could, possibly, save me from something so big. I unfolded it, and there was the Drivers' address, which was now my address, too.

'What are these Processing Centres?' I asked him.

'Just more of Varick's bullshit,' he said. 'What's for dinner?'

He always tried to change the topic like that and usually I wouldn't let him off so easy. But he looked tired and I knew it was my fault. Stressing him out. Making him ask for favours and who-knows-what to get me this ID.

'Thanks, Diggs,' I said and stuffed the paper into my pocket.

'Think nothing of it,' Diggs said and tried to sound like his usual self. But he didn't. He sounded defeated or something.

We all fell silent for a moment. There were crumbs on the table. Mum would have lost it if we'd left crumbs on our table. She was such a clean freak. That's where Astrid got it from. Usually it drove me crazy. But now I swept the crumbs into my hand.

'Thanks for doing all that, Dad,' Z said finally.

I dusted the crumbs from my hand into the bin.

'It's fine. Just don't think I haven't noticed you two lovebirds, all right?' Diggs said, and laughed.

'Lovebirds? Dad! No-one has said *lovebirds* since the 1950s.' Mila whacked her dad playfully on the arm.

'What? That's what they are,' Diggs said, and did stupid kissy noises, which made Mila shriek with laughter, and he chased her around the house.

I looked at Z. Were we? It felt so wrong to even think about love when all this shit was happening around us. I desperately needed to talk to someone about it but there wasn't anyone. Mila was mature and super smart but that would be way too much information for her. I didn't really have anyone else. Not like that. What I really wanted was to tell Mum and Astrid about him. To stand around in our kitchen while we made dinner and talked and joked and gossiped about the day and then just casually mention it – *So, I have a boyfriend now.* And Mum would ask me a heap of questions and Astrid wouldn't approve but she would when she met him cos he was Z and they'd love him. That's what I wanted to have happened. That's how it should have been.

'I'm keeping an eye on you two,' Diggs said as he lumbered back into the kitchen, out of breath.

'Dad, no, what the hell?' Z said.

'No sneaking into each other's rooms at night. Doors open. Always. Except the bathroom. And when you do go to the bathroom, you go there *on your own*. You hear me?'

'Dad, please, stop talking,' Z said.

Diggs started going on about being careful and not getting carried away and using protection. *Protection?* He actually said that and I almost died and we covered our ears and sang really loudly to drown out him and his awkward advice. It was embarrassing but it was also kinda nice that he seemed to care, and that we were all joking around again.

Even with Diggs's parental advice fresh on my mind, I hoped Z would sneak into my room again that night. I'd brushed my teeth and was heading to bed. Z's door was closed. *Maybe*, I thought, *I could slip in there.*

'Santee.' Diggs stood in the hallway.

Sprung.

'You know I'll do whatever I can for you, don't you?'

I nodded, unsure about where this conversation was headed.

'You mean a lot to Zac and it's his fault you're in this mess, so we should help,' he said.

'I'm really grateful,' I said.

'Just ... you gotta remember to always keep that ID on you, all right?'

'Of course,' I said, confused. Hadn't he already told me all that?

'Those Processing Centres, they're not good places, Santee,' he said, and left abruptly, before I could ask any of the thousand questions that started swirling around me.

Suddenly the thought of slipping into Z's room didn't feel like such a great idea. I went back to my own room, sat on the bed and wondered what Diggs wasn't telling me. I took another look at the temporary ID, searching for some kinda clue. I'd only scanned it earlier and noted my new address. But now – now I saw it. Listed as my guardian, my official, registered guardian, was Douglas Driver. What the hell?

CHAPTER 21

I didn't want to tell Z what his dad had done cos I didn't want things to be any weirder than they already were. I had a heap of questions for Diggs to answer, but he was never around. He left early, got home late and I was sure he was avoiding me. Logically I think I got it; him registering as my guardian must have been the only way to keep me there. And logically, I knew I wasn't suddenly Z's sister, adopted or fostered or whatever, but there was something that felt weird about it, and that stopped me from telling Z. I still wasn't sure what his deal was with his dad. Z never talked about Diggs's outburst from that first night. And it hadn't happened again. But still. There was something unsaid between those two.

Diggs had gone back to work well before the rest of us had the all-clear to return to whatever it was we'd been doing before the wall appeared. Whatever that was. Who could even remember anymore? Diggs's job was considered an essential service because apparently TV was important. Once, we'd had heaps of channels but slowly, very slowly, they were all shut down for breaching some law or not abiding to standards and other things I didn't get. Now we had three channels, and none of them were that great. Even Diggs said they were shit. And he worked there.

Anyway, the time came for all Citizens to report to school or work or some building in the city called the Futures Office to receive Further Instructions. I thought that third option sounded kinda terrifying. What did *Further Instructions* mean? Mila said they'd just be handing out jobs but I wasn't so sure. Not after everything we'd seen.

'They want to keep everyone occupied,' she said, cos of course she had this all figured out. 'Get things back to normal.'

But nothing was normal anymore. Not with a wall splitting everything in half. Along with the Safety Border there were new rules about what we could and could not read or watch or listen to. Travel had to be preapproved. Curfew was strictly enforced.

Z and I walked to school together. Mila went her way.

It was weird walking to school without Astrid. I couldn't stop replaying our last walk together. It was one of those moments I wanted to go back to, somehow, and redo and make right. I wondered if maybe Astrid had the same regrets.

A plane flew overhead. What did those people think from up there when they looked down and saw that scar, the wall, splitting up our city?

'People are getting out,' Z said.

'What?'

145

'If you've got the money you can go overseas, or anywhere, really. Bas is going today.'

I couldn't believe he was only just telling me this.

He showed me the text message Bas had sent: HOLIDAY! HOLIYAY! SEE U IN 2 WKS. SUCKERS. And there were emojis of a palm tree and the sun and a cocktail and a beachball and …

'OK, Bas, settle down, we get the idea,' I said, and tried to laugh. But I was boiling inside. I couldn't even get to the other side of the *city* and here was this jerk going on some international holiday just cos he could.

'I don't reckon he's coming back.'

We crossed the park in silence. The wet grass seeped through the holes in my shoes and made my ankles itch. My trousers were too short. Or I was too tall. Mum always said, *Why don't you stop growing already?* and laughed, but it wasn't her real laugh. It was a worried laugh. Stuff wasn't cheap and we had to make do, but somehow we did. Or Mum and Astrid did.

'I can't go to school.' I stopped. Right there. In the middle of the park.

Z stopped too and looked at me like I was kidding around. Until he realised I wasn't. 'You have to,' Z said. 'It'll be OK.'

No, it wasn't about it being OK or not being OK or whatever Z meant. I tried to explain it, tried to tell him how I'd left things with Astrid and how Mum had grounded me and I was supposed to be home, and that I had this sick feeling in the pit of my stomach and it wouldn't go away.

'I'll be there,' Z smiled, and went to put his arm around me.

I ducked away. I didn't need his protection.

'I've gotta try to get home. I can't just give up. I can't pretend this is normal.' My voice grew louder. 'This is not normal.'

'Yeah, I know, but –'

'You don't get it.' I took a deep breath. Looked up at the sky. I wanted to be on that plane, but I didn't need to go as far as Bas seemed to be going. I just needed it to drop me off on the other side.

I didn't know how to make him understand. So I didn't. I just ran. Away from him and towards the wall. I heard him shouting out after me. 'Sorry!' I called over my shoulder, but I didn't slow down. I kept running. Because sometimes that's easier.

If I ignored the wall, I could almost imagine nothing had changed. Cars and buses filled the roads again. People in suits and uniforms hurried across pedestrian crossings. The screens screamed News headlines. Unit Officers stood in pairs on the corner. It was almost like I was just running home.

I slipped in among the regular citizens doing their regular things in the city. I pretended I was meant to be there, that I was a Good Citizen like them. It was easy to hide in the crowds in my boring school uniform.

At the traffic lights, the green-man signal flashed and buzzed and we all crossed together. And there, on the other side, was an old, bent-over man with no shoes, his heels cracked and thick with dirt. He was talking to himself. Swearing and yelling into the wind. The others quickened their pace, diverted their eyes, their faces full of pity or disgust. I watched him peer into rubbish bins in case there was something worth rescuing, but there was nothing. He rubbed his neck and moved towards the expensive stores that lined the footpath and I imagined all the shop assistants quickly putting up their CLOSED signs and locking the doors. But he didn't try to go in. He sat against the window of a boutique, knees up to his chin, head bowed, like a tiny ball. The mannequins in their pretty dresses looked down their plastic noses at him.

I had a sandwich in my schoolbag, and I took it out and headed towards him. I wondered what his story was. Who he might have been before the wall ripped our lives in two: Before and After.

'Here,' I said and held out the sandwich.

He lifted his head, opened his bloodshot eyes. 'Piss off,' he growled.

I slowly put the sandwich on the ground in front of him, like some kind of peace offering to a dangerous animal.

'Piss off,' he said again, louder this time. The people around me moved back even further.

I wanted to help. Didn't he get it? I smiled at him. 'Stay safe,' I said, which was a dumb thing to say, but I couldn't think of anything else.

As I walked away, the sandwich hit the back of my head. I didn't turn around. He yelled, spewing out words I couldn't understand or didn't want to, and I walked a little faster.

A woman with almost blue hair touched my shoulder, gave me a sympathetic smile. 'Don't worry, sweetheart,' she said. 'They'll take care of him. The Unit are quick to remove these types now.'

'What types?' I said.

She looked surprised. 'The ones who should be over there,' she said, and motioned to the wall. 'Threats.'

As she walked away I wondered what she'd have thought of me if she knew I was meant to be on the other side, too.

'ID.' An officer stood right in front of me. She made me jump but I tried to look calm and said, *Yes ma'am*, the way we were meant to, even though she looked about the same age as me.

I fumbled around in my backpack for the temporary ID. New address. New guardian. Same name. The officer took it. Studied it. 'You're meant to be at school,' she said, still looking at the ID.

'On my way, ma'am,' I said, and smiled the way Z always did when he was trying to make a good impression. Or to get himself out of trouble.

She smiled back. It didn't look quite right, seeing an officer smile. Still, I thought I'd have to tell Z that his stupid smiling thing had worked. And then I thought about Z. His face when I'd ducked away from him. His voice when he'd shouted after me. I felt terrible. I shouldn't have run off like that. Again. Idiot, Santee.

'Go,' she said, and handed me back the ID, 'or you'll be late.'

CHAPTER 22

I was late. Of course.

Last time I'd stood out the front of school, Z had been right next to me. The school looked exactly the same now as it had then. I don't know why I'd expected it to be different. Probably because everything else in my life was. It felt strange to stare at something so familiar.

I wanted to talk to Beth about it. Which was weird cos I never wanted to talk to her. But now I had a list of things I needed to figure out. Like, how was I going to survive this? And, what is a Processing Centre? And, can you get a message to my mum? And, how can I feel so lonely and sad but also be sort-of-maybe-possibly falling in love? I imagined her not wanting to give me answers and instead making me do annoying exercises to figure it out for myself. But this time, I would do the exercises and find the answers. I had to.

The school corridors were quiet. Too quiet. I wondered (actually, I wished and hoped) if perhaps we weren't meant to be back at school yet. If we had the date wrong. I made it to Beth's office without one teacher seeing me and knocked at her door and waited. She had a bright poster stuck on the door that said: *All feelings are OK, it's what you do with them that matters.* I hated that poster.

A man stood where Beth was supposed to be. Tall. Bald. Pale. With glasses that made his eyes look huge. I hated him the moment I saw him. He frowned at me.

'Come in,' he said, and held the door open a little wider.

I didn't want to *come in* but there was something about him that made me think I didn't have a choice.

There were people in Beth's office, but none of them were Beth. One sat at her computer and scrolled through the screen. Others went through the endless paperwork that filled her drawers and filing cabinets. Pages and pages of scribbled notes. I knew there had to be a file or three of notes about me.

'Sit,' the bald man said. I sat. 'Name?'

I told him. And someone shoved some files into his hands. My files. He flicked through them as if I wasn't even there. Every now and then he made this *hmm* noise and then kept scanning the pages Beth had written about me. Those notes were private. Personal. My face grew hot. He put the papers down and stared at me. It felt like he could see right through me. Through my clothes. My skin. And into me. I wanted to rip his stupid, ugly glasses off his stupid, ugly face and smash them into pieces. He'd just read about my *impulse control issues* and *meltdowns* and *physical violence*. He should be ready for it.

I stood up quickly.

'Sit,' he said.

'Why?' I said. It felt like the office was pulsating and moving and the air was thick and I wanted to get out. But someone stood at the door, blocking my way, and I realised they'd all stood up and were watching me with big eyes and open mouths. Except him. The bald man. He sat in his – correction – Beth's chair and smirked at me, like I was a joke.

'Sit down, Santee.'

I didn't want to sit down. The room closed in. I needed to breathe and I tried to, *slowly, slowly,* and counted one to ten and let my brain catch up with my body. I didn't want to prove him right. All those things he'd read about me. All those judgments he'd made. He didn't know me. None of those people did. Neither did Beth. Even with all her notes.

So I sat.

I twisted my fingers into knots as I waited for the bald man to speak. I wondered if this was it. The Unit would burst in and handcuff me and send me to the Processing Centre and I'd never get to tell Z how sorry I was.

'You're a long way from home, Santee,' the man said. He'd perched on the end of Beth's desk. I suppose it was meant to make him look friendly and approachable. It didn't work.

'Not really.' I shrugged.

'We are aware that Douglas Driver is registered as your guardian. He has taken responsibility for you, yes?' The man was taking his own notes now, on a tablet.

'Yes.'

'He's a well-respected citizen. A Good Citizen. You're very lucky that someone like him has, how should I say this … accepted you.'

'I am, yes.' I knew I was lucky. I also knew Diggs was not a Good Citizen, but if they thought he was then I wasn't about to correct them.

The room fell silent. The bald man nodded and looked at me expectantly. Like he was waiting for me to say more. I knew this trick. It was one of Beth's specialties. I was not going to keep talking. No way. I sat back and pretended to be a lot calmer than I felt.

'So?' the man said, finally, and shifted in his chair. 'Do you agree? Mr Driver is a Good Citizen?'

'Of course,' I said quickly, but an uneasy feeling surged through me. Why were they so interested in Diggs?

'We are asking out of concern for your safety, Santee. Please take your time. Consider your response.' He made some more notes, but I didn't add anything more. I just waited for his next question. It seemed to take forever. My heart thumped in my ears. 'Do you notice if Mr Driver keeps, how should I put this, irregular hours? Does he go out during Curfew? Anything like that?'

'No,' I said. I tried to keep my face neutral but the room was stinking hot and I was nervous and sweaty and nothing made any sense.

'Have you heard him say any –'

'Where's Beth?' I interrupted.

He acted like I hadn't even asked. 'Mr Driver's job, does it take him away from home a lot?'

'Who are you?' I said. If he could ignore my question, I could ignore his.

He adjusted his tie. Cleared his throat. Tried to smile, which really didn't suit him. 'My apologies,' he said. 'Julius Warren. From the Department.'

'What Department –'

'Does Mr Driver's job take him away from home a lot? Notice anything unusual about the hours he keeps?' Julius Warren lost the smile and any patience he'd pretended to have with me.

I let a pause fill the room.

'Dunno,' I said finally.

He took off his glasses. Rubbed his eyes. 'We know you want to get home,' he said. 'That's perfectly understandable, Santee. And we'd like to help you achieve that goal. We really would.'

I stared at my hands.

'We could get you some information about your mother and your sister. Would you like that?'

I said nothing, but inside I screamed – *Yes, yes, tell me, tell me everything.*

'How about your father, Joseph Quinn? It's been a long time since you've seen him. Would you like to? I can make it happen.'

I couldn't tell if he was playing me. He gave me nothing. He was expressionless. Cold. I wanted to see my dad so bad. The prison was on the other side and it sounds dumb but I missed going there, cos when I was there I felt a bit closer to him. He was just inside that building. Only metres from me. But now? Now I might be able to see him? Actually, physically see him? I wanted to say sorry, tell him I loved him, make sure he was OK. I nodded, slowly.

Julius put his glasses back on. 'Anything odd, anything that stands out to you as ... different ... about Mr Driver?'

'Sometimes he gets home late. After Curfew. But he's allowed to. He has a permit. Cos of his job.' I didn't think that would get anyone into any trouble. And I'd get to see my dad.

'We already know that,' he said.

My mind raced. What was he after? There had to be something I could tell him that might help me out and not hurt Diggs.

'What do you know about my dad?' I asked.

'A low-grade Threat. Nothing special. A bit ... how should I put this? Pedestrian? A bit beige? You understand what I mean?'

I understood, but I didn't agree. Not at all. He wasn't a Threat, and he definitely wasn't beige. Not my dad. He was colour and stupid jokes and bad dancing and mess and ...

'He's also very stubborn,' Julius said.

And that got me. Right in the heart. How did he know my dad was stubborn? What had he seen? Had Dad given them hell in an interview? Gone on a hunger strike? I could imagine that. I really could. Because he *was* stubborn. Hope filled my chest.

'You can visit your father and go home to your family,' he said. 'You help me, I help you. How does that sound?'

It sounded unbelievable. It sounded too good to be true, which is something my grandma used to say. *If it's too good to be true, it probably is.* And this, most definitely, was. It had to be. The hope faded away. But it was clear I wasn't getting out of there without giving him something. So I gave him something.

'He drinks a lot,' I said.

Julius Warren shuffled forward. 'Interesting,' he said.

So I told him how Diggs had been drunk that first night and the way he'd gone at Z. I figured it was family stuff, personal stuff, nothing that would get Diggs into any trouble. But it might just be *interesting* enough to get me a visit with my dad.

'If you think of anything more, let me know.' Julius stood. Meeting over. 'I am here to help you, Santee. Any time.'

CHAPTER 23

One of Julius's creepy assistants walked me, silently, to the gym and pretty much shoved me through the big double doors. There were rows and rows of students inside, heads down, writing frantically. They set up like this during our exam period but this version was way more crowded and tense. It looked as if they'd somehow managed to squeeze every student in there. What the hell was going on? Everyone was so focused they didn't even notice me walk in. I stood there, confused, until Mr Lo motioned at me impatiently to *sit down, sit down*. I sat at the nearest empty desk and looked at the paperwork in front of me. GENERAL EXAMINATION was written across the first page, followed by pages and pages of equations and numbers and patterns and complicated-looking questions. I thought about walking out. Could this day get any shittier?

Mr Lo crouched next to my desk and whispered, 'You don't have much time, Santee. Get started.' He handed me a pencil and genuinely looked like he cared, which was weird for Mr Lo.

I printed my name in the boxes provided (at least I could answer that section correctly) and stared blankly at the first page. I could do this. I wasn't terrible at maths. I just had to focus. That's what Astrid always told me: *You know this stuff, Santee. You're good with numbers but you have to try, you have to want to do well.*

I took out my calculator, which had once been Astrid's, and hoped that some of her genius might magically find its way through the buttons and into me. The first section was multiple choice, which should have made things a lot easier except that my answers didn't even appear as choices. I chose way too many As in a row. Then too many Cs. But, still, I got to the end of the section and thought how Astrid would be pleased that I hadn't completely given up. And maybe I'd actually done OK, too. I turned to the next section feeling a whole lot better until a buzzer rang and someone shouted, *Pencils down.*

I looked around. People were shaking out their hands and rolling their shoulders, stretching. They snuck looks at each other, silently saying things like, *How easy was that?* and, *Finished!* I slowly closed my not even half-finished exam and sat there staring at nothing. It felt as if I'd just finished a long-distance race and come dead last.

'You can stop apologising now,' Z said.

I'd said sorry about a thousand times, cos I was. I felt terrible about running off and being an idiot but he said he understood and that it was OK and he meant it. I pulled him into a tight hug, which surprised me as much as it surprised him. I wasn't one of those hug-and-kiss-and-squeal-like-a-moron types like some of the other kids at school. But right then, I needed someone to hold onto. Someone real and there and a friend. A boyfriend. And I was lucky. I had Z.

The whole school had escaped outside and everyone was standing around in groups talking quietly. It was surreal. Like the volume had been turned right down on everyone. There were no footballs flying around or screams of laughter or anything like that.

Z and I found the only empty table. It was the one that was permanently covered in bird crap. No-one ever sat there cos you never knew when they'd strike. A lot of people had learned that the hard way. I didn't care. Things couldn't really get any worse and anyway, what was a bit of bird poo? Wasn't it supposed to be lucky or something?

'Do we go back to the normal timetable now?' I said as we sat down, carefully avoiding the mess. I never imagined I would actually look forward to Mr Lo's class.

'Nah, we've got exams. All day.' Z took a bite out of his apple.

More exams? Hadn't we had enough already?

'They're streaming us,' he said.

'What?'

'The exams. They're using them to work out where we

159

fit. You know – Low, Moderate or Advanced.' He continued eating, like this wasn't completely new information. 'You gotta get in the Advanced stream, Santee.'

'Shit,' I said. I didn't want to tell him that I hadn't even finished half of that first exam.

'It gives you more opportunities …' and he kept talking and I pretended to listen but I'd heard it all before. From Astrid. It wasn't the first time, or the last, that I wished I'd listened to my sister.

Tash was sitting nearby, at her usual spot – the table where I'd once sat. She was on her own and her hair was a bit of a mess and she looked so … sad. We made eye contact. I wanted to say, *You OK?* but we didn't do that anymore – talk or care. She rested her head on the table. Something was very wrong.

Seeing her like that made me feel awful, which was stupid. I should have been happy seeing her upset, considering what a bitch she'd been to me for the past couple of years. But I couldn't help it. Cos for years before that she'd been my best friend, and I'd been hers. I knew more about Tash than she liked to remember.

I remembered the sleepovers and the stupid dance routines we made up, and the night we snuck booze from her parents' cabinet and made ourselves sick and got in heaps of trouble (but she took the blame cos she was like that back then), and the times we lay on the scratchy picnic rug in her back garden and stared at the stars and made up great futures for ourselves. She'd wanted to work with kids, be a kindergarten teacher, and I wondered if she still wanted that. If she still saw that future for herself. And I couldn't imagine how the girl I'd once been so close to, who made me laugh and stuck up for me, had turned into this person. Or maybe I *did* know and it hurt too much to think about it.

Even so, I stood up. I couldn't just ignore her when she was like that. And Z stood with me.

As we approached Tash's table, a bunch of her friends swooped in from nowhere and gathered around her. They were all, *Oh no, you poor baby,* and *Don't cry, you'll ruin your mascara,* and *Oh honey, it's so sad.* They were so fake. All of them.

They saw me watching.

'Piss off, Santee,' Chloe said. Me and Tash had always thought she was the worst. Stuck up and mean and a bit of a moron, actually. Tash had clearly changed her mind on that.

'You OK, Tash?' I said, ignoring Chloe completely.

Tash wiped her eyes. She really had ruined her mascara. Chloe handed her a tissue. 'If you really want to know, her dad is stuck on the other side of the Safety Border,' she said. 'It's tragic.'

'Shit,' I said.

'Sorry,' Z added.

'Thanks,' Tash said. To Z. Not me. 'I'm just so scared for him, you know? It's not safe over there. With all those Threats. They're bad people over there.'

'What?' I said.

'Come on, Santee. You know that's why they built the Safety Border. To keep people like you away from us. Separating the good from the bad, Good Citizens from Threats,' she said. 'It's a good thing. It's keeping us safe. But my dad ...' and her voice broke and she was crying. Again.

It might have been what she said or how she said it or

the shitty day I was having or D (all of the above), but I lost it. This fire went up inside me and before I realised what I was doing I was right in her face, screaming at her, *Stop, stop, stop*. And then she was up and smirking and shoving my shoulders, *Come on bitch, hit me, bitch, come on psycho*.

So I did.

And she stumbled backwards and looked shocked, like she couldn't believe I'd actually done it, and I couldn't believe I'd done it either, and we stood there looking at each other and I went to say, *Sorry*, because I was, but Tash ran at me and grabbed my hair and pulled it, hard.

Trust Tash to pull hair in a fight. Typical.

'Break it up!' the principal's voice boomed across the schoolyard.

Tash and I sat outside Mrs Rook's office. Our principal had to make a Very Important Call. 'Can I trust you two to be civil for five minutes?' she'd said, and we'd nodded and were left alone together.

Tash moved one seat over as if she didn't want to get too close to me. It was so immature. Something you'd do in primary school. I was waiting for her to tell me I had cooties. *Idiot*, I thought, but I said nothing. It wasn't worth it.

I glanced around the office. The usual receptionist wasn't there. Some other person sat at her desk now, typing away loudly. Tap, tap, tap. Smashing the keys like they'd personally offended her and this was their punishment.

The bald man appeared. Julius Warren. I lowered my eyes, shrank into the seat. I could feel him watching me.

'Who's that?' Tash said.

I shrugged and started to hum, very softly. A tune I'd remembered from Mila's violin practice. It was another one of Beth's weird ideas. *Go to a happy place*, she'd once said. *What's the soundtrack to that place?* I'd never tried it cos I thought humming would made me seem even crazier than usual.

'What the hell is wrong with you?' Tash hissed across the empty seat.

I ignored her and stared at the clock on the opposite wall. I watched the seconds tick around and around. It had taken me ages to learn to tell the time. Astrid had helped me. She'd drawn all these clock faces on scraps of paper. I tried to think about that and not the bald man or Mrs Rook or anything else.

But Tash wouldn't give up. 'Do you know that guy?' she said.

I ignored her.

'He's totally staring at you,' she whispered. 'It's creepy.'

He knew he was making me uncomfortable. I could feel it.

'Sir?' Tash called to him. 'Can I help you?'

I didn't know if she was trying to stick up for me or hurt me. I just wanted her to shut the hell up.

'Santee has been helping me with some important ... how should I say it – investigations,' he said.

'Right,' Tash said and gave me a weird look.

'I'll see you later, Santee, yes?' he said, but I didn't answer him. He waited a moment before adding, 'Maybe your friend would like to help out, too. You know where to find me.' He handed a file to the receptionist, who sweetly said, 'Thanks for that, Julius,' and then he was gone.

'What the hell was that?' Tash said, and moved closer. 'What a creep.'

For a moment I saw a little, teeny piece of the Tash who'd been my friend. It disappeared pretty quick.

'You gotta stop drawing attention to yourself. Play the game, that's what they say, right? That's what you gotta do,' she said.

'What?'

'I thought you were smarter than this. Seriously.' She rolled her eyes. 'You can be such an idiot, Santee.'

I resisted the urge to slap her.

She grabbed my arm. I pulled away, but she leaned in close. 'This is a good thing, Santee. You're going to be safe now. You're out of there.'

'What are you talking about?'

'The Safety Border. It's great. You got out of there and now we can hang out, maybe, if you want.' She smiled.

My heart pushed itself right up into my throat and I was scared that if I opened my mouth it might just fall out, bam, onto the floor. I ground my teeth and concentrated on the patterns in the carpet.

Tash had been so awful to me the day Dad was taken. I was like her, crying at the table, waiting for some friends to gather around and tell me it was OK. But they didn't. Instead she announced, in front of everyone, that my dad was a Threat. *We're all a bit safer now*, she'd said, *thanks to the Unit cleaning up the place, right?* They all agreed. And she ignored me. Everyone did. It was like I had become invisible. And that was it. We officially weren't friends anymore. I had no-one. Until Z. I tried not to think about how my fight with Tash would have looked to him. How crazy and messed up I must have seemed.

'Dad was visiting my aunty over there. Near your place. That's how he got stuck. But I can't tell Chloe or anyone. And you can't say anything. OK?' she went on and on and I mumbled *Sure, I won't say anything,* cos apart from Z I didn't have anyone to tell.

'Mum says we gotta keep that quiet, you know? Otherwise we could look like Threats,' she said. 'Like you did – do … sometimes.'

'I'm not a Threat,' I said. 'You know that.'

'But you have to admit you act like one. Sometimes. Like just now, when you lost it at me,' she said. 'Mum reckons you're dangerous.'

'Dangerous?' How could her mum think that? I'd known Tash's parents since I was a kid. They knew me. They knew my family.

'You're the reason your dad ended up … well, who knows where he is. But it was your fault, Santee. That thing you did … I mean, come on, what did you think would happen after that?'

Tash's words stung like she'd just slapped me across the face. Tears filled my eyes.

It was your fault, Santee.

You're the reason …

Your fault.

165

I knew it was my fault. I'd carried it around with me for a long time. I'd tried to visit him so I could explain, so I could say sorry, so I could make it better.

'I didn't do it on purpose, Tash. It was a mistake.'

Tash shook her head like there was more she wanted to say but she couldn't find the words.

We sat in silence until Mrs Rook called us into her office, Tash's words swirling around and around in my head.

The principal didn't care about all the shit I was going through. She kept saying, *Things have changed, things have changed,* as if I hadn't noticed the wall or the fact I had no family. She wasn't interested in my questions. Her only advice was Pull Your Head In. Which was pretty shitty advice. Tash looked all serious and said, *Of course we will.* I said nothing.

And I stayed silent for the rest of the day. Through all the exams, which were so hard they made my eyes burn. I said nothing on the walk home. Or back at the apartment, which the Drivers insisted was my home – they were always saying, *Make yourself at home, help yourself to whatever you want, this is your home* – but it wasn't. Not really. It never would be. I said nothing as we ate dinner and watched the evening News. I overhead Z telling Mila that it wasn't her fault. *Santee just needs space, she's upset.* I went to bed feeling more alone than ever.

To make the day even worse, I got my period. Bam. I didn't know what to do. I had nothing. I had no-one. I couldn't ask Astrid for help. I couldn't go out to the store. I folded up some toilet paper and put it in my underwear and hoped for the best. Mila found me in the bathroom. I was washing my hands and crying and cramping all at the same time.

'Don't cry,' she said, and hugged me. 'We're here for you.'

And the words all rushed out because it was easy to forget Mila was only ten, and she listened and took my hand and said she knew what to do. She took me next door to Pip, who made me peppermint tea and sat me down in her lumpy old armchair with a hot water bottle.

'Give me a sec, sweetheart,' she said, and out she went.

Mila talked and talked about her first day back at school and cracked me up with impersonations of the kids in her class and the new, serious teachers who had turned up and started changing everything. Before too long, Pip came back with tampons and pads and I never thought things like that would be such a wonderful gift.

'Thank you,' I said.

'We girls have to stick together,' Pip said and she put the kettle on for another round of tea.

CHAPTER 24

It was no surprise to find out I'd been put into the Low Stream. They didn't even try to hide the fact we were losers by giving the group a nice name. Like in grade one we all knew the kids in the Eagle Group couldn't read that well, but they were Eagles and Eagles are tough and no-one messes with them. But I wasn't an Eagle. Or in 'Group C'. Or even 'Basic Maths'. I was in the Low Stream. Z made it into the Advanced Stream, of course, and he tried to make me feel better but it didn't help.

The whole school gathered for an assembly. Once, everyone would have been talking and Mrs Rook would have shouted at us to settle down. But now there was an eerie almost-silence as we filed into the gym. Everyone seemed to be covered in their own personal fog.

Mrs Rook welcomed us to what she called the New Beginning, and droned on and on about our new curriculum and new teachers and a new standard of behaviour expected from each of us. I was sure she was staring directly at me as she said that part.

The outdated curriculum (her words, not mine) was being thrown out along with a whole heap of *inappropriate library books* and *unreliable text books* and *dangerous websites* and *harmful words* and teachers who did not fit the New Direction of the School (*but we wish them all the best in their new endeavours*). Beth was not sitting with the other staff so I suppose she didn't fit with this New Direction. Julius Warren was in her place, observing us and taking notes.

'We're getting back to basics,' Mrs Rook announced and we had no idea what she meant but she seemed pleased about it.

At the end of the assembly we had to line up to collect our updated school uniforms, which were almost identical to the old uniforms except now it was compulsory for boys to wear trousers and girls to wear skirts and they decided which one you were and there was no arguing or complaining because they didn't care. Some tried, but it was no use. Their names were taken, and appointments were made for them to see the bald man. Julius. We were also given sports uniforms for the compulsory gym class we would take every second day – it was the only thing about this New Beginning that sounded any good to me.

Walking past the library, I could see piles of books being loaded into trolleys and removed.

People were installing screens in the corridors.

Cameras were being mounted to the classroom walls.

And a security checkpoint was being set up at the entrance of the school.

The New Beginning had begun.

I felt sick.

Our new teacher was Mrs Emery, and she stood at our classroom door to welcome us. She was younger than a lot of the teachers we'd had before and she wore cool glasses and smiled as we entered and said, *Good morning, good morning,* and I thought maybe things wouldn't be so bad.

I'd been allocated the middle seat in the middle row, which was the worst place to sit. I needed to be by the window or the door – I hated the feeling of being surrounded, especially by people who hated me. Some of them had been my friends, before, but now they pretended I didn't exist. Except Tash, who always liked to remind everyone I was there. Tash had gotten into the Advanced Stream, of course, so I didn't have to deal with her, but her pain-in-the-arse friend Chloe was given the desk next to mine. She sighed loudly when she sat down, as if that was the worst thing that had happened to her, ever.

'Hey, Santee,' Imara whispered and gave me a little wave from the row in front.

I waved back. At least some of Z's friends didn't hate me.

Mrs Emery stood at the front of the class. She smiled and said, *Good morning,* again and we said, *Good morning,* back.

'Good morning – who?' she said.

We all looked at each other like, *What does she mean?* A couple of people giggled. Her smiled turned into something more like a snarl and she stared the gigglers down until there was absolute silence.

'You will say, "Good morning, Mrs Emery" – got it?' Even though she didn't raise her voice it still felt as if she were shouting. 'Got it?' she repeated.

'Yes, Mrs Emery,' we said, our voices quiet and unsure.

'Better,' she said.

Mrs Emery was here, she told us, to teach us about the Government, History and English. We would read what we were told to read. We would respond the way we were told to respond. Opinions would not exist in Mrs Emery's class.

Mr Lo was still my maths teacher and I never thought I'd be happy to walk back into his classroom. But I was.

'You might find this a little easy, Santee,' he whispered to me as he handed out the new textbooks we'd be working from. 'I'll see what I can do.'

I was happy to have an easy maths class. I couldn't have dealt with parametric equations as well as everything else that was going on. And I thought how Astrid would be annoyed at me for thinking that – she'd tell me that I was lazy and I wasn't trying hard enough and maths was The Most Important Thing. But Astrid wasn't here.

'You all right, Santee?' Mr Lo asked as I was leaving class.

'No,' I said.

'You're a smart kid. You'll get through it.'

He spoke as if that was the final word on it – like I'd be all right because he said so. He had no idea. I wanted to yell in his face, to tell him nothing would ever be all right ever again.

'You don't realise it yet, but it's going to be a lot better this way,' he said.

I raced out of class before I said something I shouldn't, pushed through the crowded corridors and out into the fresh air to find Z. What the hell was wrong with everyone? Why were they going along with this? I needed people to see, actually *see* what was happening. What we were losing. What we were giving up. I needed them to open their eyes.

I walked towards my so-called-home alone that afternoon. Z was hanging out with his friends and I needed some time on my own. No. That's not true. What I *really* needed was my own home and Mum and Astrid and everything to go back to how it was. But that wasn't about to happen. Instead, I headed towards the piece of the wall that was the closest I could get to my real home. Being there made me feel like I hadn't given up on them.

The streets were less crowded than ever before. The shops were empty or closed, the restaurants deserted and lots of windows were boarded up, just like the storefronts on my side after the riots. The usual bustle of the city had just … gone. People moved around like zombies – they were there, but not really *there*. I wanted to snap my fingers in front of their faces and say, *Wake the hell up*. Why were we all going along with all of this?

A kid, tiny, probably only four or five, rushed out from nowhere and pulled my arm.

'Have you got any money?' he half whispered.

I didn't. But before I could say sorry or check that he was OK he'd run off to ask the next person. They ignored him. Another swatted him away as if he were a fly, not a human who needed help. And it was then that I noticed them.

People like the old man who had thrown my sandwich, but different, somehow. Less obvious. Quieter. Sitting in doorways. Crouched in the shadows of alleyways. Waiting, watching, with nowhere to go. Perhaps I'd spent too much time inside the apartment or in my own head to actually see them, all these people with no guest room or substitute family, people with absolutely nothing and no-one. I tried not to stare. I could have been one of them. Instead, I'd gotten lucky. I had Z and Mila and Diggs and food and a bed and I didn't know, would never know, what I'd done to deserve that kind of luck. I was safe. These people were not safe.

I saw the van but didn't think much of it. Not until I saw an identical one following it. And then another, and another. Four of them. White. Tinted windows. They squealed up onto the footpaths and out jumped Unit Officers. In full riot gear. Guns out.

My insides turned to mush.

'ID. ID,' the officers barked.

But they weren't talking to me. They'd found their targets. The lost people. The people with nowhere to go. A man shouted, *Let me go home!* A baby cried. Others kept their heads down and didn't say anything. And then they were gone. Bundled up and shoved into the vans. Driven away. It was as if they'd never been there in the first place.

I kept my head down, like all the other zombies, and made my way towards the wall.

I think I was hoping for some sort of sign. For a note from the other side. A feeling. A sense that my family still existed

173

and were OK and that somehow I'd be OK too. Cos right then, after all the stuff at school and Julius Warren and then seeing those vans, I wasn't so sure.

Up ahead I could see a group of kids. No. I heard them first. A bang, followed by cheers and shouts of laughter. As I got closer I realised they were throwing stuff at the wall. Rocks and things like that, which they'd collected in an old trolley. I headed towards them more quickly. That was what I needed: to throw something. To shout and scream and leave a mark on the smooth concrete face of the ugly wall. Maybe that would help shift the feeling that had settled in the pit of my stomach. I checked for drones, scanned nearby buildings for surveillance cameras, looked over my shoulder for the Unit. The way we did on the other side. We always checked. Just in case. I couldn't see anyone or anything watching, but that didn't mean they weren't there.

'Hey!' I called to the kids.

There were six of them, rummaging through their stockpile of homemade missiles. Bottles and bricks and chunks of concrete. They were there to do some damage. *Good*, I thought.

The smallest one launched half a brick at the wall. 'Take that, arseholes,' she screamed with a voice that didn't match her tiny body.

The brick sailed over the top of the wall and they all clapped and cheered and patted her on the back. 'Kill the Threats!' their little high-pitched voices screamed.

I stopped.

They didn't want to hurt the *wall*, they wanted to hurt the people on the other side.

Something inside me broke into hundreds of little pieces and suddenly I was running towards them shouting, *Piss off, stop it.* I don't know what I was thinking. Neither did they. They didn't move. They just stood there with these looks on their faces like, *Who the hell is she?* They weren't scared of me even though I was bigger and older and quite possibly crazy.

'What do you want?' One of the boys grabbed a bottle and held it high above his head.

'Stop it!' I said. 'You could hurt someone.'

'Yeah,' he said. 'That's the point.'

They laughed and moved in closer. These little shits. All arrogant and used to getting their own way. Spoilt rich kids.

'Piss off!' I shouted.

But they didn't.

We stared each other down from a few metres away, me and the boy with the bottle. He made like he was going to throw it at my head and I ducked and moved back. It only made it worse. The boy looked very impressed with himself – like he was suddenly the most powerful person in the world, and I was just an ant.

'They're people,' I said. 'Like us.'

'Explain yourself,' the boy said, and he didn't sound like a little kid anymore. He sounded like a Unit Officer.

I said nothing.

'Show us your ID,' he said, still using that Unit voice.

'No,' I said, cos there was no way I was going to let a bunch of kids start ordering me around.

A rock sailed through the air and bounced off my shoulder. The sting of the impact rushed down my arm. I tried to keep my face neutral, normal, as if it hadn't hurt at all.

I kept my eyes on the boy with the bottle. Whoever had thrown that rock had shown him up. They'd had the guts to throw their missile when he'd just stood there, threatening me with it. He raised the bottle again. The air buzzed and tightened around me. He had to do it, had to throw it at me *now*, or he'd lose his position. He'd be just another ant, like me. He narrowed his eyes and steadied himself and I stood there and waited. I was not going to make this easy for him.

The bottle flew through the air and I shut my eyes and tried not to flinch.

It smashed apart at my feet.

Close.

The glass sparkled on the ground.

The kids laughed at the boy and he ran towards me, arms swinging and swearing his head off. He was much younger close up. Tiny. Like those little kids I'd see walking to school, holding their mothers' hands, their backpacks almost as big as them.

He shoved me hard in the stomach and I stumbled back and I didn't know what the hell I was supposed to do cos this was a little kid. How could I fight a little kid?

'Traitor!' he shouted in a high-pitched whine.

The other kids joined in. All of them as small and angry as this boy. The girl with the good arm gave me a little shove as she said, *ID, ID, show us.* She pushed me again.

And that was enough.

I pushed her back. She fell. The boy went at me again and I punched him, hard, just in the arm, but it must have hurt cos his face went all blotchy and red and I thought he was going to start crying.

A drone hummed overhead. I looked up to see it hanging above me, watching us. I'd never felt so relieved to see one of those things. The kids scrambled to their feet and took off, leaving their trolley of missiles behind. I watched the drone hover, collecting our images, recording us for future reference.

My legs stung. Little specks of blood bubbled to the surface and ran down my shins.

I stopped at my section of the wall. I blocked out the noise of the traffic, the sirens, the people who passed by. I placed the palms of my hands onto the surface of the wall and closed my eyes and imagined that Mum and Astrid were doing the same thing on the other side. In my mind the wall disappeared and the three of us stood there, palm to palm, and I said something like, *This is weird*, and Astrid laughed and Mum said, *It's a moment, Santee, don't be so cynical*. That didn't happen. Of course. But imagining things like that kept me going.

CHAPTER 25

I was in my bedroom trying to finish an essay that just didn't want to be written, so I was happy to hear Mila calling my name. I headed into the kitchen, where she had rearranged the chairs into a neat row. Pip was already sitting there, waiting.

'You're my test audience,' she said, and pretty much shoved me into a chair.

'What?'

'I have to do a speech for school and I need to practise,' she said before running off to find Z.

'She's just like her mum,' Pip said, and chuckled quietly to herself.

'Is she?' I said.

'Enthusiastic, full of energy and far too smart for her own good.'

'Sounds like her mum was pretty great.'

'She was,' Pip said. 'And she would have thought you were pretty great, too.'

There was so much more I wanted to ask her, but Mila came back, dragging Z with her.

'This better be good,' he said as he flopped into the chair next to me.

'It will be,' Mila said, and took her place in front of us, palm cards in hand. She took a deep breath. Smiled. She looked calm and composed and this vision of her in ten years' time flashed through my mind: Mila standing at a podium, inspiring the crowd and being in charge and doing something good.

'Good afternoon students, teachers and honoured guests,' she said in a voice that was hers, but also not hers. 'Today I will be discussing the Safety Border. Our city had been plagued by Threats for decades. Countless leaders attempted to curb these heinous acts; however, it was not until Magnus Varick's unprecedented and courageous move to build the Safety Border that real change occurred.'

Pip shifted in her seat, but Mila didn't seem to notice.

'Research proved that in our city, Threat activity originated in the area now known as Region Two. In order to contain and limit the movement of this activity, Varick and his government implemented the Safety Border. Essentially, it separates two distinct cultures growing in our capital. That of Region One and that of Region Two.'

'I need a snack,' Pip said loudly. 'Anyone else want a snack?'

'Pip,' Mila said, 'it's a three-minute speech. You can wait for three minutes, can't you?'

179

Pip sighed. 'Yes, love, sorry.'

'That's OK.' Mila smiled again and returned to her palm cards. 'The Safety Border provides an efficient and effective way to monitor movement and Threat activity while also keeping Good Citizens safe and secure. Citizens from both Regions have welcomed the Safety Border and the protection it –'

'Have they?' Z interrupted.

'This is a speech, Z,' Mila said. 'You can't interject like in a debate or –'

'Does Santee welcome the wall?' Z said.

I reached over and squeezed his arm and tried to say, *Leave it*, but he didn't get it.

'Does she, Mila?'

'Um.' Mila shuffled through her notes. 'My speech isn't about Santee.'

'But it kinda is, right? I mean, she's stuck here cos of that wall,' Z said.

'Yes, I know, but …'

'But what?'

Mila looked confused; she wasn't used to her work being criticised, to getting the answer wrong. 'This is what we're learning in class,' she said.

'Doesn't make it true,' Z said.

'I know that, Zac,' she said. 'I'm not stupid. I know exactly what's happening. I also know that if I give a speech about greed and abuse of power and fear-mongering and the truth about this regime, we're all going to end up in a lot of trouble.'

Everyone fell completely silent.

That image of Mila in her twenties got a whole lot clearer in my mind.

'I'm sorry, Santee,' she said finally. 'I don't want to make you upset.'

'It's OK,' I said, even though it wasn't. It wasn't OK that her school would make her regurgitate that crap. Mila was smart. She could think for herself, could smell bullshit a mile off. Those kids I met at the wall? They ate up all that bullshit. And that wasn't OK, either.

'Can I keep going?' Mila said.

'Well, I don't know about the rest of your audience, but I'm learning a hell of a lot,' I said. 'Keep going.'

She took a moment, straightened her back and cleared her throat. 'Citizens are required, by law, to remain loyal to their Region as movement of any kind has been proven to have strong links to Threat activity.'

'I'm sorry, love, but I can't listen to this,' Pip said quietly, and left the room.

'Me neither,' Z said as he followed her out.

We heard the front door slam.

Mila stared at the empty seats. Her eyes were glassy and her lip was trembling, just a little.

'Hey,' I said gently. 'Don't worry about them. We all know you're way too smart to just believe whatever some teacher tells you.'

'Our new teacher is a moron,' she said, smiling.

'Same here,' I said.

She gave me a hug, planted a kiss on my forehead. 'I wish it was under different circumstances, but I'm glad you're here, Santee,' she said.

'Me too,' I said. 'Now, come on, practise this speech. You need to get an A-plus, or whatever it is you geniuses get.'

'A-plus-plus-plus,' she said, and laughed, and started her speech from the top.

CHAPTER 26

The next morning I woke before the sun was up. I was in a shitty mood and didn't want to go to school. I kept thinking about Mila's speech and the kids at the wall and the zombies in the city who just ignored all those nowhere people as they were thrown into vans and taken away.

I turned on the bedside lamp and grabbed my sketchpad, but I'd used up most of the pages and there wasn't enough room for all the things I wanted to draw. I needed to create a mess. A huge mess. I wanted to scribble over everything I had sketched cos it all seemed so pointless now. I felt trapped. Useless. Like a tiny speck just getting thrown around wherever, whenever, with no say in it. At all.

I needed a bigger canvas. I needed room to scream, but not with my voice. With my pens. My markers.

I changed, packed my bag and snuck into Z's room. I was sure Diggs would catch me, that he'd set up some kind of surveillance in the hallway. But it was worth the risk. Z had to be a part of this.

He was all rolled up in his blankets like a cocoon and he looked kinda cute and funny and I thought about taking a photo of him, but that would be super weird so I didn't.

'Hey,' I said, and shook him.

He murmured something and tried to roll away from me, so I shook him harder. He opened his eyes and freaked out when he saw me standing above him in one of his old hoodies.

'Shhh,' I said. 'It's me. Get dressed. We're going for a run.'

'No,' he said, and pulled the blanket over his head.

'I need to do something, Z,' I said. 'I feel so useless.'

He groaned a bit as he sat up and said, 'For you? Anything.'

We slipped out of the apartment and into the morning. I wanted to run. Really run. Sprint through the park until my legs screamed and my chest ached. Smash and destroy everything in my way. Instead I jogged slowly with Z, who kept telling me, *Go ahead, go ahead,* but I stayed right beside him. This guy who hated running, who was so crap at it, had agreed to come just because I'd asked him. Why would anyone do that? I didn't get it. But I knew I wanted him there, with me.

I led us to an alleyway. We'd walked past it on our way to school and I knew it would be perfect. It was enclosed by walls that were clean and smooth. There was no way walls like that would be left so clean back at home. Where

I grew up every surface was tagged, stickered, stencilled and painted. The Unit had stopped caring about it, stopped trying to cover it up. I liked it. It was way more exciting than the stuff in the art gallery. Over here, the walls were grey or white or brick or glass and they were blank. Which was good. It meant my message would stand out.

We stopped, and I waited for Z to catch his breath. The alleyway was deserted. There were no windows looking onto it, only fire exits and loading docks. I'd seen the cameras as we'd entered but it didn't look like there were any more down the long cobblestone passageway. That didn't mean a drone wouldn't fly overhead, or a patrol car wouldn't drive past, but it was worth the risk.

I took a marker from my pocket and stood at the wall. I'd been thinking, over and over, about what I could write. This could be it. The one chance I'd get to leave some sort of mark, get the voice out of my head, that feeling out of the pit of my stomach. I drew a cartoon face. Big, bold lines. A girl's face. Screaming. A speech bubble. Help me!

'Shit, Santee,' Z said quietly.

The streetlights buzzed and clicked off.

'I had to do something, you know?' I said.

He didn't say anything. I thought he was pissed off at me for dragging him into this, for making him part of something so stupid. Then he took the marker and wrote, under my picture, DOWN WITH THE REGIME.

He smiled at me. 'You're amazing.'

We walked back to the apartment with the secret of what we'd just done bubbling inside me. I thought about the people who would walk past it on their way to work. Would they notice? What would they think? How would Varick react? Would he ever know? I couldn't believe I'd done it. After they took Dad away I did a lot of crazy, stupid things, but they all seemed a bit childish now, compared to what we'd just done. Back then I'd done things like smash up the pot plants in our concrete yard. I'd just needed to destroy something, to get back at the neighbours. This was so much better than smashing pot plants.

My whole body trembled with every step, but I wasn't scared or nervous. I was happy. For the first time in the longest time.

'You OK?' Z said.

'I want to make people think,' I blurted out. 'About the wall and Varick and my dad and your mum and just ... everything.'

He murmured, *Yeah, me too,* and smiled and put his arm around me as we continued through the park.

'I want to do more,' I said. 'You in?'

'You kidding me? Of course I'm in.'

I kissed him. Pulled him in close and felt his heart pounding through his chest and into mine.

CHAPTER 27

We watched the News every night, both hoping and dreading that there'd be something about the graffiti. Diggs wanted to know why we were so interested in the News all of a sudden.

'Mrs Emery quizzes us on it,' I said. Which was true, even if it wasn't the reason I watched.

It didn't matter, anyway – the graffiti never got mentioned on the News. And out there, on the walls, our messages were painted over and covered up and it was like they'd never existed.

One night the News included a segment about a family who lived close to the wall. They could see it from their backyard. It shadowed over everything. But they didn't mind. They explained to the reporter how much better life was with the new Safety Border. *It's a relief,* the mother said. *We never really felt safe with all that Threat activity so close by,* the father added. The children nodded in unison. *They stole our bikes once*, the middle child said. The mother looked sad. *I'm sure there are some nice people over there, but most of them are criminals and it's about time something was done about it.*

'Shit,' Diggs announced loudly, 'we've got a bloody criminal in our house. Lock up your bikes, kids!' And he laughed and they laughed and I knew he was being funny and trying to cheer me up. I knew he didn't believe what those people were saying, but still, something about it hurt.

I wanted to break into that family's yard and write all over their fence, take my pens to the part of wall they could see from their house and write on it too, so no matter where they looked they would see my messages. *Help me! Let us out / Let them in. Freedom!* Maybe then they'd wake up to the fact that the wall was wrong. None of us were safe. People on both sides were trapped. All of us. The Drivers understood that. And so did Pip. So it made me think that, maybe, there were more people like them out there somewhere. And maybe other people, one day, would work it out.

I started to call the Drivers' apartment *home*. I felt so guilty every time the word slipped out because it couldn't be home – not really, not without my family. But I'd just have to think about those vans picking up lost people to remember how lucky I was. The vans, like the graffiti, were never mentioned on the News.

'Who decides what makes the News?' I asked Diggs late one night.

Z shot me a look that said, *Don't say anything*. As if I would. I told Diggs about the vans I'd seen and how people were taken away in them. 'Do you know where they took them?' I asked. 'Is it that Processing Centre thing?'

He turned the TV up loud. Way too loud.

'Tell me again,' he said, and I did.

He wanted to know when it had happened and what the vans looked like and who was taken and I couldn't answer all his questions.

'Santee.' He spoke in that kind of whisper that wants to be a shout. He got close to my face. 'This is bloody important.'

One of his eyes was bloodshot and I wondered if that meant he was drinking again. Since my first night there things had calmed a little inside the Driver home. Or maybe, compared to what was happening outside, it just seemed that way. He said he had something important to do and stormed out, slamming the door behind him and making the walls shake, and Z just shrugged at me and Mila said, *He gets like that, don't take it personally.*

Anyway, I decided right then that I'd never tell him about Julius Warren – if he got this angry about the vans I didn't want to see his reaction to that bit of news. I didn't like the way his face seemed to change, the violence in his body that he could barely keep inside.

Diggs didn't come back that night. That was the start of seeing even less of him than usual. He was always working and said it was easier to stay at the office, so Pip would come around to make sure we were eating and sleeping and doing all the things that kids supposedly can't do without an adult being around. They hadn't figured that we had Mila. And Mila was more responsible and grown-up than most of the actual adults I knew.

Without Diggs around it was possible, although banned, to sneak into Z's room. Or he'd sneak into mine. I thought it was a rule worth breaking. And who could stop us? I'd wait until I was sure Mila was asleep, tiptoe across the hall and quietly open his door. Most of the time he'd still be up drawing. He was obsessed with lettering and kept going on about finding his style. His sketchpad was full of different ways to write DOWN WITH THE REGIME.

'Time to get a new sentence,' I joked.

'I like it,' he said. 'Simple, easy to remember. And not all of us can be as creative as you.'

'Shut up,' I said and shoved him.

'You're an artist,' he said. Again. Just like he did that first day we'd hung out. He always said it. And I always told him to shut up cos I was embarrassed by how happy it made me.

He sat on his bed, hunched over his sketchpad, and I lay beside him. He had this serious expression on his face, like he was constantly judging the work he was doing and none of it was good enough. I reached out to touch the back of his neck, feel where the hair was shaved and short, trace my fingers down his spine. He threw the sketchpad on the floor and turned to me and we kissed and it felt like my whole body was alive with electricity as he pulled me closer. I wanted to touch him and feel him touch me and it was as if we couldn't get close enough. My skin turned to goosebumps as he slid his hand under my shirt, his fingers running up and down my back and me falling, falling into this rhythm, this moment.

I tried not to wake him as I slipped out from under his arm and out of the bed. It was early. Very early. But I couldn't sleep. I looked over at Z and part of me wanted to get back into bed, climb under the sheets and curl up next to him

190

and just go with it, forget everything else except being there with him. But I couldn't. Not now. I snuck out of his room and back into mine, got changed, grabbed a pen and headed outside.

I was an artist.

And I had to keep going. I didn't want to fall in love with Z and the Drivers and life with them and forget everything that had led me to this. It would be easy to get used to the wall and everything it stood for. I could get comfortable with the nice house and the perfect boyfriend and the surrogate Dad and cute little sister. I could pull my head in like Mrs Rook told me and I could be the smart kid Mr Lo seemed to think I was ... or I could be me.

I ran and ran and it felt like I could go on forever.

CHAPTER 28

Diggs was actually home for once when we got in after school. We could hear him chatting and laughing with Pip as we walked in.

'I made cupcakes,' Pip announced. 'Come get one before your dad eats them all.'

They were both in a really good mood, which was nice after a crappy day with a psycho teacher. We sat down and Diggs ran around making us coffee and tea and pouring orange juice for Mila. I wondered if he was feeling bad about being so absent.

Julius Warren had asked me again about Diggs's activities (his words, not mine). He'd called me to his office over the loudspeaker and I dragged myself there as slowly as possible. He had made heaps of changes to Beth's office. Removed the posters I'd once hated but now missed, got rid of her filing cabinets and comfy armchairs. I had sat opposite him at his large desk.

'Any news?' he had asked, smiling like we were best buddies. Gross.

'Any news for me?' I replied, and flashed him back the same fake smile.

'We're working on it.'

Liar, I thought. I repeated the stuff I'd already told him. He sighed loudly and sent me back to class, where Mrs Emery was waiting with a lunchtime detention. Perfect.

Pip's cupcakes were just what I needed.

'Santee,' Diggs said, and motioned to a couple of plastic bags on the chair beside him. 'Those are for you.'

'Me?'

He nodded and Pip said, 'Open them.'

They were full of clothes and shoes and stuff like that and I couldn't believe it and didn't know what to say, so I just kinda stood there like an idiot staring at all the stuff. New stuff. My own stuff.

'Thought you could do with some new things,' he said. 'Pip helped. No biggie.'

I didn't know whether to laugh or cry and I ended up doing both at the same time.

'Don't get all weird about it,' Diggs said as I gave him a hug, which was definitely not the sort of thing I usually did. But it seemed right.

That night felt like some kind of celebration. Diggs made this fancy pasta thing and the five of us sat around the table eating and talking and laughing with classical music booming from the stereo. We missed the News and for a moment I worried about what the neighbours would think, except our neighbour was there, with us, also not watching the News.

Pip said, 'Did you hear about the random checks?'

And Diggs said, 'Pip. No. Not in front of the kids.'

Of course then we really wanted to know, but Diggs insisted that Mila go to bed and she tried to argue with him but it was no good and in the end she went to her room as if it had been her idea all along anyway. (She said something about needing eight hours' sleep to be at her *optimum*. Her words. Not mine.)

The random checks didn't sound like anything new. The Unit would turn up and take people away. Just like they'd done to my dad and our old neighbour from number four and heaps and heaps of people. No-one talked about it back then but it didn't mean it hadn't happened. And according to Pip it was happening again now.

'But it's not just people. They're checking everything. Going through cupboards and pulling up floorboards and checking under beds.' Pip moved in close and spoke like she was telling us some sort of scary story at a campfire. 'They'll use anything against you.'

'Against you?' I said.

'For crimes against the State,' Diggs said. 'Bull. Shit.'

'What stuff are they looking for?' I looked at Z to see if he was thinking the same thing. Our pens and markers and sketchpads. What if they found them? We didn't even hide them. Z kept his head down, his eyes away from everyone.

'A banned book,' Pip said, 'or film. Maybe you'd left it on your shelf. Forgotten about it. I mean, that can happen, can't it?'

'But they don't really care – they can make anything look bad,' Diggs said. 'It's all about context.'

CHAPTER 29

We walked to school together every day. Me and Z. I thought it might get awkward, like maybe we would run out of things to say to each other, but even when we walked in silence it felt right. And it wasn't like Z was all that quiet. He liked to talk. A lot. He talked while we did the housework, which was something I wanted to do on my own as a way of thanking the Drivers but he always insisted on helping with. He talked to the checkout operators when we bought groceries from the nearby supermarket. He talked in his sleep. But he was a good listener, too, and he never got annoyed with how much I went on about missing Mum and Astrid or my frustrations about not being able to contact them or anything. He always listened.

We kept going on our morning runs, even though it made the days long and exhausting. It was worth it. It felt like we were the only people trying to do something, anything – the rest of the world kept their heads and eyes further down than before, their ears and mouths shut. No-one questioned anything. And it seemed like the words we wrote never lasted long enough to get through to anyone. When we felt really brave (or stupid) we'd walk by the building or fence or rubbish bin or spot on the footpath a few hours later to find our graffiti had been scrubbed away. And I'd wonder if, maybe, the whole thing was just in my head. But Z would squeeze my hand or smile his smile and I'd know it was real. DOWN WITH THE REGIME. Z added it to every picture I drew or sentence I wrote. I wanted all of it to come down – the wall, the school, the Regime and especially Magnus Varick.

'You wanna go the long way?' Z said.

'We got time?'

'Always.'

The long way meant the weird detour Z had taken me on all those months ago. It was a thing we did. We'd talk about that first day together and remember (or misremember) how everything went down and we'd notice the way the city was changing.

The Unit had started setting up security checks all over the city. It made things really slow but because it also made things 'extra safe' people didn't mind. They said things like, *If you're a Good Citizen you've got nothing to worry about.* And they lined up, patiently and quietly, as their bags were scanned and their movements questioned by Unit Officers.

A line had already formed at the security check they'd set up at the far end of the park, by the gates that led into the city. Sometimes the check could be really quick – you'd show them your ID and everything would be fine and through you'd all go. Other times, not so much. It all depended on the officers' moods. And today they were all in really shitty moods.

We pushed our bags through the scanner, showed our IDs. I had my permanent ID now, plastic and official and keeping me safe. But I still hadn't told Z the bit about his dad being my guardian. It felt too weird. The officers made us empty our bags and, as they went through every single item, asked what we were up to. The interrogation went like this:

Where are you going?

School.

What are you doing there?

Learning.

What's this?

That's a calculator.

Why do you have a calculator?

For school. Maths class.

Show me.

And I showed him it was just a calculator and nothing to worry about and he turned it over and over for ages before shoving it back at me.

When we finally got through the security check and there was enough distance between them and us, Z put on his stupid (and kinda funny) officer voice and said, 'Tell me everything you have eaten for dinner for the last month.'

'And how many times you went to the toilet,' I said in my attempt at the officer voice thing.

'Do you prefer dogs or cats?'

'Sweet or savoury?'

'Magnus Varick or Magnus Varick?'

When we were stupid like that it was almost like things were normal. Like I could almost imagine Astrid walking with us, telling us, *Stop being idiots,* and, *Hurry up or we'll be late.*

Suddenly Z grabbed my shoulder and did this weird motion with his head.

'Stop it, weirdo.' I laughed and went to move away, but he pulled me close and whispered, *Look up.*

I did and there, up high on an old building with a restaurant downstairs and teeny offices upstairs, were the words: *DOWN WITH THE REGIME.* Red block letters. Spray-painted and messy, but readable. And right in the middle of the city. Not hiding down some alleyway. The words were out in the open for everyone to see. If only they'd look up.

I took Z's hand, squeezed it tight and didn't let go until we reached school.

CHAPTER 30

Peter was in my classroom.

I kept staring at him to make sure. Part of me wondered if I was losing it. But the more I stared at him, the more I knew it was him, and then he was introduced and it was definitely him and I wanted to stand up and shout, *Hey, Peter, it's me!* But I didn't. Of course. I just stared and tried to send him a message with my mind: *Look at me, look. I'm right here.* But he avoided my eyes completely.

He stood in front of the class with another officer. Mrs Emery wrote the name of the class across the whiteboard in sprawling black letters – *Futures: Your Life with the Unit.* The week before we'd had *Futures: Your Life in Agriculture* and listened to a dairy farmer and someone who worked at the abattoir try to convince us that our lives would be so much better working out of the city. *You're making a real contribution to society*, the farmer had said, and we'd all nodded.

'It's great to make a real contribution to society,' the officer said. And we all nodded. Again. I wondered if anyone else realised we were being read the exact same script.

The officer, who was all pimples and eagerness, told us his name was Baxter. He didn't look like an officer, he looked like a kid playing dress-ups. He could have easily passed for one us. *Baxter*, I thought, *I could outrun you and outfight you any day.* If Z and I were ever caught doing graffiti, I hoped it would be Baxter who found us. We'd be fine.

'You can't take Safety and Security for granted,' Baxter said. 'It's up to us to protect it. Our Safety ensures our Freedom.' He went on like that for ages. I couldn't follow his argument but he was really into it and lots of the guys in class were nodding along with him.

Peter shuffled from one foot to the other. He'd always been kinda shy. Astrid and I would always force him into our stupid make-believe games. *Let's pretend to be pirates,* we'd say, and he'd get all self-conscious about putting on the voice or acting out the fantasy world we'd created. It felt like a lifetime ago. It probably was.

We locked eyes. I smiled. He didn't. He looked right through me and I wondered if he'd forgotten me. I squished my face at him, squinted, stuck out my tongue, and finally, there it was. A very quick sideways smile. A slight nod. Then he looked at Baxter as if he were really interested in what he was saying.

Peter. I couldn't stop looking at him, trying to read his mind, his expression, his body language. Anything. Last time I'd seen him he'd pulled me from the crowd at the Checkpoint. Pushed me. Yelled at me. Saved me. There was so much I needed to ask him but it wasn't like I could just blurt out, *Hey, Peter? Can we talk?*

Everyone started clapping and I realised the presentation was over. Baxter looked very pleased with himself.

'The officers have agreed to answer your questions. Ask something smart. Don't embarrass me,' Mrs Emery said.

Everyone sat quietly, eyes forward, hands on desks. We never asked questions. We weren't used to doing that anymore. Mrs Emery pointed to some poor kid at the back of the class and demanded they ask a question. They stood and stumbled over their words until Mrs Emery had had enough and put them out of their misery.

'You,' she said, and pointed. At me.

I pushed the chair back and stood. My knees were like jelly. I couldn't ask my questions out loud. Not in front of all these people. I needed to get Peter alone, but I had no idea how to do that.

'Do Unit Officers work on the other side of the Safety Border?' I finally said.

'We work across both Regions. You get placements and are deployed to areas that need you most,' Peter said. He looked right at me. I searched his eyes for something more, a hint or a secret code or anything about my family. Anything. 'And, just so everyone knows, the people on the other side of the Safety Border are doing OK. They're all OK.'

My heart jumped. He held eye contact for a little longer than he probably should have. I was scared Mrs Emery might intercept his message. *They're all OK.* My mind raced as I tried to come up with another question. Something that could get me some more details. But the guy in front ruined everything.

'Who cares how they are?' he said loudly. 'They're all Threats over there!'

'My mum reckons they should be cut off completely,' another said, and people murmured in agreement. 'We're propping them up with our resources and taxes and what do they do? Riot and attack us cos they always want more. Nah. Let them fend for themselves. We're better off without them.'

Mrs Emery nodded like all this shouting was suddenly allowed, and the rest of the class took that as a chance to start talking over each other in angry voices about how bad the other side was. It was like they wanted to outdo each other with who had the loudest, most stupid opinion. Peter and Baxter gave them more ammunition with their well-rehearsed lines about Threats and Security and how the Unit makes a Difference and why the Safety Border works.

I sat quietly and let Peter's words sink in: *They're all OK.* My eyes grew hot with tears and I blinked and blinked to stop them breaking through. Mum and Astrid were safe. They were OK. What else could he have meant?

CHAPTER 31

I needed to do something. I had that butterflies-in-your-stomach feeling, like you get when you're a kid before your birthday party. Maybe it was the news about my family. Or the fresh graffiti we'd seen. Or maybe I was just fooling myself into thinking things could, possibly, be OK.

I lay in bed and stared into the dark and wished Diggs wasn't home so I could go into Z's room. I had weird, half-asleep and half-awake dreams where I felt like I was falling and just as I was about to hit the ground I'd feel a jolt and find myself in bed.

When Dad was taken from us, we all slept in the big bed with Mum for a while. Me on one side, Astrid on the other and Mum in the middle. She would twitch in her sleep, cry out sometimes, and we would help her fall back to sleep again. Tell her we were there and that it would be all right. She said we shouldn't have to do that, that she was the mother and she should protect us and not the other way around. And then she would cry. She cried a lot back then. We told her we loved her and climbed into her bed every night for months. I wondered if she slept in my bed now, to be closer to Astrid. I wondered if she was having the same dream where she was falling. Maybe we were falling together and jolting to consciousness at the exact same time.

As soon as the first signs of morning appeared, I snuck into Z's bedroom. He was already awake, a pile of pens and markers on his bed. He said he'd been collecting them whenever he could.

'What do you mean, "collecting"?' I whispered.

'Better if you don't know,' he said, and smiled. He was lucky he had that smile. It really got him out of so much trouble. Or into it.

'Let's go for a run,' I said.

'Now?' He yawned.

'I think we should put our mark somewhere people will actually see it. I mean, Z, come on – we started this whole thing –'

'No, we didn't. You did. I was just coming along for the exercise.'

'You're part of it! They copied *your* words. I just think people should see it, our stuff. The original.'

I wanted to be braver than whoever had copied us. I wanted to watch people reading our words. I needed to know we were doing more than inspiring copycat graffiti.

'I dunno, Santee,' he said.

'We need to make stickers.'

'Stickers?' he said. 'Really?'

'Really,' I said, and showed him. I'd taken some of those sticky label things that Diggs had in his study. I'd been snooping for new markers when I found them. 'We just need to decorate them.'

I thought it was best to keep the message simple. Just DOWN WITH THE REGIME, written in the quick style we'd gotten pretty good at by now. We sat on the bed and wrote it out on label after label.

'Do you think Diggs will notice we've taken all his labels?'

'No,' Z said. 'Anyway, I think these would have been Mum's.'

'Shit, sorry, I didn't – I didn't think.'

'She would love it, Santee. She'd probably be out there with us if she was still here.'

We walked out into the early morning darkness. It felt as if it were just the two of us against the world. But, somehow, Z's mum and my dad were with us, too. Urging us on. I liked that feeling.

My idea sounded better in my head than when I tried to explain it to Z. The basic idea was this: stick our message on all the trees in the park. OK, maybe not *all* the trees, but the big ones that lined the paths. The ones people would walk past or sit under. The ones they couldn't miss.

'They're trees, Santee,' Z whispered as we slowly jogged through the park. 'We can't do that to trees.' He looked at me like I was some kind of psychopath. 'Don't you care about the trees?' he said. And he looked so sad.

I felt awful and tried to take it back.

He cracked up laughing. 'I'm kidding.'

I whacked him on the arm.

'It's a great plan,' he said. 'You're a genius.'

Problem was, I wasn't a genius. Not even close.

There were security cameras in the park but Z was pretty confident he knew where they were and how we could avoid them. We would jog along the winding paths and one of us would stop to catch our breath or stretch or tie a shoelace and the other would slap the stickers onto the tree. Simple. We would hit as many trees as we could across the entire park. I had this idea that if we spread them out, the Unit might miss a couple and then our message would remain and maybe someone would actually see it.

It worked. The stickers stuck to the trees and Z even added some to the park's signs and plaques and statues. It was quicker and easier than writing and we covered way more ground than we'd been able to before.

I was pretending to stretch at a tree and was about to plaster a sticker to its smooth bark when I heard Z whistle. A loud, piercing sound that made my heart stop. The whistle was our sign. Something wasn't right.

Someone was coming. Or already there. I froze. I was supposed to act casual. That's what Z had told me to do when we made our getaway plans. Act casual. Walk away. Like you hadn't even been there.

'Run, run, run,' Z said and ran past me, grabbing my arm and pulling me along with him.

It felt like I was watching myself in a movie cos there was no way this could be true. Z was running faster than he'd ever run in his life. I knew there were officers chasing us down but I couldn't tell how many or what they looked like or anything. All I knew was the sound of their boots hitting the path behind us. Their voices shouting, *Stop or we'll shoot.* Shoot? Shoot what? Us? I kept my eyes forward. Maybe if I didn't look at them we'd be safe.

Z suddenly swerved off the path and onto the grass and I stumbled as I followed him and my ankle twisted and a sharp sting shot up my leg but somehow I managed to stay up and kinda ran kinda limped and ignored the whir of a distant helicopter getting closer and the sounds of the officers shouting, *Go-go-go.* Z led me into a garden thick with trees and bushes and onto a hidden dirt path that wound through it and we pushed through the bushes until Z stopped and pulled me to the ground with him.

My whole body was thumping, thumping, thumping as we crouched in the dead leaves and dirt, hidden by the bushes. What the hell was he doing? They were close, they must have been close. I tried to shove him, keep him moving, but he wouldn't move. I waited. I tried to hold my breath. To stop my heart thumping. My blood flowing. My mind racing. Everything inside me was too loud. I was sure I was going to give us away just by existing. Z found my hand and squeezed it. I looked into his eyes. *We're safe*, he seemed to be saying, and I tried desperately to believe him.

We huddled together and waited.

Bang.

We both jumped. A gunshot. Then another and another. Shit. They were going to kill us. I started shaking and couldn't stop, even when Z put his arms around me and held me tight. *This is it*, I thought, *this is the end*. And I didn't want it to be. It wasn't fair. It wasn't right. I was trying to breathe but I'd forgotten how to and suddenly, without thinking, I pushed Z away and stood up and … there were no officers. No guns. The helicopter was hovering above another section of the park, not right overhead like I'd thought.

We took off our hoodies and hid them in the dirt, just in case someone had noticed two terrified idiots running from the Unit – even though the Unit wasn't chasing them. Of course they weren't. We were nothing. We weren't doing anything that needed guns and helicopters to make it stop. They could stop our messages just by covering them up.

CHAPTER 32

As we finally made our way to school, exhausted and sore and feeling more empty and useless than ever, it wasn't a surprise to see all our stickers had been ripped down. Little bits had remained, tiny streaks of white paper stuck to tree trunks and things, but there were no words left on any of them.

Except for one.

A lonely sticker had stubbornly remained, stuck to the trunk of a big old tree on the main path. My writing stood out clear and strong. DOWN WITH THE REGIME. It might have been small, but it was there.

And it lit something inside me. Made me less tired. More determined. It felt like we were invincible. Like we could do anything.

'How's your brother doing?'

It was lunchtime and I was sitting at the bird-crap table, on my own, sketching some ideas for our next graffiti attack. I wanted to source some better-quality stickers – some that were really, really sticky and hard to remove. And I was already dreaming about covering the whole city: sticking them to cars and buses and letterboxes and shop windows and Unit patrol cars. I was lost in all of this when Tash approached me.

'How's your brother doing?' she asked again.

I shut my sketchpad and looked at her. I knew exactly what she was trying to do. Make me feel stupid and embarrassed. I wasn't going to let her. I just stared at her. Waited.

'Z,' she said. 'I mean, you're like their foster kid or something, aren't you? So that makes him your brother.'

'What do you want, Tash?' I said, and started packing my bag like I had somewhere to be. I didn't. Z was off with Riley and his friends playing basketball. He said I should come but I wasn't going to sit on the sidelines like some dumb girlfriend cheerleader. No way.

'Look,' she said. 'The girls sent me over cos Chloe is into him and wanted to find out what his deal was. You know.'

The Tash I had been friends with would never have said that kind of thing. We would have laughed at girls like that. We had.

'Go away,' I said.

'She really likes him and we think they'd make a cute couple.'

I heard her friends laugh. It was so ... high school. I mean, it *was* high school, of course, but it just seemed so out of place with everything that was going on. Who could honestly care about crushes and gossip and popularity when the world was like this?

'He's my boyfriend,' I said. Calmly. Or as calmly as I could. I hadn't said it out loud before. It made me feel a little sad to tell Tash like that when, once, she would have been the first person I'd told.

'So weird,' she said, and backed away like I smelled bad. She headed back to her friends and they laughed, then made a big deal of looking over at me and laughing some more.

My face burned. It wasn't weird. Was it? I liked him. He liked me. What was weird about that? My brain raced with all the things I should have said to Tash – all these smart comments that would have shut her up straight away. Perhaps even made her cry. But it was too late now. So, I kept drawing as if I didn't notice Tash and her friends – as if anything they said didn't bother me. At all. I had way more important shit to deal with.

'Santee Quinn, may I sit down?'

It was Julius Warren.

First Tash, now him. I just needed Magnus Varick to show up for the perfect trifecta.

'Lunch break is almost over, sir,' I said with a smile, and repacked my bag quickly.

'You had quite a morning, didn't you?' he said, and sat across from me.

I kept the smile on my face but my insides were churning. What did he know about my morning? I said something about my morning being pretty boring, actually, and that I had to get to class early, but he ignored all that and leaned forward.

'I have news,' he said. 'About your father. If you want it?'

'Why?' I said quietly.

'You helped me with some information so now I'll help you. That was the deal. Remember?'

What had I told him? I ran through all our meetings, tried to remember everything I'd said about Diggs. There was nothing I'd said that would get him into real trouble. Was there?

'You've been so helpful,' he said.

I felt like I'd snapped, disconnected from myself. I was hovering above, watching this all unfold to someone who looked and sounded just like me but wasn't me. No. No way.

What had I done?

'I don't want anything from you,' I said with a determination I didn't know I still had in me.

And I walked away without getting any information about my dad, and possibly destroying the only sort-of-Dad I had in my life right now.

I was stupid. So stupid.

I sat out the front of school waiting for Z. He'd texted me to say he had to stay behind for a bit and I should go on without him. I assumed he'd heard that Julius Warren had talked with me at lunch, assumed he knew I'd betrayed everyone and that he was done with me.

I texted back: *I'll wait.*

And got a smiley face, kiss and thumbs-up back. So he didn't know. I was going to have to tell him, though I wasn't sure what to say cos I wasn't sure what I'd done. Maybe it was the stuff about Diggs's drinking? Or the way he'd physically gone at Z? Perhaps something like that would be enough to be considered a Threat ... hadn't Diggs said it was all about context?

Shit.

'Hey,' Z said as he approached me.

I didn't want to look at him but I couldn't help it. My heart twisted itself into a heavy lump.

'I got you something.' He grinned and handed me a paper bag. Inside there were markers and those 'Hello, my name is' nametag stickers and it was just so perfectly Z that I almost cried. 'That's why I was late. Had to make sure Karen had gone for the day.'

'Karen?'

'The receptionist,' he said. Smiled.

I didn't care what Tash thought. This guy was everything. And I kissed him. Right there. In front of the whole school. I didn't give a crap who saw it.

On the way home I told him that Tash thought it was weird we were together and that Chloe had a crush on him and he cracked up laughing like it was the funniest thing he'd ever heard. It made me realise I should've just laughed it off, too. I had to stop letting Tash get to me and promised myself I'd do better.

'How 'bout the rest of your day?' he said.

I took a deep breath. Steadied myself.

'You know that Julius Warren guy?' I said.

'That weird bald dude?'

'Yep,' I said, and was about to tell him everything, but I never got a chance. Because we were home. And sitting outside the apartment block was one of those white vans. Its hazard lights were flashing. Its doors had been left wide open.

I thought I was about to throw up.

This was it. They were taking Diggs. I knew it cos I'd caused it.

'Shit,' Z whispered. 'They know about the graffiti.'

That stopped me. Of course it could be that. Of course they would know who we were. Julius had pretty much said as much. The Unit must have watched some security footage and traced us back to the apartment. We weren't invisible or invincible; we were idiots. And I felt a little relieved then, cos they *should* have been taking me away. If anyone was going to suffer, it should have been me. Not Diggs. He'd done nothing wrong except take in an ungrateful, stupid idiot.

The neighbours stood in their open doorways. Their whispers turned to silence when they saw us. Their icy stares followed us as we rushed upstairs.

Z opened the front door.

They were there. Of course. Unit Officers. And my worst fear was playing out in front of my eyes.

CHAPTER 33

The officers dragged Diggs down the hallway towards us.

'Dad!' Z ran to him.

'Stand back,' an officer yelled. Z didn't, and the officer slammed him against the wall. Hard. I saw him gasp and struggle as all the air was knocked out of him and it felt like I'd been hit too.

'I'll be OK,' Diggs kept saying. 'I'll be home soon.' And for a second I thought I was hearing my dad telling me it would be OK and watching my dad getting pulled away from me forever. It was happening all over again. But this time, I stepped in.

'Why are you taking him? What's the charge?' I shouted.

The officers ignored me and kept marching Diggs towards the door. I backed out of the apartment as quickly as I could. 'What's the charge?' I shouted again. Louder this time. But still, they ignored me.

'Santee. Tell the kids I'm OK. Tell them –' but he was cut off by the officers yelling, *Get back! Stand aside! Move!*

'Santee!' Diggs tried to yell over their shouts and I saw him twist and turn like he was trying to get to me, like he wanted to tell me something, and an officer raised his baton high above his head and hit Diggs and he staggered and fell and everything sparked and fizzed and I screamed until my voice disappeared. And then an officer was right in my face, his nostrils flaring, his skin red and sweaty and flaky. He swore at me: *Little slut, dirty mongrel dog, fuck off.* So much hate. Spit exploded out of the corners of his mouth and foamed and dripped like *he* was the dirty mongrel dog that needed to be shot in the head.

And then he was gone. And Diggs was gone. The neighbours disappeared back into their homes.

I stood outside the door. I could hear Mila crying. Softly. Softly. And I thought I should go to her but my whole body was shaking and shaking and there was nothing I could do to make it stop.

'Santee.' The voice sounded really far away. 'Santee.' I opened my eyes and there was Pip and suddenly I was crying these huge, heaving sobs that wrenched themselves out of my gut and it hurt so bad but I couldn't stop. She wrapped her arms around me and whispered things I needed to hear but didn't deserve.

We were told to get whatever we needed from our bedrooms cos we were moving in with Pip.

'But –' Z said.

'Your dad and I worked this out already. No arguments,' she said, and held up her hands like she wasn't going to hear anything more about it. 'Check your rooms carefully,' she added. 'Don't leave anything you don't want those arseholes to have. Understand?' She looked right at me and Z then, as if she knew exactly what we were hiding. *Understand?* We nodded and I followed Z to his room.

'I can't believe this is happening,' he said, closing his bedroom door.

We hadn't hidden anything because we hadn't thought we'd needed to. Everything we used was stuff we were legitimately allowed to have. Pens and markers and sketchpads and stickers. Office supplies. Nothing that screamed *Threat.* But in a different context, who knew what they'd make of it? I couldn't stop thinking about the context I must have supplied the Unit for their arrest of Diggs.

Z started ripping out pages from his sketchpad and tearing them into tiny pieces. I shouted at him to stop, but he wouldn't. He was crying and ripping up the paper and I joined him until the floor was covered in sad confetti. We broke our markers and destroyed our pens and ruined all the stickers. For a moment, I wanted to set the whole lot on fire.

But then, as I looked at the stuff in my room, it came to me: everything was from them. The Drivers. I'd never asked for any of it, but somehow they just knew. The sketchpad Z had given me. The pile of clothes from Mila. All the things Diggs had bought, like it was no big deal. Except it was. I made a pile of all my stuff. I didn't want any of it to burn away to nothing. I didn't want any of it going to the Unit. It was mine. And I'd keep it forever.

CHAPTER 34

Pip's apartment was small and messy and not made for four people. We crowded into her dusty-smelling lounge room that had way too much stuff in it: three mismatched, lumpy armchairs and a little table surrounded by wobbly looking chairs and a whole jungle of house plants that curled towards the light streaming in from the window. I didn't know how we would all fit in there but Pip said, *We'll work it out*, and she sounded so cheerful I almost believed her. Mila curled up into one of the armchairs, surrounded by her bags, and stared at the wall. She hadn't spoken for hours. Every now and then tears would slide silently down her face.

'Let's bake a cake,' Pip said.

Mila didn't respond.

'I don't think Mila wants to,' Z said.

'I'll need more butter.' Pip kept right on talking as if everything was normal. 'Zac, Santee – you two can get butter and we'll get started. Won't we, Mila?'

But still Mila didn't move.

'I think I should stay with her,' Z said.

Pip gave him one of those looks and said, 'Butter.' She shoved some money into his hand and pretty much pushed us out the door.

Everything looked the same. How was the world carrying on as if nothing had happened? It should have been all over the News – *Douglas Driver: Falsely Arrested!* – with his face on screens across the city. People should have been crying and demanding that the Unit fix it, bring him back.

But, just like when my own dad was arrested, there was none of that.

Me and Z walked in silence. I didn't know what to do, what to say. Should I hold his hand? Comfort him? Tell him everything would be all right even though I knew that was a lie, and so did he? But the biggest question circling and circling around was: should I tell him this was all my fault?

We walked through the familiar sliding doors and into a silent, almost deserted store. There was no crappy music playing over the speakers. No kids throwing tantrums or stressed-out parents or impatient shoppers in long queues for the checkouts. And there was hardly any food on the shelves. It felt as if we'd missed something – a big sale or a massive riot. The dairy section was nearly empty. I picked up a lone tub of yoghurt.

'Remember that cartoon cow?' I said.

'What?'

'When we had to hitchhike from the National Park. Remember? The truck had a cartoon cow painted on the side. I thought we could trust the driver cos of that cow, remember? Turns out I was right. And you kept asking her all about cheese and stuff ...' I rambled, trying to get something out of him. A tiny smile. Just a glimpse of the Z I knew. A sign that he was going to be all right. But his brain was somewhere else entirely. I didn't blame him.

We stared into the refrigerators. I reached for some butter but a woman swept in from nowhere and grabbed it from me and before I'd realised what had happened, she was rushing to the cash register, her arms full of whatever she could carry. There was a time, not that long ago, when I would have chased her down and yelled at her and got my own way. But now? It didn't seem so important.

I asked the guy who worked there if there was anything more out the back, any stock that hadn't gone out yet.

'Nope,' he said. 'That's it.'

'When are you restocking?'

'Dunno.'

How could he not know? They needed to restock right then and there. If they didn't ... I looked at what remained on the shelves. There wasn't much to choose from and I figured if we didn't buy food now, we might be waiting a while for our next chance. I copied the woman who'd stolen our butter and filled my arms with whatever I could manage. Z followed me around in a daze.

We had some supplies, but no butter, and I wondered if we should try another store just in case.

'No,' Z said. 'I'm going to HQ. I've gotta find out what's going on.'

I didn't argue or tell him it was pointless, cos I understood. I was the girl who stood outside the prison, week after week, waiting to visit her dad even though there was a good chance he wasn't even there.

I'd always tried to avoid Unit Headquarters. It had those windows you couldn't see through, but that they could see out of. That was the point, I suppose. The windows reflected everything back in this distorted, slightly golden way. I suppose it was meant to be impressive but it just made me feel uneasy.

I think Z thought we'd just walk up the stairs and into reception and ask for his dad. Like visiting someone at their office. Simple. But it wasn't going to be like that. People like us weren't meant to go inside that building. Threats would be marched inside by people in uniform and that was that.

They'd put up a fence. A wire thing that stretched across the front of the building and blocked the stairs and entrance. A heap of people peered through the wire, called out to the officers who stood guard on the stairs. We joined them, even though I knew it was useless.

'Douglas Driver!' Z added his voice to all the others who shouted the names of their missing people. 'Douglas Driver! I need to see Douglas Driver.'

The officers did a good job of pretending we didn't exist. All the voices bounced off them and didn't even leave a mark. They blocked out all our desperate faces and just stood there, still and expressionless, machine guns in hands. They were like robots. It didn't bother them that people kept shouting and pleading and crying and rattling the fence.

Z kept on shouting and every time he did – *Douglas Driver! Douglas Driver!* – it sounded like the words were being ripped from the back of his throat. I couldn't stand hearing him like that. I added my voice to his and Z reached out and took my hand. And we stood like that, shouting.

There must have been a hundred people there, maybe more. Enough to push the fence over. March up the stairs. Demand something be done. How could they stop so many of us?

'Step away from the barrier,' a voice boomed.

More officers had appeared on the stairs. One repeated into a megaphone: *Step away from the barrier, move along, step away from the barrier, move along.* But it wasn't until the officers started moving towards us that the shouting faded and people walked away. I was still holding Z's hand, and I said something like, *Let's go home,* and he said nothing as I gently dragged him out of there.

CHAPTER 35

There was cake because Pip had enough butter to bake, after all (*I realised after you'd left*, she said, *sorry about that*), and we ate it in front of the News. We crowded around the little television on the mattresses we'd dragged in from next door that now filled Pip's floor. We had taken whatever we could from the apartment and Pip had locked the door behind us.

The Unit had turned up later, as Pip knew they would, to find whatever they thought could be evidence of whatever it was they'd taken Diggs in for. We could hear them turning the place inside out even though Pip turned the volume up on the TV extra loud.

I stared at the screen but I wasn't really watching. The images blurred in front of my eyes. I could still see the look on Diggs's face as they dragged him away. The sound of his voice. The way he'd collapsed when they'd hit him. My thoughts of Diggs got all mixed in with my memories of Dad. *My fault, my fault.* The guilt kept surging and growing inside me.

I replayed my conversations with Julius Warren over and over. What if I'd given something away with a look or my silence? What if I had accidentally given them that one piece of information they needed to make their arrest? I was to blame. For my own dad and now Diggs. I knew it. But there was no way I could explain any of that to them – not after everything they had done for me.

The Government would move a new family into the apartment. Pip said that was what they did now. This was an area where people wanted to live, which meant someone important, a family of Good Citizens, would inherit the place.

'That's not fair,' Mila said.

'No,' Pip said. 'But it's the way it is, my love.'

'Can't we change it?' There were no tears in Mila's voice anymore. She was all cried out, I suppose. In their place was the Mila I was more familiar with. The Mila whose brain was constantly tick-tick-ticking over and running ahead and outdoing all of us.

'Maybe,' Pip said. 'But not for a little while yet. We have to be patient.'

'When's Dad coming home?' she said.

'Soon, love. Soon.' Pip looked at me and Z. 'And in the meantime, no more going for runs in the morning, either. You two have to be patient, too.'

I looked at Z – *Does she know?* He shrugged. Pip said nothing more about it.

The Unit kept searching through the Drivers' apartment well into the night.

We slept like sardines on the mattresses. Mila cushioned herself between me and Z and took up most of the room, which was fine. I wasn't really expecting to sleep anyway.

In the grey morning light, I carefully stepped over Mila and snuggled in next to Z. He was already awake and staring, blankly, at the ceiling.

'How about a run?' I whispered in his ear. 'It might make us feel better.'

He shook his head.

'Come on,' I said. 'We've got to do something.'

He shook his head again and I realised tears were streaming down his face and I thought, *Shit, Santee, you've done it again.*

'I think it's my fault.' He spoke quietly, his eyes still focused on the ceiling. 'That stupid graffiti ... they must have known it was us and come here and he must've said something he shouldn't have said cos he's got a bloody big mouth and – and ...' His voice trailed off to nothing.

I said I was sorry, so sorry, because I was. Because it wasn't his fault. It was mine. And I didn't know how to tell him. I lay beside him, rested my head on his chest and listened to his heart thump, thump, thump.

CHAPTER 36

Mila was crying. Sitting on the stairs in her neat school uniform with her backpack on. But she wasn't going anywhere.

It had been a week and we had hardly left the cramped apartment. We sat around in a weird sort of daze, lost in our thoughts of Diggs. I helped Pip out as much as she would let me. I cleaned and cooked and checked on Mila and Z constantly and tried to make myself useful. I wasn't part of the deal she'd made with Diggs and she had no reason to take me in. But any time I said anything about it she'd tell me, *Shut up and stop being so silly.*

After a week in the fog, Pip announced we had to go back to school. And we were all too exhausted and sad to argue.

The reality of going back hit Mila when we were halfway down the stairs, on our way out of the apartment block. She suddenly just stopped. And sat. Right there on the step.

I sat beside her. Put my arm around her. I could have told her it would get better and easier and although she'd miss him every single day she'd get on with her life and be just fine. That's the sort of stuff people who have never been through anything bad think is comforting. It's what people said to me when my dad was taken. And it would boil me up inside. Mila was too smart and too special to be fed any of those lies. And so I said nothing. I just let her cry.

'This is the worst,' she said, finally.

'I know.'

And she blew her nose, wiped her eyes and headed back into the real world.

I went outside at lunchtime to find Z at our table, deep in conversation with Tash. She was doing all the talking and he was leaning in close and listening, really listening, to everything she was saying. And it looked like she had a lot to say.

I was stuck to the spot. I knew I wasn't supposed to be part of this conversation. The two of them had built this invisible force field around themselves and there was no way I could get through it.

It was Z who burst their little bubble. I must have been standing there for ages, staring at them like a weirdo, when he finally looked over and saw me. We held eye contact for a moment and I tried to send him a *what's up?* but he didn't give me anything. No smile. No shrug. Just this strange expression. He dropped his gaze, which made Tash turn around to see what he'd been staring at. Me. She waved me over and it kinda looked like Z was telling her not to. I ignored it. Told myself I was being stupid. Z was my boyfriend.

'We were just talking about you,' Tash said.

'No, we weren't,' Z quickly said, but he wouldn't look at me.

'I was saying how sad it is about his dad. So sad. Right?' she continued.

'Yeah –'

'Anyway,' Tash interrupted me, 'I was like wow, at least you have Santee. I mean, she's been through all that before, you know? And then I thought, that's kind of strange, right? Like, you were pretty much the reason your dad was taken, and now Z's dad's been taken. Just feels like there's a common denominator, don't you think?'

The common denominator. Me. Always me. I froze.

'I'll let you two talk. I find it's always best to be honest, Santee,' Tash said. 'Oh, Z, Chloe wanted me to say hi. From her. To you. Cool? 'K. Bye.'

And then she was gone.

Z sat on the table and stared up at the sky. It wanted to rain. The clouds were thick and heavy and the air had that smell to it. I sat next to him, but he wouldn't look at me. He was concentrating hard on the clouds.

I twisted my fingers in knots that matched the ones in my stomach. And then I told Z about my dad. The full story this time, because last time I'd left some parts out – the parts I didn't like remembering. I suppose I thought if I left out those bits for long enough then maybe they would no longer be true. Like I could rewrite history if I tried hard enough. Thing is, I always remembered the bad part. Not talking about something doesn't mean you forget it. No matter how hard you try.

The part of the story I didn't like to remember happened before Dad was taken away. When I'd been a loud, stupid brat. *Even more than I was now.* I said that to make Z laugh, but he didn't. He didn't even look at me. So I took a deep breath. This guy who thought I was an artist and a genius and special ... I didn't want him not to think those things anymore. And there was no way he would after I told him the truth.

The truth.

The truth was, I was the reason my dad was taken away.

I said it. Just like that.

He didn't ask why or how. He didn't say, *No you didn't, I don't believe you.* He kept his eyes down. Played with a loose button at the bottom of his shirt.

I'd never told anyone apart from Tash. And once I'd told her, she'd stopped being my friend. I didn't want to think about all the things that would stop once I told Z. But I told him anyway. I owed him that.

'My dad is a bit like your dad,' I said quietly. 'He hates this government, and Varick, and everything they stand for ... And, he did things. Like organised protests with his students at the Uni. And he made signs cos he was an artist, you know, and he was smart and people liked to hear him talk at rallies and whatever. Anyway, they'd started shutting down all these departments at the Uni. You remember that? And Arts was one of the first to go and that meant Mum and Dad were fired and they were angry, really angry about it and they organised a protest and they made all these signs and banners. And I brought one to school. One of the signs. Cos I was confused and upset about how everything was changing at home and in the world and here at this shitty school ... they'd taken away the Art Room and Ms Francis just disappeared and I couldn't deal with it. So I stole one of Dad's protest signs. A real bad one. The stuff it said about Varick – it was really bad, stuff no-one would say out loud – and I snuck it into school and I was going to stand up in assembly and start my own protest with it, to get the Art Room back, but ... I never .... They found out about it, Mrs Rook and some of the other teachers, before I'd even ... And I had to sit in her office and they all wanted to know where I'd gotten it and who had made it. And I told them. I told them it was my dad.'

I spoke fast and quiet and I couldn't tell if Z had heard me or not cos he didn't react. But I kept going. I'd gotten this far. 'Later that night the Unit took Dad away. And it was my fault.'

I wanted the sky to open up, for the rain to start thundering down. Right there. I wanted to feel those heavy, fat raindrops burst against my face, my arms, my legs. I wanted the rain to pierce through my skin, sting me, hurt me. But nothing happened.

Finally, he spoke. 'Am I supposed to feel sorry for you?'

'No, that's not –'

'And how about my dad, Santee, how about Diggs? Why did they take him? What did you do?' He turned to look at me.

'They just asked me questions.'

'Who?'

I couldn't speak. I hadn't meant for any of this to happen. I wanted to go back, way, way back, to before. Before me and Z. Before the Wall. Before Tash hated me. Before Varick.

'Who?' He grabbed my arm. Not hard. Not mean. But pleading. Like he thought I had the answer he was searching for.

I steadied myself. 'Julius Warren. I told him Diggs worked late and could sometimes drink too much and how he tried to punch you that time.' I watched Z crumple and it felt like my heart was splitting apart. 'He told me he had information about my dad and he could help me get home and …'

My voice got stuck in the back of my throat. I'd run out of words.

'You know what? You're still a brat. Selfish and full of shit and a fucking brat.' His voice was low but it pounded in my head as if he were shouting. I couldn't look at him with his face all twisted like that. I focused on the clouds. They were angry and grey. In them I could see the faces of all the people I'd hurt. Dad, Mum, Astrid, Diggs and now Z. And Mila.

'I wish I'd never met you,' he said.

And he left.

CHAPTER 37

I had to prove Z wrong. Show him I had changed and I was sorry. I apologised over and over by text message but got no response, and thought of how Mum would say, *Actions speak louder than words.* It made sense now. I had to *do* something. So, instead of going to Pip's after school, I headed to Unit HQ. I was going to get information about Diggs. I thought that could help, at least a little. It was the not knowing that was the hardest. Living with all those what-ifs and endless scenarios and questions, questions, questions. It could drive you crazy.

There were no crowds at Unit HQ. The wire fence was still up but no-one was shouting through it or shaking it or anything. They'd all given up, I suppose.

And just one officer was standing guard. 'Good afternoon, sir,' I said as politely as I could, considering how much I despised them.

He looked above my head like I wasn't even there.

'I would like to see my brother. He's an officer. Like you. You might know him?' I was doing that thing my mum did. Talking and talking and talking cos I was nervous. I stopped myself. Took a deep breath and gave him Peter's name.

I don't know why I hadn't thought of it sooner. Peter would help me. He'd helped me before and he would know where Diggs was, or at least find out for me. He might even be able to get us a visit with him. Of course he would. He was Peter.

The Officer held his ear and spoke into a device I couldn't see and I smiled at him because I thought this meant my plan had worked.

'No,' the officer said. 'He doesn't work here. Move along.'

'He does,' I said. 'He works here.'

'You talking back?' The officer stood taller, bigger, rested his hand on his gun as if to remind me he had one and I did not.

I said nothing. My heart thudded in my chest. He stepped closer to the fence. I thought he was going to shove his hand through the wire and grab me by the throat and kill me, right there, with his bare hands. No-one would have stopped him. 'Piss off,' he said.

And I did.

I could hear him laughing as I ran and ran and ran.

I walked back to the apartment and into a family moving into the Drivers'. They looked like the kind of family we always saw on the News: two girls, one mum, one dad, and an annoying, yapping dog that might have been cute if its humans hadn't just taken our home. I pushed past them as I climbed the stairs and they didn't say anything to me. And I said nothing to them.

Pip said it would be better to ignore them.

'What would I want to say to them anyway?' I said, but Pip just shrugged. I wondered if she didn't trust me either. If she thought Diggs's arrest was my fault, too. It felt like she was being distant. I could feel the panic rising up in me. Maybe they all knew what I'd done and they were going to kick me out, send me off to the Processing Centre.

'Why did you get our house?' Mila said.

'What?'

'That's what I want to say to them. That's what I want to know. Why does *that* family get *our* home?'

'They proved themselves to be Good Citizens. So they get the house. It's all part of the deal,' Pip said.

'What deal?' Mila said.

Pip started humming a little tune, which always drove us crazy cos it meant that was the end of that. No more questions. No more answers. Pip never answered questions. And we had a heap of them: When did you meet Diggs? How do you know him? Why did you take us in? Do you work? Where do you work? Her response was always to hum that irritating song.

Z got home right on Curfew. Mila told him off cos that was her job now.

'I don't want to hear it,' he said, and stormed off into the bathroom for a really long time.

'What's up with him?' Mila said.

'He hates me,' I said, cos there was no point in lying to Mila.

She sighed. 'No, he doesn't.'

I wanted to tell Mila what was going on. How I'd stuffed everything up. Again. But I couldn't handle her hating me, too. That would be too much.

Z finally emerged from the bathroom and threw himself onto his corner of the mattress, pulled the blanket over his head and went to sleep. Or pretended to.

I couldn't even pretend to sleep. When the apartment fell into a soft snore, I carefully untangled myself from Mila's arm (she was like a little koala, clinging to us in the night like we were trees) and tiptoed to the front door. I sat in the corridor with George the Gnome and the pot plants and tried to think about nothing. But my thoughts went from Dad to Tash to Diggs to the new family in the apartment to Mum and Astrid to the Unit Officers shouting, *Stop or I'll shoot*, to the man on the street with no shoes to the explosion and the smoke and then to the Safety Border. Every thought led me back to the wall.

One thing at a time, that had been one of Beth's lessons. *Focus on the here and now, that's all you have to do.* But the here and now was the problem. I wondered what Beth would say about that. I wondered where the hell Beth had gone. And all my jumbled thoughts cycled around and around again.

The front door opened and Pip slipped out. She said nothing and for a moment I wondered if she'd even noticed me. She pulled a battered packet of cigarettes and a lighter from the pocket of her dressing gown.

'Are you allowed to smoke out here?' I said.

'No,' she said, and lit up. 'Want one?'

I almost laughed. 'No,' I said quietly.

Smoke curled out of her mouth, her nose. She smoked slowly, like she was really thinking about each drag she took. The tip of the cigarette glowed a brilliant red.

'It's not your fault, love,' she said.

'What isn't?'

'Your dad. Diggs. Any of that. Not your fault.' She dusted the pot plants with cigarette ash. How did she know?

'But –' I started.

'No. No *buts*. That's the truth,' she said, and started to hum very, very softly.

CHAPTER 38

I had been living with Pip for a month. It felt like heaps longer. Probably because in all that time Z pretended I didn't exist. Even though we lived together, I missed him. And I missed Diggs. And Dad. And Mum and Astrid, who I still kept trying to contact even though it never seemed to work. I constantly had this nauseous feeling, which made it difficult to eat and sleep and think and even draw. I didn't want to do anything. Except maybe curl up on the street and wait for the white vans to take me away. It would have been better that way. That's what I thought.

I hadn't done any homework for ages. I knew I should but it was hard to find the motivation. Even Mila didn't seem as into her assignments and projects as she used to be. And she barely did any music practice. She spoke about Diggs a lot, wondered what he was doing, where he was, sat at the bottom of the stairs for hours just waiting for him. It was hard to watch. But at least she was still there, with us. Z was always with Riley, doing whatever he could to avoid being in the same room as me.

I walked to school alone, through the city that was desperately trying to hold on to some version of what it had been. The good side. The clean, shiny city for people who could afford it. But every day there were more people lining up at the Futures Office, and more of those fancy stores and nice restaurants were boarded up, closed. It started to remind me of home.

The security check at the school entrance was hectic. Long queues and stupid guards who seemed to like the tiny bit of power they'd been given. They weren't Unit Officers, but they wanted to be. They were even worse than the real ones.

In maths class, Mr Lo was pissed off at me. He'd moved beyond disappointment and now he was just plain annoyed. When I told him I hadn't finished my homework he didn't check to see how I was holding up, or if I was finding the work too easy or too difficult. He just sighed. He was over it. And over me.

I hung back after class cos I felt I owed him an apology. I mean, he'd tried with me and I'd let him down. I hated that he was suddenly treating me with the same contempt he showed the rest of the class. I had to promise that I would do better.

'Mr Lo –' I started, but was cut off by the loudspeaker.

'Mr Lo to the office. Mr Lo to the office.'

He started packing up his desk, throwing pens and papers and the chipped coffee mug he always carried into his tattered satchel.

'Mr Lo?' I tried again.

'Not a good time, Santee.'

And he walked towards the office, just like that. I stood there for a moment before packing up my own bag and heading to the bathroom. It was lunchtime. I was back to hiding there during breaks.

Back when everything had gone wrong at school, when I'd lost Dad and my best friend and my whole world felt like it was collapsing in on itself, Mum had let me stay home. I had my uniform on and was sitting on the couch, trying to tie my shoelaces, and they wouldn't work and I threw my shoes across the room and burst into tears. *Hey, hey, hey,* Mum had said but she wasn't angry even though I'd left a black mark on the wall. She sat beside me. Rubbed my back. *Let's all stay home today. What do you think?* And we had. Mum made us hot chocolate and the three of us cuddled up on the couch and everything felt like it was going to work out somehow. I longed for my mum to appear, take me home and tell me it was all going to be OK. I really needed her, and I wiped my eyes and blew my nose and hoped no-one could hear me crying, alone, in the cubicle.

'Santee?'

Shit.

'Just a sec,' I said, and flushed the toilet as if I'd been doing what people were meant to do in there. I unlocked the door and there was Imara.

'Thought that was you,' she said.

I washed my hands, splashed some water on my face.

'I was gonna chill in the library, you want to come with?' she said, like it was no big deal. Perhaps it wasn't a big deal to her. But to me, at that moment, it was kinda like Mum's hot chocolate.

On our way to the library we almost collided with Mr Lo. He was storming down the corridor, red-faced, angry, satchel banging by his side. We watched him as he shoved everyone out of the way and yelled at the security guards to let him through and disappeared out of the school.

'What was that about?' Imara said.

Mr Lo wasn't there the next day, or the day after that. And he wasn't the only one. There were rumours that they'd quit, that they hated the New Beginning and had argued with Mrs Rook and walked out. Or been fired.

'I hope he's just gone on holiday,' Imara said during one lunchtime. We had been hanging out more often and I was grateful for her company. Even if she sometimes said the dumbest things. 'Hawaii or something, have you been? We love it there. As soon as our papers are in order we're going, maybe you could come with?'

She was clueless. Absolutely clueless. Like so many of the people at that school. I saw Z across the courtyard. Kicking the soccer ball with Riley and Gen and Will and pretending I didn't exist. Z would have got it. My heart ached as I watched him, and I longed to talk to him.

'Here,' Imara said, and shoved a muffin into my hand.

'How the hell did you get these?' I said. Muffins were like gold. With the lack of supplies and stores closing down and people full-on fighting over the last carton of milk, it was crazy to see Imara's full lunchbox.

'Your face!' she laughed, not in a cruel way, but in her out-of-touch-with-the-real-world way.

'Imara's got muffins!' someone shouted, and suddenly she was surrounded by people all pushing and shouting and bargaining for a muffin. She was like a queen handing out gold to the peasants. If it wasn't so shitty it could have been funny. I gave my muffin to a couple of younger kids who stood back from the pack. I wasn't hungry anymore.

Varick had promised everyone that things would get better. And once, people would have accepted that. But when I watched him on the big screen in the city, I overheard people mumbling about how much money he was spending and words like *corruption* and *power-hungry* were thrown around and even though I knew the Unit Officers must have heard them, too, they stood back and did nothing.

CHAPTER 39

Pip made us all gather in front of the television way before the News began. Which was strange. Even for Pip.

'We can't miss it,' she said. And she sounded like she was kinda looking forward to it, which was weird, cos we never looked forward to the News.

The TV show *Real Life* was on. Mila pretended to vomit. 'Ugh,' she said. 'This is the worst.'

She was right. It was this stupid show everyone watched except, it seemed, our little family. Along with whatever they'd seen on the News, *Real Life* was all anyone talked about at school. This stupid show about idiotic people going about their Extraordinary Lives. Cameras followed them everywhere, these rich people who were pretty awful to each other but *totally loving life in Region One* (their words, not mine). People were obsessed with it. Although I reckon Mum and Astrid would have hated it as much I did. Just imagining Astrid trying to watch *Real Life* made me smile.

The show ended with a close-up of one of the characters crying and it looked so fake we all burst into laughter. I snuck a look at Z but he wasn't looking at me. As usual.

I was still trying hard to prove to him (and me) that I wasn't a brat anymore. I helped Pip with housework and chores and cooked dinner with Mila and even talked her back into regular music practice and we did our homework together every single night and I promised Pip I'd get a job to pay my own way. Not that there were any jobs, but still. I was trying. Z wasn't. Sometimes I wanted to shake him: I AM HERE. But what would be the point?

The News began the way it always did and I closed my eyes and let the droning voices wash over me. The reports were always the same. Something about the Threats contained on the other side, something about how successful the Regions were and then something cutesy and sweet and not really news at all.

'Good Citizens,' I heard Magnus Varick say.

'Our Leader.' I said it without thinking, along with everyone else.

But Varick's voice suddenly cut out and I opened my eyes as the screen went black. And then, suddenly, there were images of a mass of people walking beside the wall, all of them holding candles. They looked like a thousand fireflies. There was no sound, but you could tell they were chanting and shouting something. And I held my chest cos I thought my heart was going to explode right out of it when I realised where they were. They were marching on the other side.

My side. My home. I frantically scanned all the faces in the crowd, trying to spot Mum or Astrid or even one of our annoying neighbours. But as quickly as the scene appeared, it disappeared. To nothing. A high-pitched buzz rang out through the television.

'That was home. My home. What were they ...' I couldn't keep talking because I was crying. Mila put her arm around me. Leaned her head on my shoulder.

'They were protesting. That was a protest!' Z leapt to his feet.

'OK, OK,' Pip said. 'Let's get rid of this awful noise, huh?' And she turned off the TV but it still felt as if everything was buzzing and humming around me.

Mila started to say something but Pip gestured for her to wait and switched on her little stereo. Dramatic piano music blasted from the speaker. My heart thumped, thumped, thumped out of time. *A protest?* Like the ones Dad had tried to organise? I needed to know more, but my brain was scattered and no words would come.

Finally, Pip turned to us. In the glow of the lamplight I could see tears running down her face. But she didn't look sad. 'I can't believe they did it,' she said, more to herself than us.

'Who? What?' Mila was bursting with questions. *What had we seen? Why had we seen it?*

I closed my eyes and replayed the footage in my mind: the crowd, the candles, the wall. I added Mum and Astrid into the images. Imagined I'd seen them there next to an old man with a walking stick and young parents pushing their baby in a pram. I had to believe they had been there.

Pip cleared her throat as if she was ready to tell us something important. I could feel us all move in closer to her. 'Your dad should've been here,' she said. 'Diggs should have seen that.'

'Why?' Z said.

'He made that happen,' Pip said quietly.

It felt like everything tilted a little bit. What? Diggs did that? Mila and Z started talking over each other, demanding that Pip tell them more.

'Nope.' Pip smiled. 'I've said too much as it is.'

'You've said nothing!' Mila said.

'The less you know the better.' And that was all she'd say about it.

The next morning, Pip announced we were going to do something fun.

'What did you used to do? Before all this?' she asked.

We were sitting around the apartment. That excited, hopeful feeling from the night before had disappeared with the new day and the realisation that everything was exactly the same. I don't know what I'd expected – to wake and find they'd removed the wall, apologised for the whole experiment, put things right, and that everything was OK with me and Z again too, oh and maybe even Dad and Diggs had returned home? Yeah. Sure.

I tried to tell Pip I didn't feel like doing anything, but she wouldn't listen.

'Find a picnic blanket would you, Santee,' she said. 'Please? It's a beautiful day so we'll eat outdoors.'

I didn't want to go on a picnic. I wanted to go back

to sleep. But I dragged myself up and pretended to be enthusiastic about it for Pip's sake.

'Don't worry, I'll do it,' Mila whispered to me and I flopped back onto the mattress and watched her rush around gathering whatever crap she could find. She actually got pretty psyched about the picnic and started going through her things cos she was sure there was a frisbee in there. Why she'd kept a frisbee I didn't know but, sure enough, she had one.

She found some big, floppy hats in the back of Pip's wardrobe and said, *Please, please, please can we wear them?* and Pip thought that was the greatest thing she'd ever heard and so we all had to put on a stupid hat. Mila chose the ugliest one for me. It was covered in bright flowers and had a stupid feather thing on one side and it was way too big and kept slipping down my forehead but Mila said I looked beautiful.

'You are evil,' I told her.

I caught Z's eye, under the big straw hat Mila had put on him.

'You laughing at me?' he said. The first thing he'd said to me since calling me a brat.

I felt my heart flip-flop but tried real hard to play it cool.

'Never,' I said. Why did he have to be so cute? It was infuriating.

Our neighbours were returning home as we were leaving. It felt so weird seeing them head into the Drivers' old place. I could only imagine how awful it must have been for Z and Mila. The neighbours were quiet and perfect and obviously in favour with the government cos they never seemed to be without food or petrol or bright shiny uniforms for their bright shiny school.

'Bastards,' Pip whispered in my ear and then turned brightly to them with a very fake, *Good afternoon.*

They smiled a little but didn't say anything. Mila kept her eyes on the ground, as if she couldn't bring herself to look at them.

'Race you to the park,' I said, and started running.

'You got a head start! Not fair!' Mila called behind me.

As much as I didn't want to admit it, Pip was right; it was a nice day for a picnic. If you were into that kinda thing. And maybe I was. The sky was that perfect blue that seemed to go on forever and you could almost forget there was a wall splitting it in two. It felt good to be out of the tiny apartment and strolling in the sunshine, even with drones shooting across the sky and Unit patrol cars cruising down the streets.

It was as we were trying to find the perfect spot (Mila had a very strong opinion on it) that the officer approached. 'It's unlawful to gather in groups of four or more,' she said. 'You'll have to break this up.'

'Sorry, officer,' Pip said. 'We're just having a family picnic.'

We all motioned to our bags and outfits and smiled at the officer, who didn't smile back.

'This is a punishable offence,' she said.

It felt like it had suddenly dropped ten degrees. We all looked at each other like, *What are we supposed to do now?* It was Mila who stepped up. Of course.

'Terribly sorry, officer. We were unforgivably ignorant of that fact,' she said. She was good. All sweetness and smarts. And it worked. I actually saw a bit of a smile on the officer's face. Maybe Mila reminded her of her own kid sister or her daughter, or maybe that was just the effect Mila had on everyone. 'It won't happen again.'

'Right, well, all right then,' the officer stumbled. 'It better not.' And she shuffled away to harass another group heading into the park.

'You guys should still have your picnic,' I said, and walked away quickly. This wasn't my family. If anyone should leave, it should be me. It would always be me.

I hadn't gotten very far when I heard Z call my name. I turned around and there he was, out of breath, but smiling. 'I'd rather hang with you,' Z said. 'If that's cool?' And my heart soared.

We sat in Red because Z said he'd been neglecting her and he felt bad. She was almost out of petrol and we had no way of getting any more. Petrol, like lots of things, was way too expensive now. But even if we could have filled her tank there was no way I'd trust Red to get us anywhere. So we just sat out the front of the apartment block, going nowhere. Me in the driver's seat cos I wanted to at least pretend I could drive her, and Z next to me, his feet on the dashboard.

'So, it's groups of four now,' he said.

'Oh, yeah, those groups of four terrorizing the Regions. Gotta get them under control.' I laughed nervously. It was a relief to be talking with him again like that but something had shifted. I put my foot on the clutch and jammed the gearstick from first to second, from second to third and back to first.

Things always seemed to sneak up on us. Stuff we could do one day was suddenly unlawful the next. Like the gathering in groups of four, or the banning of certain movies and music and websites and words. Like Curfew. And we all just went along with it. Except, I realised as I stared through the windscreen, those thousands of people on the other side with their candles and marching and chanting.

'The fireflies!' The words burst out of me.

'What?' Z said.

'The protest on the other side. All those people. I reckon it got the Regime scared. Scared of groups getting together and protesting like they were.'

'So, no more groups?' he said.

'And no more protests.'

'I don't reckon it'd be that easy to stop them.' He had that same sort of look he used to get before we went out on our morning runs. 'Anyone who's gonna protest won't let something like that get in their way. I mean, graffiti isn't exactly lawful, is it? Didn't stop us.'

I felt the butterflies come back to my stomach, only now I didn't think of them as butterflies, but fireflies. All bright and glowing. We sat in silence. Me with my fireflies and Z with whatever went on in his head.

Then he took my hand. Just like that. Like it was the easiest thing in the world to do. I pulled away.

'I'm sorry,' he said.

'OK.' I didn't know what else I was supposed to say.

'I've been a jerk.'

'Yeah,' I said, cos it was true. He had been. I'd apologised my guts out and tried to show him how sorry I was, and he'd ignored me. At school. At home. At times when I really needed him.

'I blamed you and it wasn't your fault and I was angry, and I took it out on you and I shouldn't have. I shouldn't ...' his voice trailed off. The fireflies stopped dancing in my stomach and in their place sat this weird, twisty feeling. 'I'm really sorry,' he said again.

'It wasn't my fault what happened with your dad,' I said.

'I know,' he said. 'I think it was probably my fault ...'

'Ever think maybe it was Diggs's fault?' I said, and went to get out of the car.

I felt his hand on my shoulder but didn't turn around. 'You're not a brat,' he said to my back.

'I know,' I said as I got out the car. My eyes felt hot and I hated myself for even thinking about crying. I was not going to cry. And I didn't. I closed the car door gently behind me and went back inside the apartment. Alone.

CHAPTER 40

The weeks rolled by and Z stopped avoiding me and we talked more and started holding hands again and it felt like things were kinda getting back to how they'd been. But no more fireflies appeared on our screens or in my stomach.

The new law banning people from gathering in groups of four or more meant no-one could queue outside the Futures Office, or wait at Unit HQ for news about a loved one ... or protest. Our school took it seriously, too.

'We support the Government,' Mrs Rook said, 'and this shall always be reflected in our rules and policies.'

Being in class with thirty other people was acceptable. Sitting in assembly with the whole school was fine. But hanging out with more than three friends at lunchtime? That, according to Mrs Rook and her New Beginning, was prohibited.

And then there were the blackouts. They said they were forced to do it, *To conserve energy,* but Pip called them liars and worried about food going off in the fridge.

Every night after the News the power would go out. Mila would light candles and say, *Isn't this cosy?* It made me think of how Mum had liked to light candles that smelled like vanilla even when Dad would tell her not to. *It stinks up the place,* he'd say, and she'd say, *Don't be such a grump – it's nice and cosy.* The candles here didn't smell like anything, but they still reminded me of home.

I'd scrunch up on a lumpy armchair and try to get some homework done by candlelight. I had to be a good role model for Mila (but it was far more likely that she was a good role model for me, to be honest). Z would sit near us with his sketchbook. I hadn't felt like drawing in the longest time. It felt kinda pointless now. Plus, I was all out of blank pages and sketchbooks weren't really a priority. Anyway, doing homework made me feel like I was actually achieving something, and even though she couldn't see me I knew Astrid would be proud. There was something nice about that.

Our lives had become so much quieter without Diggs. There were times I'd expect him to burst through the door with some crazy story about where he'd been. Mila would sometimes cry out for him in the night. I'd tell her it was, *Just a nightmare, just a nightmare,* and soothe her back to sleep. Just like my big sister had always done for me.

It felt as if things would go on like this forever. Like this was our life now. Curfew, blackouts, boredom, fear. The blue skies disappeared and the days got shorter and colder and there didn't seem to be any point. To anything.

And then the graffiti started up again.

It wasn't me or Z who created the spray-painted letters, all in red, shouting at everyone from everywhere: PROTEST TONITE 2100. It was bigger and braver than anything I'd ever seen. Or attempted to do. As soon as we walked out of the apartment block we saw it – sprawled right across the road. And on signs and fences and buildings, and even on our school. They'd sprayed it right across the main doors. People in fluoro overalls tried to scrub it off or blast it away with high-powered hoses or paint over it. But it didn't matter. There was way too much of it and they couldn't get rid of it fast enough to stop us from seeing it.

'This is incredible,' I said to Z. He put his arm around me and I put mine around him and we slowly walked to school. I longed to reach up and kiss him, like I would have done in the past. But something stopped me. It always did.

In the hallways and in the bathrooms it was all anyone was whispering about. PROTEST. Mrs Rook banned the word, but that didn't stop people from talking about it.

The screens in our school hallways made no mention of the graffiti. There were just the regular warnings about not using prohibited words or being in groups of four or more and reminders to Always Be A Good Citizen! (Their words, not mine.)

In class Mrs Emery made us do a dictation test. Back before all of this, someone would have made an immature but kinda hilarious joke about dictation and the rest of us would have laughed. But not anymore. We sat quietly and wrote out the sentences as she spoke them, and it wasn't until she started throwing in the word *tonight* that I realised what she was doing. They were looking for someone to blame the graffiti on.

'Tonight I will watch the News with my family,' she said. 'Tonight ...'

Seriously? I couldn't believe the teachers thought that would work. There was no way the people responsible would slip up and write 'tonite' in a stupid dictation test. And there was absolutely zero chance that a high school student in *Low Stream* with poor spelling skills was going to be the mastermind behind that huge graffiti attack. I snuck a look around the class to see if anyone else thought this was bullshit. They were all heads down, as usual. Doing the right thing. Except the girl behind me. She had never looked at me before. I don't think I even knew her name. But at that moment she made eye contact and half smiled and raised her eyebrows as if to say, *What the hell?* And I nodded and shrugged and felt a little less alone in that classroom.

Mrs Emery banged her ruler on my desk, making me jump. 'Stand up,' she said.

I slid my chair back and stood. So did the girl behind me, even though she didn't have to. 'Sorry, Mrs Emery,' I said.

'No,' the girl said. 'I'm sorry. It was my fault, Mrs Emery. My pen is out of ink and I just –'

'I just, I just,' Mrs Emery mimicked her. She laughed and looked at the class so they'd laugh, too. Some of them did. 'That's enough. Sit down. And next time, detention. For all of you.'

I heard her sigh as we sat back down.

'Give her a pen,' Mrs Emery snapped at me as she returned to the front of the class.

I kept my eyes down and put a pen on her desk. I wanted to say, *Thank you,* or smile, but I put my head down and carefully wrote out the next sentence: *Magnus Varick shall make a formal address to the Citizens tonight.*

I was washing my hands when I heard someone trying not to cry in one of the cubicles. I thought about ignoring them, just heading back outside to eat lunch with Z, but it hadn't been that long since I'd sat there, and I remembered how much Imara's company had meant to me that day. I knocked and Tash said, *Go away.*

'Tash?' I said.

There was no response.

'I know it's you,' I said. 'Let me in.'

She must have been desperate because eventually she unlocked the door and I pushed it open to find her sitting on the lid of the toilet pulling apart what might once have been a sandwich.

'Come eat lunch with us. They haven't banned groups of three ... yet,' I said.

'Seriously?' she said. Her mascara had run a bit. She looked so pathetic it was hard not to feel sorry for her.

'If you don't mind being seen with me,' I said. 'And my boyfriend.'

'You worked it out?' she sniffed.

'We did.'

'That's good. That's really good, Santee,' she said, and suddenly she was crying again and I handed her some toilet paper. 'Why are you being nice to me?'

'I can't let you eat in the toilet. You always told me it was unhygienic,' I said.

'I think I said more than that.'

We sat at our table because even though it was cold, it was better being outside than stuck in the building with teachers and security cameras listening in. As soon as Tash was out of the bathroom she changed – she was all chirpy and chatty as if she hadn't been crying at all.

'It's this whole groups-of-four crap, that's all,' she said. 'There's too many of us in the group so I offered to leave ... you know ...'

'Really?' Z said.

'Yeah.' Tash flicked her hair the way I'd always hated her doing. But at that moment I just felt sorry for her. She still thought she had to be that fake Tash. Or maybe she had been that version of herself for so long she'd forgotten what the real Tash was like. I hadn't forgotten. And I realised how much I wanted her back.

'Tash,' I said. 'You can tell us the truth. It's just us.'

She relaxed her shoulders a bit and dropped the fake smile and stared into space for a while. 'They don't want me in the group anymore. They kicked me out ... because Dad is on the other side,' she said. 'With my aunty. And that makes him and me and all my family Threats. According to Chloe.'

I waited for the apology. For the, *Now I know what I put you through, Santee, and I'm soooo sorry* bit. But it didn't happen.

'Can I fix your hair, Santee? It looks terrible,' she said.

'Fine,' I said. 'Go for it.'

Back in class with my Perfect Ponytail (Tash's words, not mine), I only half listened to whatever Mrs Emery was droning on about. It was a bit of a relief when the alarms sounded and we all moved into lockdown mode. No-one laughed about it anymore. We'd gotten really efficient at closing blinds and locking doors and hiding under our desks. I smiled at the girl who sat behind me. She mouthed the word PROTEST and I nodded and she gave a thumbs-up and so did the guy who sat behind her. I looked around, which was harder than it sounds when you're crouched under a desk. Most of the class kept their heads down or their eyes closed but the ones who didn't passed on a thumbs-up sign. Around and around it went.

We were going to protest.

The fireflies burst back to life in my stomach.

CHAPTER 41

Mrs Rook spoke over the loudspeaker to inform us that a very real, very serious warning had just been issued. 'All after-school activities have been cancelled. Early Curfew is enforced. Citizens are to go directly home and await further instructions,' she announced.

The sky was alive with drones and helicopters. The ground crawled with Unit Officers. People crowded the paths and roads, impatiently trying to get home. It wasn't easy with cars and buses jamming the streets and Officers stopping anyone they wanted for random checks. A car backfired and everyone screamed and dropped to the ground. Including Z. I helped him to his feet.

'You all right?' I said as he dusted himself off.

'I just wanna get home,' he said.

As we walked I got lost in thoughts of the protest. The fireflies were going mad in my stomach, excited and eager to burst out and do this thing. But another feeling kept tugging at my brain. The memory of the last time I'd attempted a protest. And how badly it had ended. But this was different, wasn't it? I mean, this time I wouldn't have my dad's anti-Varick placard and I wouldn't be alone and even though it was a risk, it was worth it. Right?

At home we were greeted by booming classical music, which meant Mila and Pip were discussing something important.

'She won't let me go,' Mila said as soon as she saw us.

'What?' I said.

'To the protest. *Protest tonight nine o'clock*. You saw it? Yes? You're going? Everyone is going. It's important.' She was talking super-fast, her words falling over themselves.

'Yeah, I'm going –'

'No-one is going,' Pip said. 'It's dangerous.'

I started to argue but she did that annoying humming thing. I wanted to shout at her, tell her just how frustrating she was. But I didn't. I took a deep breath and went to the bathroom, locked the door and sat on the cold tiles. I closed my eyes and tried to think of the right words to say to make Pip change her mind. No shouting. No slamming doors. I was going to *use my words* – Beth would have been impressed at my progress.

Pip turned on the News. It didn't mention the graffiti that had blanketed the city. Instead, it was filled with endless stories about the Serious Threat.

'For your safety, all Citizens are required to stay indoors. Anyone found breaking the emergency Curfew measures will be arrested on sight,' the anchorman said. The reports continued. There was something about the Safety Border requiring further reinforcement and another informing us that random house checks would take place. Tonight. For our Safety and Security.

The report ended and the power went off and Mila lit the candles and the clock said nine and I thought, *It's now or never*. But as I went to recite the speech I'd prepared, we heard shouts and bangs from the street below and Mila raced to the window to see what was happening. A handful of people were walking down the street, heading towards the park. Some carried candles, others banged pots and pans, and they all shouted, *Down with the Regime!* People were shouting the words we could barely write. They were saying it, out in the open, loudly, so everyone could hear. *Down with the Regime!* A helicopter rattled overhead. Close. Watching. Always watching.

There weren't many people out there. They wouldn't get far before they were arrested. Or worse. And then the whole thing would be written off as another Threat incident and they'd put some new laws in place and our lives would go on getting smaller and smaller until there was nothing left. It felt like they were trying to suffocate us to death. And succeeding.

I turned away from the window.

'What?' Z said.

'I'm going outside.' I didn't care that nobody else had bothered to show up. I just knew I needed to be out there, doing something.

'No,' Pip said. 'I can't let you do that, Santee.'

'I think Diggs would want us there. Don't you?' I said.

It wasn't quite what I'd rehearsed but it was all I was able to get out. Because at that moment, we could hear a mass of voices and shouts and whistles and horns and noise, noise, noise. A huge crowd. Fireflies.

'Diggs would never forgive us if we missed this.' I tried again. 'Please.'

'Please, Pip,' Mila added.

Pip studied our faces, as if she were afraid she might forget what we looked like. It felt like the minutes clicked by – one, two, three – as we waited for her permission. The crowd got louder and bigger and I was just about ready to jump out the window to join them if I had to.

I watched Pip as she watched the crowd. Watched her eyes get a little teary. Watched the creases in her forehead relax. 'Diggs should be here to see this,' I said, echoing her own words from before. It was a cheap shot, but it was worth a try.

'We'd better get moving, then,' Pip said. Finally.

Mila wrapped the ends of the candles in old dishcloths so we wouldn't burn our hands cos she was Mila and she thought about stuff like that. Pip gave us three rules: *Stick together, leave when I say we're leaving, and no arguing.* We agreed and ran downstairs and Pip yelled behind us, *Wait, what did I say?* So we stopped at the entrance and Mila hopped from foot to foot as we waited for Pip to make her way down the stairs. Our neighbours opened their door. We all noticed it. They didn't come out but others from our building did. I knew their faces. Recognised them from months and months of sharing a staircase. Pip greeted them all by name and introduced us properly and it felt almost like a party.

The protest was one of those things that once, a long time ago, people would have taken photos of and shared with their friends – *Hey, I was there too!* A river of candlelight flowed through the park and merged with more and more people until there was an entire ocean of light rippling through the city. It felt like there were thousands and thousands of us.

We made our way past the apartments and office blocks and boarded-up storefronts. No-one stopped us. Some joined in. Some just watched. Others stayed away from their windows and locked their doors and pretended nothing was going on.

I could hear bits of conversation shouted between old friends or partners or complete strangers over the noise of crowd: *About time we did something. Enough is enough. How did this happen?* I heard someone say, *I don't know what took us so long,* and when I turned to find out who'd said it I saw an old man, much older than anyone else there, leaning heavily on his walker, which he'd decorated with a string of fairy lights. The man who shuffled along next to him nodded solemnly and then they both shouted, *Down with the Regime!*

I wasn't entirely sure where we were going, we just moved along with the crowd. The four of us linked arms and walked in time and it reminded me of Dorothy and the Scarecrow and the Lion and the Tin Man in *The Wizard of Oz.* The four of us skipping down the yellow brick road, except with less singing. *There's no place like home* looped over and over in my mind. I wanted to explain what I was thinking to Z but the noise had gotten way too loud for talking and the crowd seemed to tighten around us, so we unlinked and Mila took my hand and we all tried our best to stay together.

Everyone stopped outside Parliament. A place where Citizens had once been allowed to enter and watch debates and voting and see decisions being made, until they decided we weren't welcome there and fenced it off and patrolled the perimeter with guns and barking dogs so that, over time, it became Strictly Off Limits and no-one went near the place. Except that night. That night, it felt as if we'd surrounded Parliament and could send our message straight to the heart of the Regime, right into Magnus Varick's ears. 'Down with the wall,' the crowd shouted in time and we added our voices to the chorus. 'Down with the Regime!' And we raised our candles high so Varick and his friends could see the light, the fireflies, enclosing him. We were a crowd of strangers but, at that moment, we moved as one and it made the air ... electric.

'Amazing!' I shouted to Z and then immediately wanted to stuff the word back into my mouth cos I wasn't one of those people who said *amazing* but he grinned that grin and, before I'd even realised it, I kissed him. Right there. My lips tingled and the electricity from the air whooshed through my entire body.

He tried to tell me something but everyone was shouting and chanting and I couldn't hear him and he kissed me again and we clapped and shouted and cheered and danced. It felt like cracks were appearing – not in the wall itself, but in people's belief in the Regime. There was a warmth inside me. I'd felt the same thing when we'd watched the other side protesting, but there, in the midst of this crowd, it grew even larger. A glimmer of something. An image of Mum and Astrid and even Dad, somehow, and Diggs and my home and all of us living happily ever after. Something like that. Something amazing.

And then they turned their guns on us.

And fired.

And the cheers became screams.

We dropped our candles. A helicopter shone its searchlight back and forth across the crowd. Crack, crack, crack, the guns blared. *Rubber bullets, they're rubber bullets*, people shouted and held their ground and put their hands above their heads but still it didn't stop and I saw a flash of Pip's panicked face and I spun around and around and there was Z but where was Mila? People were shoving and pushing and running over the top of each other. Something hit my leg and my knees buckled and a sting spread up my body and Z held me up and I kept saying, *I'm OK, I'm OK,* because if I said it maybe it would come true.

'Mila!' we screamed and pushed against the retreating crowd.

She had been right there with us the whole time. Hadn't she?

The sound of guns and screams filled the air. And there, in a flash of the searchlight, a man stood in front of me holding his head and the blood poured from between his fingers and his mouth hung open and I felt a wave of vomit rush up my throat. Those bullets weren't rubber. Another flash of light and there were people on the ground, people in each other's arms, people screaming and holding onto their faces, their legs, their chests and all of them were gushing red. Blood. Everywhere.

'Mila!' I screamed.

People were carried out like sacks of meat or left crumpled on the ground and still the shots continued. At every crack we ducked as if that was going to save us. In the next flash I saw a tiny figure. Mila? I tried to run but my feet kept slipping. She was just standing there in the thick of it all. Someone scooped her up and ran, head down, and as they passed me I realised it wasn't Mila at all.

Something hard and sharp hit my back with a whack. The air emptied out of me. I couldn't breathe. There was nothing. I gulped and gulped. It felt like I was on fire, like something was burning across my shoulderblade. I saw those kids from the wall with their trolley of missiles even though they couldn't have been here. They couldn't have thrown that ... and then I don't remember anything.

PART THREE

CHAPTER 42

Someone was talking to me. A voice I didn't know. I wanted her to stop talking. I wanted to go back to sleep and stay there, in the dark, forever, but she wouldn't stop. *Santee*, she kept saying in this soft sing-song voice, *wake up now, Santee*, and I finally forced my eyelids open and the woman smiled and said, *Good girl*, and I wanted to shove her right in the face but I couldn't lift my arm.

'Go away.' I tried to speak but the words were stuck in my dry mouth. She held out a plastic cup with a straw and told me to take a sip and I did.

I had no idea where I was. I was alone, on a hard bed with a drip in my arm hooked up to a bag and the low light from a lamp made weird shadows on the walls that sometimes turned into people screaming and then I'd hear a voice I thought I knew say, *It's OK, it's OK*.

I don't know how long it went on.

I opened my eyes and found Pip and Z. They were curled up in chairs beside my bed. There was no Mila. I tried to tell myself she was having a shower or making a sandwich or practising her violin but I listened and listened and couldn't hear her music.

Z stirred and lifted his head and we looked at each other and neither of us said a word, but I knew.

Mila was not here.

Mila wasn't anywhere.

She had gone.

And a sob escaped from the bottom of my gut and it spewed across the bed and the room and the whole wide world and I didn't give a shit who heard it. Pip said, *It's OK, it's OK,* but she was lying. My body twitched and shook and I felt hot and cold and sick and numb. Z said nothing. I think it was better that way.

People came in and out of the room. They brought food and chunks of ice and needles and pills. They all looked like versions of Beth, these people, with calm faces and sad smiles and words that meant nothing cos they hadn't known Mila and they didn't know me. They wanted to make me comfortable, make me feel better. But I didn't want to feel better.

Pip told me I would be OK. I told her I didn't want to be. She squeezed my hand and told me I'd been shot. A real bullet. Not rubber. Left shoulder. I'd lost a lot of blood, but I was alive. Mila was not. She had lost a lot of blood, too. More blood than me. I was there and she had gone. I said, *Why me?* I said, *She was a kid.* I said, *It's not fair. She was better than me. Than all of us. It should have been me.* Pip said, *You can't think like that.* I said, *Piss off.* Or something like that. But she didn't listen. She stayed right there, by my bed.

'We're in a safe place now,' she'd say when I'd wake up crying and sweating.

But I didn't feel safe.

They told me I had to eat but I wasn't hungry and I'd push the tray away or throw it on the floor and Pip would have to clean it up but I didn't give a shit, even when she apologised to the doctors or nurses or whoever the hell they were. 'She's not herself,' she would say, and I'd think, *Nope, this is me. This is exactly what I am like.*

I didn't see Z again for a long time. Thinking about him and what he was going through ... it plunged me even deeper into a black hole. Pip told me he was helping out and I didn't ask her what that meant cos I didn't care. I couldn't care. About anything. It hurt too much to care. I slept. I woke up. I stared at the blank wall. My nightmares felt like real life. And real life felt empty. I wanted my mum. I wanted to rewind. I wanted to close my eyes and have all this be over and done with. Finished.

One night, at least I think it was night, I heard the violin. The song was one Mila had practised over and over. My feet touched the carpeted floor and I slowly stood up. My legs were wobbly and it took me a moment and a few deep breaths but I eventually managed to shuffle to the door. I pushed it open and found myself in an ordinary hallway. Not a hospital. Just a house. I followed the music down the hallway of closed doors. I think I must have known it wasn't Mila. That it couldn't be her. But still, I let myself pretend I'd see her, standing so perfectly poised with her little violin and serious face.

'Santee!' Pip rushed towards me.

I was in a room full of strangers and no Mila.

'Where's Mila?' I said, even though I knew the answer by now.

Pip looked old and tired. She cupped my face in her hands. Tears filled her eyes.

'Sorry, Pip,' I said, cos I was.

'You have nothing to be sorry for, my love.'

The strangers turned out to be Pip's friends and the house turned out to be where we were staying.

'Just for the time being,' Pip said, and I wondered how long that would be, but I didn't ask. Pip was never big on details, anyway.

I fell asleep on the sofa listening to the classical music and the whispered conversations happening around me. The next morning I woke up in the bed without crying or screaming out. I won't say the nightmares had gone because those kind of things never leave. Not entirely. But that night they'd left me alone. (I liked to tell myself that was Mila's doing. Somehow.) There was toast on a tray and something that was supposed to be orange juice in a cup and I actually ate and drank and didn't throw my food or refuse it like a big baby. I half expected to see Mila in the doorway, hands on hips, telling me, *It's about time.*

Someone had left a sketchpad and pencil at the foot of my bed. The book had some pages torn out of it and the pencil was chewed at one end but they both looked absolutely perfect to me. I could only use one arm, for obvious reasons, and I wasted pages and pages with lines and circles and threw the book across the room and scribbled nothing all over a page and let the pencil get blunt. And then it happened. I started drawing. And the drawing turned into a picture of Mila. It was her face, because it had to be her face. She was all I saw when I closed my eyes, when I slept, when I woke, when I did anything. Mila. My drawing didn't look like those almost-photograph drawings Z did, but it was definitely her. I drew a frame around her face of music notes and flowers and the words: *She Was Ten*. Because it was true.

'That is a beautiful drawing,' Pip said.

'No,' I said. I hadn't got her eyes right. I couldn't quite capture them. I suppose I never would.

'I want to show this to someone,' she said. 'Just sit tight.'

I sat because there was nothing else to do. I stared at the television. It was silently playing footage from the night of the protest. Words scrolled along the bottom: *Region still reeling from violent Threat attack. Hundreds injured. Magnus Varick announces State of Emergency measures.*

'Arseholes,' someone said.

It could've been Diggs, the way he said it. But it wasn't. It was Z. I forgot all about my arm and ran to him and ignored the pain as we hugged.

It felt like I hadn't seen him in forever. His face looked thinner and there were dark rings under his eyes. I stared at him and tried to think of the right thing to say but nothing came out. I don't know if there ever could be the right words for all he'd gone through. Z had lost everybody. Everything.

'How you feeling?' he said cos he was Z.

'Better,' I said, because I *was* better. Heaps better. Even though I felt like I shouldn't be. Not with Mila gone.

'That's good,' he said, and he tried to smile but it crumpled into a sob and my heart broke all over again. It hurt to see him like that. To hear the sorrow in his cries. Feel the heat of his tears. I wanted to take away all of the pain he was feeling, but I couldn't. All I could do was hold him. So that's what I did.

Z stayed around the house more after that, which was good. For me, anyway. We didn't talk much but it was nice to feel him there, in the same space. To not have to worry about losing him, too. He slept next to me, the two of us crowded into the little bed. It helped. To wake up from a nightmare and feel his heartbeat, hear the even rhythm of his breath, feel his tears on my cheek, hold his hand and never let him go.

CHAPTER 43

Pip and her friends were constantly coming and going. Her friends never spoke to me. They kept to themselves and whispered their secret conversations under the blare of classical music.

'It's better this way,' Pip said. I had learned by then not to ask why.

But still, I knew things were happening out there. Big things. There was something in the atmosphere of the house. The music, being played louder and more frequently. The almost-smiles on the strangers' faces. The sound of faraway sirens. The smell of smoke that filled the night air.

Z wanted to go for a walk and Pip thought it was a good idea. I hadn't been outside in weeks and wasn't sure that I wanted to. But they both insisted and I was so much better that I really had no excuse.

So we went out. Me and Z. The house was a house, not an apartment, and it was out of the city a little, on a quiet street of nondescript houses and dying gardens. We walked on the footpath even though no cars were on the roads. We saw no-one. Heard no-one. It felt like we were the only people in the universe. It brought back a long-ago memory of being in the bush with Z in his broken-down car. Just the two of us.

Z said he needed me to see something. The further we walked, the more people and cars and life appeared. Every step got us closer to civilization. We reached the end of one street, turned left, right, left and then we were on a street of stores and offices and cafes left over from when people had been allowed to use those sorts of things. But that wasn't what he wanted to show me.

It was Mila.

She was everywhere. I mean, it wasn't her, of course, but my drawing of her. Her face. Everywhere. And the words *She Was Ten*. Her face was printed onto pieces of paper that could be stuffed into letterboxes or thrust into passing hands or pasted onto walls or stuck up in windows. And that's where they were. On walls and telegraph poles and bins and trees and in windows. *She Was Ten*.

But she wasn't alone.

Alongside her were other faces. *He Was 50. They Were 19. She Was 38*. All these people. There were so many of them. Face after face after face.

Z took my good arm cos he was Z and he just knew I needed some help keeping upright. 'We've put them everywhere,' he whispered. 'All over the city. Even on the Safety Border – the wall. Everywhere.'

'What is this?'

'We call it the Reminder.'

I stopped and stared at Mila. I wished I'd gotten the eyes right. People should have had a chance to see her eyes. I touched her cheek. 'Why haven't they taken them down?'

'Not enough of them and too many of us,' he said. 'Not worth their effort, so they've given up.'

That didn't sound like the Unit. Or the Regime. Maybe the tiny cracks of the protest had grown. Become fractures. Fractures that might, in time, make it all fall apart. I didn't want to get my hopes up, but a small spark lit up inside me.

A couple of Unit Officers walked by and Z casually led us in the opposite direction.

'This was all you,' he said. I shook my head. I hadn't done anything.

We walked back to the house in silence. I thought about forever ago when we'd get a rush from writing *Down with the Regime* wherever and whenever we could. When we thought we were making some kind of difference. *Waking people up.* Maybe we had. But we'd lost Mila. And I would have given all that up to have her back.

Pip was waiting out the front, pacing back and forth across the dead grass. She looked so much smaller than she had when I'd first met her and I wondered if maybe we had all shrunk a bit. Collapsed in on ourselves under the weight of everything that had happened. She broke into a smile that didn't quite reach her eyes when she saw us.

'We're going home,' she said.

For the tiniest second I thought she meant my real home. But she didn't, of course. She meant her apartment, and we bundled into a car I'd never seen before, and haven't seen since, and left the unknown house and the quiet street behind for good.

We'd left everything in the apartment as if we were about to come back, cos I suppose that's what we'd thought; that after the protest we would have come back, the four us, and Pip would have made us cups of tea and we would have chatted in the candlelight about the night until, one by one, we fell asleep. The plates in the kitchen sink had a layer of fuzz growing on them, and so did the coffee in the cup one of us had left unfinished on the counter. Mila's backpack was on an armchair, the homework she'd completed that afternoon sitting on top ready to be handed in on time, as usual. I packed her homework into her bag and stuffed the whole lot under the chair.

I opened the windows to get some fresh air into the apartment. It had been closed up for so long that the whole place smelled like dirty socks. We all kept busy that day. Cleaning and putting things away and not talking about the thing we all needed to talk about the most.

That night, after the News, which we all stared at but didn't really watch, there was a knock at the door. It didn't sound like the sort of knock you'd expect from the Unit, but it still made me catch my breath and wait and listen for a moment before saying, *I'll get it.*

There was nobody there. I looked up and down the corridor but the light was already fading. Maybe someone was watching me from the stairs, but I couldn't see them. What I did see was a handful of flowers on the doormat, arranged on top of a piece of paper. I picked it all up and took it inside. The paper had SORRY scribbled on the front and when I opened it I saw they had used the Mila poster. I found some empty jars in Pip's pantry, filled them with the flowers and placed them around the apartment. Mila would have thought they were pretty.

'You mad at me?' Pip asked me later that night.

'Why would I be mad?'

'Your picture of Mila and those words ... maybe I should have asked, but everyone was so taken by it, and it's working, love. You're making a difference. Your voice, people are hearing it.'

'It's just a drawing,' I said.

'A voice can take many forms, Santee. It can be more than words.'

I couldn't sleep that night. Instead, I lit a candle and, in the flickering light, I tried to draw Mum and Dad and Astrid. But I couldn't hold their faces in my mind long enough to get them on the page. I don't know why I hadn't tried to capture them sooner. Why had I waited so long?

CHAPTER 44

U OK?

The text message beeped through in the early hours of the morning. It was Tash. In all that had happened I had forgotten about school and Tash and all that stuff. It seemed so unimportant. I had no idea what to write back to her. It wasn't as if we were going to fall back into the best-friends routine we'd had all those years ago. We were well past that. But it was kinda nice that she cared. Or seemed to. Maybe she just wanted some gossip.

Yeah. That's all I wrote back. What else was I supposed to say?

She wrote back, real quick, *When U back at school?* And I knew why she'd messaged. She didn't care about me. She was just concerned about being alone at lunchtime and wanted to know when 'her group' would be back.

But I didn't want to go back. Ever. School seemed completely irrelevant.

'We have to get back to normal sometime,' Pip said.

'Normal?' I almost spat out the word. I could feel that familiar blood-boiling, fizzing, popping feeling rising up in me. 'What the hell is normal?'

I stormed out of the apartment and sat on the stairs to cool down. From the surrounding apartments I could hear televisions and muffled conversations and yaps from the sad dogs locked indoors all day.

I heard them before I saw them. For a moment, the girl's voice sounded just like Mila's and I caught my breath. They came in the front entrance. The perfect-family neighbours. The people living in the Drivers' home. School must have finished. They thumped up the stairs with their backpacks and I made them squeeze past me. Their mother stopped in front of me. I thought she was going to yell at me for being in the way.

'We all miss her dreadfully,' she said, and gently touched my arm. 'We're so sorry.'

'Thank you,' I said quietly.

'Please let us know if there is going to be a funeral and if we can help with anything, anything at all …'

I looked at her. This woman who'd taken the Drivers' home without so much as a, *Sorry*.

There wasn't going to be a funeral, not until Diggs came home. Z was determined about that. I wondered if I should tell her that was how she could help: Get Diggs back and get out of his apartment. But before I could say anything they'd gone inside. I heard the door shut and lock behind them.

Something shifted inside me and suddenly I was up and out the door and heading towards the park. It was filled with memories of Mila – in Pip's floppy hat, playing soccer, holding my hand – but still I walked. Breathed in the air. Let the tears slide down my face.

There were Reminders plastered all over the park – more faces of people lost in the protest. I noticed a Unit Officer standing, staring at one of the posters. A wave of panic washed over me and for a moment I thought he was going to rip it down or cover it up but as I edged closer I realised he was crying, too. A Unit Officer. Crying over the image of a man with the words: He was Twenty-Three.

That night I told Pip what I'd seen and she nodded knowingly. 'They're people, too,' she said.

'Who are?'

'The Unit Officers.'

I couldn't believe what I was hearing. Those monsters who'd killed Mila were not people.

'They've stopped paying them. Part of Varick's Economic Plan,' she said, and then added with a laugh, 'let's see how well that goes for him, huh?'

I wanted her to tell me more but she was already humming, a sly smile on her face.

'Oh my god, oh my god,' Tash squealed and then burst into tears and hugged us and worried about my arm and Mila and then cried again.

It was our first day back. Pip had insisted and I was too tired to fight about it.

'I was there, at the protest,' Tash whispered as we headed into the building.

'You were?' I was surprised. I couldn't imagine her mum ever agreeing to that.

But it turned out Tash's mum more than agreed to it – she went along, too. She wanted her husband back. 'It's a joke. Varick has let the power go to his head and he's ruining everything. It has to stop.' She said it with such authority that it was hard to imagine she had once told me Varick was the leader of the greatest and bravest government in history.

Imara had gone. Turned out her family managed to get the paperwork they needed for their Hawaiian holiday. Not that anyone believed it was a holiday. Muffins and international flights. Imara's family really were connected.

Riley raced up to Z and gave him a tight hug. I headed off to let them have their moment. Riley wasn't exactly my biggest fan. I thought he'd probably find a way to blame me for everything.

But he didn't. Instead, he caught up with me. 'Glad you're all right,' he said, and gave me an awkward pat on the shoulder. Still. It was something.

Mrs Rook wanted to see me and Z in her office. At once (her words, not mine). She seemed nervous, offered us water, poured some for herself, sat down, stood up, sat down again.

'I wanted to extend my deepest and most sincere condolences. To you both. It is very ...' and she stopped. Took a tissue. Dabbed her eyes. I'd never seen Mrs Rook like this. 'It is very sad.'

She wanted to know how we were and if we needed any extra support and then she suggested that, perhaps, we reconsider our decision to return to school.

'What?' I said.

'Your presence here could be a distraction. For the other students. You understand?' She looked miserable and dabbed her eyes again.

'You don't want us here?' Z said.

She lowered her voice. 'It's not me, Zac. It's bigger than me.'

Mrs Rook hugged us before we left and forced her business card into my hand in case I needed anything. *Anything at all.*

Everyone was in class. The corridors were silent. The screens played a loop of school rules and reminders. *Be a Good Citizen!* We emptied our lockers and walked out of school. Forever.

I think I was supposed to feel happy and relieved. I'd always imagined that's how my final day of school would feel. Instead, I felt kinda empty. And lost. So very lost.

CHAPTER 45

They planned another protest. The details were on flyers that dropped from the sky. Little pieces of paper that scattered across the roads and gardens and bush and rooftops. They got stuck in gutters and drainpipes and under parked cars. There were so many that the Unit couldn't stop people picking them up and passing them on or stuffing them into back pockets or hiding them in the pages of books or under cushions or inside shoes. It was almost like the officers didn't care. There were less of them around and the ones that were there just sort of shrugged when they saw us with flyers.

DAY OF ACTION, they said. A date. A time. A place. A mission: *Bring down the wall, bring back our rights!* (Their words, not mine.)

Tash came over to visit us, which was weird. I still wasn't used to being friends with her again. Part of me knew it was because she had no-one else but another part of me hoped it was because she missed me. She told us how the school had banned the flyers and anyone caught with one faced immediate expulsion and further penalties. No-one knew what *further penalties* meant. Not that it mattered anyway because, according to Tash, everyone was talking about the Day of Action, even some of the teachers.

'Are you guys going to go?' Tash said.

'No,' I said.

Z gave me a weird look but didn't say anything. He and Tash started talking about other things. I didn't want to go. I didn't want to see what I'd seen again. I didn't want to lose anyone else. Especially not Z.

I walked Tash back to her house. She lived in a big, beautiful house set at the top of a long, steep driveway. It had seemed longer and steeper when we were younger. But still. It was impressive. I remembered how we'd ridden her scooters down that driveway. How we'd gone so fast it felt like we were flying. She'd made her mum buy her two scooters for her birthday – one for her and one for me. That's how it had been.

'Please come to the protest,' she said, and gave me a quick almost-hug before heading up the driveway.

As I walked back towards the place I now called home, I thought of all the times Mum had picked me up from Tash's house. The way she was so kind to Tash's mum even though Tash's mum always acted like she didn't want us there. I wondered how she'd felt, approaching that huge house in our rundown old car. Tash liked coming to our house more than being at her own, and Mum would talk and laugh and joke and make a fuss of her like she was one of us. Tash once said she wished my mum was her mum. I said we could share her. Her own mum never came into our place. She would pull up, keep the car running and call Tash to come down.

I sent Tash a message as I walked: *I'll try to be there tomorrow. I'll try.*

She wrote back quickly: *U R braver than U know xx*

Pip told us she would not be home that night. She was working on something that we weren't to know about and said we were to behave ourselves and, *There are eyes everywhere*, and it was hard to tell if she was joking or not. The power went out, as usual, and we lay next to each other on the mattresses that still covered the floor and talked about that long-ago time in the bush. The candlelight cast weird shadows on the ceiling. I touched Z's face. Gently traced the profile of his nose, lips, chin, neck with my finger. I ran my hand across his collarbone, his chest. He kissed me. Softly at first. Like a question. *Is this OK?* It was. It really was. And I felt him move closer and our kiss grew deeper. We were breathing each other in. And the world slipped away and it was as if we were floating. Together. And I never wanted that feeling to end.

CHAPTER 46

The News before the Day of Action was interrupted by what they called a Very Special Announcement. We were all home. I was trying to get Z to sit still because I was attempting to draw him. Neither of us were paying much attention to the TV, and we didn't say anything when we heard Magnus Varick say, 'Good Citizens.' I don't know if anyone responded anymore. Still, he paused and waited as if he could hear us, and once I would have been worried that the Unit would burst into our flat and arrest us for not giving the response we were supposed to. But now ...

I kept drawing Z.

'Stop moving,' I said. He threw a cushion at me. I threw it back.

'Hey, come on – I'm trying to listen,' Pip said.

We laughed.

'No, I mean it, I am,' she said.

We stopped being stupid. I put down my drawing and sat with Pip.

Varick held onto the podium as if it might fly away from under him. 'It saddens me to speak with you this evening. However, there are a small minority of citizens who wish to undermine and destroy the Safety and Security we have built across all the Regions. We cannot allow this to happen. We cannot allow the great work we have done to be destroyed by these Threats. And so, we are imposing a forty-eight-hour lockdown, effective immediately. All events and travel are cancelled. All Citizens must remain indoors. We know that all Good Citizens will be supportive of this necessary measure. Thank you. And good night.'

The screen went black.

'Bastard,' Pip said.

But before we'd had a chance to turn off the television, numbers flashed up on the screen – counting down from ten with these loud beeps keeping in time. Once it got to one the beep got louder and louder. And then this explosion of images burst from the television. A kid being shot at the protest cut to a close-up of Varick drinking Champagne cut to a family being pushed into the back of a van cut to Varick's men in suits eating and eating and eating cut to an old woman holding a bleeding child in her arms and crying cut to someone begging on the street cut to rich people dancing at Parliament cut to … the screen went black. The power went out.

'That should have done it,' Pip said.

'Did you do that?' I said.

'I might have helped,' she said, and patted my hand. 'Just a tad.'

The next day it felt like no-one had remembered anything about a forty-eight-hour lockdown. I mean, some of them must have been following the rules, of course. But they were the minority. It felt like the whole world was outside and they were right on time.

'You wanna get out of your pajamas?' Pip said.

'Don't think we should go,' I said, and slipped back under the blanket.

'We can't miss this, Santee.'

What the hell was wrong with them? Of course we could miss this. I didn't understand how they could even want to go. Risk it all over again – for what?

Z crawled under the blanket with me. I stared at him. He stared at me.

'What?' I said, finally.

'We owe it to Mila.'

'You can't say that,' I said, and tried to roll away from him, but he caught my arm, forced me to look at him.

'Please,' he said.

My heart hammered through my chest and my arm ached even though it didn't really hurt much anymore and I couldn't stop the bad thoughts whirring through my head, but somehow I made it outside. Into the Day of Action. With Pip on one side and Z on the other and thousands of people all around us.

The Day of Action started at Parliament where Pip said there would be some speeches before everyone moved to different sections of the wall.

'To show our support for the other side,' she said.

It was overwhelming to have to walk the exact same route we'd taken last time, but without Mila. Time would always be marked by her now: With Mila and Without Mila. I never imagined she wouldn't be here. I suppose no-one ever thinks that about the people they love.

Even with the summer sun glaring down on us, I felt the hairs stand up on my arms. The closer we got to Parliament the worse I felt until we were there, back at that same spot, and I didn't know if I wanted to throw up or scream or run away or collapse, right there where she had. But Pip put her arm around me and said, *Look,* and it was then I realised I'd kept my head down the whole way and hadn't noticed the signs people were carrying.

Mila was everywhere. Her face. On banners and placards and watching me from the walls of buildings. And the crowd was huge. Bigger than last time. There were elderly people wearing nice hats and dads pushing babies in strollers and couples holding hands and kids jumping around clapping and music blaring from speakers. And Mila. Everywhere.

I looked at Pip and said, *Thank you,* and she started to cry and it was my turn to hug her. The way Mila would have done. Easily. Gently. Kindly.

There were so many people that we couldn't get close enough to hear the speeches, but it didn't matter. We got the idea of what was being said from the chants that rippled through the crowd – *Down with the Regime! Down with the wall!* We added our voices and the message was passed back and back and back to the people who stood at the very edge of the crowd.

I scanned the rooftops for the Unit. I imagined them

standing up there with their guns locked on us. Sitting ducks. But I couldn't see them. No helicopters or drones were around. I tried not to think the worst, but it was difficult not to. It felt like a trap. A cruel joke. And we were just waiting for the punchline. I couldn't breathe.

'Check that one out,' Z said, pointing to a big old sheepdog. 'What's its name?'

I shook my head.

'Fred,' he said.

I shook my head again.

'No?'

'It's definitely a Ron,' I said, my voice wobbly. He laughed and pointed to another dog and we thought of another name, and another, and I knew what he was doing and it worked and I thought, *There's Number Ten on my things-I-know-about-Z list: He is the best person I've ever met, the best person I'm likely to ever meet.*

And then we were moving again, like a huge serpent winding through the streets and down the alleyways and across the city towards the wall. I knew the section I needed to go to. And Z knew, too. We found our way to my part of the wall, the section closest to home, and stood with the crowd that had already gathered there. We shouted and cheered and whistled and hoped that the people on the other side were there. That they could hear us. A woman at the front of the crowd held up her hands to shut us up and we did. We held our breath and crossed our fingers and waited and waited. Nothing. She got us to make noise again. She was like a conductor with an orchestra. Then silence again. *Wait, wait, wait,* the conductor seemed to be saying.

And then – BAM! There it was. The other side. They were shouting and cheering and it was muffled but it was there. It was definitely there. We cheered back and waited and they answered and on it went and it was wonderful.

A couple of helicopters appeared overhead. Low. Menacing. Then the drones came out. Watching. Waiting.

'Maybe we should go,' I said.

'They can't arrest us all,' Z said. 'There's too many of us.'

I wasn't so sure. Besides, they hadn't been interested in arresting anyone last time. All Varick had wanted before was to stop the protest, and he didn't care how it happened or who he killed. So long as it stopped. As much as I wanted to believe it would be different this time, I just couldn't get rid of that feeling in my gut that kept telling me, *Get out of here, run, run.* I saw kids everywhere, younger than Mila, and I couldn't shake the image of them lying on the ground soaked in blood. I squeezed my eyes shut. Tight. Smoke billowed across the city. Something had been set alight. I could hear the high wail of the sirens as the Unit raced through the streets. The sky darkened. The helicopters remained. And still the people around me shouted. But part of me knew they wouldn't be allowed to go on like this forever.

And then they arrived. Like I knew they would.

The Unit marched into the crowd and the people booed them and I wanted to throw up cos this was it. It was going to happen all over again. Everything started spinning and my heart was banging and banging and Pip's mouth was moving but I couldn't hear what she was saying cos everything was static and she helped me to the ground and sat with me and rubbed my back and Z had found a bottle of water and was pouring it on my head and I wanted to tell them, *Stop, leave me alone, get out of here,* but nothing was coming out.

Everything went blotchy and blurry and then ... Nothing.

'You with us?' Pip's voice and face came back into focus.

I nodded. 'Sorry.'

'It's OK, love,' she said.

We sat there for a moment and Pip kept telling me it was fine, everything was fine. She scrambled around in her bag and found an old cough lolly and made me eat it and I started to feel a little more normal.

'Come look at this,' Z said.

They helped me to my feet and we pushed through the crowd to the wall where some Unit Officers stood shoulder to shoulder with some regular citizens.

'Look,' Pip said.

I could not believe what I was seeing.

The Unit Officers were breaking the wall apart. They had these heavy hammers, which they pounded at the wall, and a machine that made a heap of noise and dust as it cut through the concrete.

Real cracks started to appear. Small at first, but they didn't let up, and finally we could see through to the other side. Just a little. A glimmer. Of something. They moved faster then and the crack grew wider and taller until someone from over there was able to pull their way through to over here and we all went silent. Absolutely silent.

The young woman stood there like she had landed on a different planet. We stared at her. She stared back. Then her face broke into pieces as she cried and laughed and screamed to the sky and she shouted out names of people I didn't know and the crowd gathered her up and people filmed it on their phones and then more people were slipping through the crack, more and more and more.

'Go, Santee,' Pip said, and she gently pushed me towards the wall.

'What?'

'Go through the wall. Go home. You can go home.'

I stared at them. I didn't know what to say. I hadn't expected this. I wasn't ready for it.

'What about you?' I said.

'We'll be fine, love.'

I looked at Z. He had closed his eyes and turned his face up to the sky. I remembered him doing the same thing out in the bush and I wished I could go back there, right now.

'Come with me,' I said, and grabbed hold of his hand.

He opened his eyes and gave me that smile of his that I hadn't seen, not properly, in what felt like a million years. 'Dad's here,' he said.

'You think he'll come back?'

'Don't you think your dad's coming back?'

I nodded and he nodded and I said OK and he said OK and we just looked at each other. I didn't know how to move, how to step away from him. It was as if there was something, a real, physical thing holding me to him, and I knew it was going to hurt like hell to break it.

Pip said, 'Go, love. We'll be all right, I promise.' And I believed her because I had to.

I didn't say goodbye cos I couldn't. And I couldn't believe that this was it. Everything felt too big for words. I said, *I love you*, because it was true, and it was all I could think to say that came close to what I felt. For them both. But even that was too small for all of this.

And then I walked away. Pushed through a sea of excited faces and happy tears and shouts of joy and waited for my turn to slip through the hole in the wall.

An officer took my hand to help me over the rubble that had gathered at the bottom of the wall and as I stepped up and through the opening I thought I heard him say, *Good luck, Santee*. Peter? I couldn't be sure, and there was no chance to turn around to check. I just had to keep going. Through the Safety Border, the wall, to the other side. To my home.

The crowd cheered and clapped as I stepped through. I searched for a familiar face, for anyone I recognised, and they stared back as if trying to work out if, perhaps, I could be their lost daughter or sister or whoever it was they needed me to be. But I wasn't theirs. And none of them were mine. And I could see the disappointment on their faces, which probably matched my own. A group of official-looking people surrounded me and wanted to know, *What's your name? How old are you? Who are your parents?*

'Wait here,' they said, but there was no way I was going to wait anywhere except where I knew they'd be waiting, and so I shoved past the questions and the clipboards and ran towards that split in the road where, on mornings long ago, Mum had always gone her way and me and Astrid had gone ours.

The sky grew darker. The cheering faded away. Smoke streamed across the city. Sirens cried out. And in the distance, two figures got closer and closer and my heart thumped, thumped, thumped.

And this is the part where I'd like to tell you that everything turned out all right. That the wall came crumbling down and families were reunited and the Regime was ruined and everyone was happy. The end.

But that would be a lie. I think you knew that already.

THE END

ACKNOWLEDGEMENTS

What an absolute joy and pleasure it has been to work with everyone at Hardie Grant Egmont. Marisa, thank you for your enthusiasm and belief in this book. Luna, I don't know what I would have done without you. Thank you for your insights, feedback, encouragement, and skilful and thoughtful edits. And huge thanks to Emma, Penelope, Tye and everyone at HGE – THANK YOU!

Aviva Tuffield, you saw a book in me when I thought I only had plays and a couple of short stories. Thank you for starting all of this. I am forever grateful.

I am still pinching myself that I have the amazing Grace Heifetz in my corner. Thank you, Grace (and all at Curtis Brown) for your incredible support and for making this happen when I really thought it might not.

Thank you to all my friends and colleagues at Arts Centre Melbourne who have been so accommodating of my crazy leave requests, and genuinely supportive of (and interested in) my writing endeavours. And to all my dear friends who have offered advice and places to write (Lyall and Adam, I'm looking at you) and have been so understanding.

I wanted to be a writer because of my mum. Thanks, Ma, for a childhood full of stories and books and writing projects! Dad, thank you for instilling in me a strong work ethic and for your constant support. Thank you both for the long phone calls across the desert, for a bed in Perth, for your guidance and love.

To my beautiful sisters, Claire, Jessica and Ashleigh – early readers, cheerleaders, spellcheckers, therapists, all-round wonderful humans and my best mates – thank you. And to my equally beautiful little brother and best mate and legend, Ethan – thank you for checking in on me. To Clinton, Chris, Luke and Caitlyn – thank you for your encouragement. To the best in-laws anyone could wish for – Sue and Paul and all the Barrons – thank you for understanding why I had to miss family dinner ... again ... and for your love and support.

To my amazing nieces and nephews – this one is for all of you. Abby, you are one of the main reasons I started writing about Santee. I think you'd be friends.

Finally, Steve. Thank you for nagging me when I needed it, for making dinner, for letting me off the hook, for your unwavering belief that I actually could do this. We make a good team. I love you and I appreciate you.

ABOUT THE AUTHOR

Katy Warner always thought she wanted to be an actor and for a big part of her life that's what she did – until she realised she actually preferred writing the words herself. Now, she's an award-winning playwright and the author of many short stories and a young-adult novel. Even though she misses the costumes, Katy is much happier as a writer. Her plays have been performed across Australia and in New Zealand, London and Edinburgh. Katy lives in Melbourne with her husband, their cat and a lot of books. Her debut novel is *Everywhere Everything Everyone.*